MURDER TAK

CW01064306

Laura Lippman's novels have won many crime fiction prizes, including the Edgar, Anthony, Agatha and eDunnit Awards. Her more recent works include *Sunburn*, a Waterstones Thriller of the Month in 2018, *Dream Girl*, which was shortlisted for the 2022 CWA Ian Fleming Steel Dagger and *Lady in the Lake*, adapted by Apple TV+ in 2024. In 2025 she was named a Grand Master by the Mystery Writers of America.

ALSO BY LAURA LIPPMAN

MURDER TAKES A VACATION

A NOVEL

LAURA LIPPMAN

faber

First published in the UK in 2025
by Faber & Faber Limited
The Bindery, 51 Hatton Garden
London EC1N 8HN

First published in the United States by William Morrow, an imprint of
HarperCollins Publishers, 195 Broadway, New York, NY 10007.

Printed in the UK by CPI Group (UK) Ltd, Croydon CR0 4YY

A CIP record for this book
is available from the British Library

ISBN 978–0–571–39462–3

Printed and bound in the UK on FSC® certified paper in line with our continuing
commitment to ethical business practices, sustainability and the environment.
For further information see faber.co.uk/environmental-policy

Our authorised representative in the EU for product safety is
Easy Access System Europe, Mustamäe tee 50, 10621 Tallinn, Estonia
gpsr.requests@easproject.com

2 4 6 8 10 9 7 5 3 1

For Susan Seegar

And in memory of Madeline Mabry Lippman

They found you dead
In a safety net

—"MISSION À PARIS,"
HANS VANDENBURG

PART I

ITINERARY FOR MURIEL BLOSSOM
PREPARED BY HART TOURS

March 31: Depart Baltimore-Washington International (overnight flight).

check in 24 hours in advance

April 1: Arrive at Heathrow, transfer to Air France flight to Charles de Gaulle in Paris. You will be met by a driver from Hart Tours, who will take you to your hotel, Le Bristol.

call Hart re: driver

April 1—April 7: Enjoy several days in the City of Lights on your own, visiting world-class artistic, culinary, and cultural attractions.

April 7: Welcome aboard the MS *Solitaire*, your home for the duration of our cruise! The *Solitaire* is one of the more intimate ships in our fleet, with a maximum capacity of ninety-eight guests, a restaurant, a lounge, and a bistro that serves food from 7:00 to 22:00 hours. Please call Hart Tours for the ship's docking location.

Substance 13 Rue de Chaillot

April 8: The MS *Solitaire* remains docked in Paris, with opportunities to explore independently or participate in one of our group excursions, including a trip to the Musée d'Orsay.

No?

April 9: Travel north as part of a private excursion to charming Vétheuil, the home of Claude Monet from

1878 to 1881, where he created some of his most impressive impressionist works. The MS *Solitaire* sets sail from Paris at sunset.

April 10: Cruise up the Seine to visit Giverny, the setting for Monet's beloved water lily paintings, and then sail a bit farther to Les Andelys to enjoy a spectacular view and quaint shops.

April 11: Visit fascinating Rouen, home to world-famous cathedrals, the burial site of Richard the Lionheart, and execution site of Joan of Arc.!!!

falafel?

April 12: Travel farther upriver to Normandy, to visit the historic beaches that were home to the battles of D-Day.

April 13: ~~Return to Paris and soak up one more evening in this magical city.~~ Don't forget to join us for a special farewell dinner on board!

La Reserve 42 Av Gabriel

April 14: Depart the MS *Solitaire* for Charles de Gaulle Airport for your Air France flight to Heathrow, where you will connect to your British Airways flight to Baltimore. Bon voyage, you are now part of the Hart Family, and we hope to "sea" you again on another one of our cruises.

Check in online 24 hours in advance?

MRS. BLOSSOM HAD never been upgraded in her life.

To be fair, until this moment—the last day of March, a Baltimore March that was going out full lion, all blustery winds and horizontal sleet—it had not been a life that offered many opportunities for upgrades. A good life, yes, even an excellent one while her husband was alive, but also a rooted-to-the-ground kind of existence. It wasn't a matter of never getting past the velvet ropes, more an issue of never getting *to* them.

For one thing, she seldom flew, averaging only a trip or two a year between her native Baltimore and her recent hometown of Phoenix. She always chose Southwest, a no-frills airlines, because she was a no-frills kind of person. Once, just once, she bought a Business Select ticket because circumstances had forced her to book last-minute. The only real advantage was boarding in the first group, a novelty to her. Oh, and there was a drink coupon, but it was 6:30 a.m. She gave it to the nervous flier next to her, who ordered a screwdriver, downed it in three gulps, then fell asleep, his head lolling on her shoulder. Mrs. Blossom had the kind of shoulder that even strangers found inviting.

Meanwhile, when it came to hotels—well, she hadn't stayed in one of those since Mr. Blossom died. Even during the marriage, it had just been the occasional Hampton Inn here and there. Harold Blossom was a homebody, which meant Mrs. Blossom had been a homebody, too. If the person you love likes to stay put, you stay put with them.

Planes, hotels—what other situations offered upgrades? Mrs. Blossom couldn't think of any. Probably because she had never been upgraded.

Which explained her tongue-tied confusion when the young woman at the British Airways ticket counter asked if she wanted to be "bumped up" to business class for her flight to London.

Mrs. Blossom lowered her voice. "How much would that cost?"

She immediately regretted the question. She had vowed she would not ask the price of anything over the next fourteen days. The point was to pretend that money was no object. But who was she fooling? Money, if not *the* object, was always *an* object. It wended its way through almost every human transaction, even those we consider pure. You can marry for love, bring children into the world for your own express joy—and it's still part of the US tax code. People thought money was rational because it could be quantified, but Mrs. Blossom found money stranger than love.

And more shameful than sex.

"The upgrade won't cost you anything," the ticket agent said. "The economy cabin is oversold on this flight while business has several open seats. I'm going to have to upgrade two or three people, and you're the first to check in. Besides, you would be so much more comfortable in business. The seats are much wi—" She paused, stopped, started over. "The seats are much more comfortable."

She was probably going to say "wider," Mrs. Blossom realized. Mrs. Blossom was a big woman. Mrs. Blossom was a large woman. OK, fine, she was a *fat* woman. Her grandchildren kept telling her that the word *fat* was okay now, even preferable, that it was a factual term that should not be stigmatized. Fat was a fact, fat was neutral, or should be.

Bless their hearts.

Mrs. Blossom loved her three granddaughters, but those three petite tweens had no idea what it was like, FWF: flying while fat. Internet savvy as they were, they probably didn't even realize there was an entire subreddit devoted to the topic.

Because as little as Mrs. Blossom may have flown, the experience was depressingly, consistently humiliating. She usually boarded in the last group, when only middle seats were available because of Southwest's open-seating policy. People would avoid her eyes as she made her way down the aisle, like little children thinking they were invisible if *they* couldn't see you. When she finally chose a seat, the passengers on either side would sigh, no matter how much she tried to shrink herself. And if she dared to use the armrest, the only perk of a middle seat, they would sigh even more.

She glanced at her British Airways ticket: She was in 36-D, an aisle, but toward the rear of the plane. If an upgrade could spare her those affronted sighs, those worried glances as she walked toward her seat—*oh god I hope she's not next to me*—then it would be quite the upgrade.

"And it's—free?"

"Yes. Plus, you would be welcome to wait in the Chesapeake Lounge before boarding, which is nice given that you're here"— the young woman checked her wristwatch—"three hours before departure."

"I thought you were supposed to build in a lot of time for—" Mrs. Blossom stopped herself from saying "foreign," a tic her family had been teasing her about as she planned this trip— "international travel."

"I wish more of our fliers were like you," the ticket agent said, her eyes fixed on her screen, her fingers making all those mysterious clicks and clacks that ticket agents apparently require to produce a new paper ticket. "I'm going to put you in 2-F, Mrs. Blossom." Everyone called her "Mrs. Blossom," always had, even when she was a twenty-year-old newlywed, possibly because it was an amusing name to say: *Mrs. Blossom*. She hadn't liked this when she was young; she felt it aged her. But as she had grown older and the world had become more casual, she found she enjoyed the implicit fealty.

Besides, it was her husband's legacy to her, and every time someone used her surname, it was as if Harold, dead for ten years, lived again for a nanosecond. There could be no Mrs. Blossom without a Mr. Blossom.

Except, it turned out—there could be.

"Here's your ticket, Mrs. Blossom. Don't forget, the Chesapeake Lounge is close to the security checkpoint in Concourse E, but it's a little behind you when you enter. You have to loop back for it."

"I'm worried I'll miss my plane if I'm not sitting at the gate," Mrs. Blossom confessed. She quoted her ticket: "The flight closes thirty minutes before departure."

"Oh, the staff in the lounge won't let you be stranded." It was a man's voice, rich and resonant, coming from behind her. "There will be ample notice and multiple announcements."

Mrs. Blossom turned and saw a silver-haired man waiting patiently for his turn at the counter, a man who also had to be headed to London, as there was only one daily BA flight out of Baltimore. She wasn't the only person to arrive at the recommended three hours before, after all. *So there*, she said in her head to the ticket agent. (Mrs. Blossom said a lot of *So theres!* in her head, very few out loud.)

"They announce the flight well in advance," the man continued. "And because you're flying business, you'll be among the first
passengers summoned to the gate." He approached the counter
and showed the agent his boarding pass, placed his suitcase on
the scale, where it registered only ten pounds. Oh, wait, it was
probably kilos at British Airways. After all, the ticket agent had a
British accent. "I'm already traveling business, as it happens, but
if you can seat me close to this kind lady, I'll take good care of her
here and at Heathrow."

The man was her age, give or take, although Mrs. Blossom had
trouble judging people's ages. The silver hair—quite thick—might
be premature. She had let her hair go gray after Mr. Blossom
died, then been convinced by her granddaughters to have the
gray changed to a subtle platinum. A silly expense, $175 every six
weeks, not including tip—but here she was, thinking about money
again when, if she were judicious, she could live the rest of her life
with any hair color she wanted.

"If you'll wait for me to check in," the man said, "I'll show you
the lounge. You don't have to stay there, but I think you'll prefer it
to the gate. The international terminal here is pretty bare bones."

She gave a slight, imperious nod, as if she were familiar with
the amenities offered in various airports. She had been to exactly
three in her life—Baltimore, Phoenix, and Louisville.

He did more than show her the lounge. He narrated Mrs.
Blossom's journey through security, a process she found unnerving, despite having flown only last week. He even threw their
passports and boarding passes into the same little bowl, as if
they were traveling together, then reminded her to take off her
charm bracelet, saying it might ping the metal detector. Lovely
manners. He reminded her of Mr. Blossom, who had lived to put
others at ease.

"Brand-new passport?" he asked, handing it back to her. "The photo is quite nice. But maybe you're one of those people who can't take a bad photo."

"I've never left the country before," she admitted, blushing. "I'm embarrassed that I've waited so long to travel"—she stopped to consider the best word—"abroad."

"The important thing is that you're *starting*," he said. "It's never too late to see the world. And solo travelers are a special breed, the best and the bravest in my experience. 'Down to Gehenna, up to the Throne. He travels the fastest who travels alone.'"

"Kipling?"

"Right! 'The Winners.' I've never met anyone else who knew the reference."

Buoyed by his praise, she decided not to admit that she recognized the poem only because it was quoted in a favorite children's book that she still reread from time to time. A story, as it happened, about a young woman embarking on her first European trip. She also did not clarify that she would be alone for less than a week—and she found the idea borderline terrifying. Her best friend, Elinor, would be joining her in Paris for a cruise up the Seine. But she was doing Paris by herself, so she wasn't being *completely* deceitful.

In the lounge, her new companion seemed to anticipate Mrs. Blossom's questions at every turn, whispering that the food and drinks were free, but it was always nice to tip the woman restocking the buffet. He instructed her to take one of two overstuffed armchairs in a dimly lit corner, then fixed her a plate of crackers and cheese and brought her a glass of red wine. She had never been much of a drinker, but it seemed suitable to the occasion. This was supposed to be a celebratory trip, after all, the start of a new life—whether she wanted one or not.

They exchanged first names—Muriel, Allan—and hometowns. He lived in the suburb of Columbia, Maryland, and she decided to say she was from Baltimore because it was too complicated to explain that she was a Baltimorean who had moved to Arizona to be closer to her grandchildren, but now would be moving back to Baltimore because her son-in-law was being transferred to Tokyo, where she just didn't feel she would fit in, literally or figuratively. Mrs. Blossom had seen videos of the men hired to tuck and push people into the subway at rush hour, and she feared it would make her terribly self-conscious. She didn't like strangers touching her.

Then, of course, there was the simple fact that she had not been invited to relocate with her family to Tokyo. *Real estate is expensive in Japan,* her son-in-law had said. *We can't afford an extra room for you, much less a casita like we have here.*

"Is London your final destination?" Allan asked.

"No, I'm changing planes there and heading to Paris for two weeks. Well, first Paris, then a cruise."

"Do you speak French?"

"Only the kind of French one learned at Notre Dame Prep back in the day. I can ask where the library is and maybe order some sausages."

Allan laughed and Mrs. Blossom blushed, warmed by his—could it be admiration? She did not expect a man like this, a catch by almost anyone's standards, to be interested in her. He must be uncommonly kind, she decided. Which only made her like him more.

"Where are you headed?" she asked.

"London. I'm traveling for work."

"What do you do?"

"I'm a lawyer, the most boring kind, the one who's all about dotting the *i*'s and crossing the *t*'s," he said. "How long is your layover at Heathrow?"

"Just under two hours and all the online sources say that's cutting it a bit close," she said. "I'm a little nervous. That's why I'm traveling with only a carry-on. I hope the weather doesn't cause a delay. If we're even fifteen minutes late —"

"I'll watch over you," he said. "I know all the tricks. Allan Turner's rule number one for overnight flights: When we get on the plane, it will be very tempting to eat and drink more. They serve a full meal, and it's not bad, by airline standards. But if you can, you should try to go straight to sleep. When we land, it will be four thirty a.m. according to our body clocks. If you don't sleep on the plane, you'll be fuzzy all day."

"I've never been able to sleep sitting up," she admitted.

Again, he laughed, but—again—in a way that made her feel enchanting instead of ignorant.

"The seats in business transform into beds. Not the most comfortable beds in the world, but far superior to trying to sleep sitting up."

"How?" she asked. She imagined a wizard, snapping his fingers.

"Don't worry, the flight attendant will show you."

Their flight was called, but Allan put a cautionary hand on her wrist. "We can wait until just before the gate closes, another benefit of business class. No reason to be part of the cattle call at the gate." He looked at her bracelet. "That's so pretty," he said. "I love how one of the charms is a tiny watch. Does every charm tell a story?"

They did. "I have one for each grandchild and a disc for my twenty-fifth wedding anniversary with a sapphire chip."

"It matches your eyes," he said, looking into her eyes and paying no attention to the disc.

"It's my birthstone."

"And is that a golden fortune cookie?" Allan's fingers caressed the last charm that had been added to the bracelet.

"It is—and it even has a fortune."

"What does it say?"

"I'm afraid that's private." She had actually never read it, because Harold had given her the charm the Christmas before he died, not that either of them had any inkling that he would be gone within the year. But she still wasn't ready to read his final words to her. "As for the watch—I could never wear a wristwatch—I am one of those oddballs who scrambles the works—so my late husband came up with this solution."

She felt almost guilty, the way she leaned on that word *late*. Allan said only: "You're no oddball. Let me set it to Paris time for you." His eyes held hers while he turned the tiny stem. It felt strangely, thrillingly intimate.

Once on the flight, she was pleased to see they were next to each other as he had requested, his seat facing toward the front of the plane, hers toward the tail. He showed her the little divider that gave them privacy, then asked if she wanted it up or down. She said she didn't have a preference. She wanted it down, but that seemed too bold.

"I'll keep it down until we're truly under way," Allan said.

And, although he had told her that she should go straight to sleep, he helped himself to a glass of champagne, so she did, too. Then she required a bathroom, but she wasn't sure in which direction to go. Allan seemed to intuit what she needed. He got up and walked toward the tail. Oh, so civilized, the way each seat had its own individual pathway, no crawling over people here in business class. Mrs. Blossom's bladder had to be bursting before she risked trying to get out of her middle seat on a domestic flight.

When Allan returned, she waited three discreet minutes then made her way to the bathroom, which was occupied. She lingered in the small galley space that separated the seating areas, feeling self-conscious under the gaze of the travelers in the economy section. *I'm one of you!* she tried to telegraph, her eyes fixed on her shoes. *The only reason I'm in business is because I'm always early.* Still, it was a relief when she finally was able to use the bathroom. Was she crazy or was there something intimate about using the space that Allan had used only minutes ago?

"You are certifiable, Muriel Blossom," she told her reflection. She recalled Allan saying she probably couldn't take a bad picture. He was wrong about that, *but*—her skin was smooth and relatively unwrinkled. She wished she had put on a little mascara, but she had foregone makeup because she didn't want to sleep in it. Mascara, some eyeliner, really made her eyes pop. But it would be odd to apply it now.

Once she was back at her seat, Allan offered her a pill—a melatonin gummy, he said, a natural sleep aid. When she expressed surprise at how good it tasted, he insisted she take the entire vial, tucking it in her handbag. "You're going to be in Europe much longer than I am. I'll be home by Wednesday. There's no point in me adjusting to local time, but you should try."

She doubted anything could affect her queasy buzz of anticipation and anxiety. What had seemed like a good idea in Phoenix six months ago now seemed foolhardy. *What did she think she was doing? Who did she think she was?* She could practically hear her mother's voice asking the same questions, although her mother also had been gone for a decade now, dying a month after Harold, almost as if she hoped she could upstage him. Mrs. Blossom's devotion to her husband had always irritated her mother.

*Who do you think you are, Muriel Hummel? How can you possibly be thinking of marrying a man you met at a bus stop? Even you can do better than that, don't panic. You're not going to catch Prince Charles's eye, but you can do better than **that**.*

(It was the 1970s, and marrying Prince Charles was still seen as somewhat aspirational. Also, not unprecedented for a Baltimore girl: look at Wallis Warfield Simpson.)

Mrs. Blossom sternly told her mother to pipe down. The trip was beginning propitiously. First the upgrade, now this attentive man, Allan, who seemed determined to make sure she had the best experience possible. It had been so long since anyone had tended to her. She removed her shoes and snuggled under the thin blanket provided, sure she would never fall asleep.

"MURIEL! MURIEL! MURIEL!"

Mrs. Blossom was a cherub, drifting on pink-tinged clouds. She didn't want to leave her cloud; it was peaceful and her name sounded like a hymn as the other cherubs called out to her over and over. She opened her eyes only when she felt someone's hand clutching her upper arm. Such kind eyes, such nice eyes—oh, it was the man from the plane, Allan.

"Muriel, we've arrived late because of the weather delay in Baltimore and you won't be able to make your connection to Paris. You're going to need to rebook your flight, I'm afraid, and I don't think we can get you out until tomorrow."

"What? How?" As he had warned, she felt fuzzy and disoriented. She looked around—goodness, they were the only passengers left on the plane. She checked her watch. "My plane for Paris doesn't leave for another sixty minutes—"

Allan shook his head. "Boarding for international flights closes early at Heathrow. Plus, the line at immigration will take forever because the UK is no longer part of the EU."

"But I don't have luggage to collect, only a carry-on, and I don't think I have to go through immigration because I'm transferring—""

"But you will have to go through security again," he said. "You'll never make it. Trust me. I'll take care of everything."

Trust me—Those weren't exactly the first two words that Mr. Blossom had spoken to her, but they were close. *"You can trust me. I don't bite."* He was holding her shoulders and trying to comfort her because a dog had run into the street and been injured and the two, strangers to each other, had run into the street from different sides, trying to save the poor thing.

What would Harold have advised her to do in this situation? *Let him take care of you,* counseled the Harold who lived in her head, the Harold to whom she still spoke every day. *You have to learn to let others take care of you. Most people are kind if you give them a chance, although no one is as kind and decent as you, Mur.*

That was what he called her, Mur. He knew she hated being named for her mother, who seemed to harbor so much ambivalence toward her only child. That's why she had come to prefer Mrs. Blossom, but obviously, Harold couldn't call her Mrs. Blossom. He called her Mur or, sometimes, Murkat, a play on meerkat, an animal they both loved long before they became famous on that television show *Meerkat Manor*.

She pulled her suitcase from the overhead bin and followed Allan, panicky and overwhelmed. Thank god she had such an experienced traveler to help her rebook her flight. She should not have risked such a short transfer time for her connection.

Yet, beneath her worry and anxiety, she also couldn't help being pleased that she got to spend a little more time with Allan.

"My company has an account here," Allan told Mrs. Blossom as their cab pulled up in front of the St. Pancras Hotel in London.

"I'll cover your room for the night. I can bill it to the firm as a client expense or use my Marriott points. I have more than I could use in a lifetime."

"You shouldn't do that," Mrs. Blossom protested.

"I insist. It's the *least* I can do. I'm afraid that my gummy is what caused you to sleep so soundly."

Allan had been gently insisting on things all morning—and once she had accepted that her plans had been upended, she found that she *loved* it.

"Whenever something goes wrong," Allan said, "I tell myself that I can't be the first person this has happened to, which means there are solutions." She had filed that nugget of wisdom away, grateful for his kindness.

The first thing he did was lead Mrs. Blossom to the "Fast Track" line reserved for business class travelers, then instruct her to wait for him after she had cleared customs, as he had checked a bag and would need additional time.

She waited awkwardly in arrivals for almost an hour, but she couldn't imagine not following Allan's instructions. She tried to distract herself by thinking about the Heathrow scenes in *Love Actually,* although she didn't care for that movie at all. That girl they called plump, what was she, a size ten?

Then Allan appeared. It scared her a little, the way she felt when she saw him, swinging his old-fashioned suitcase by the handle like a schoolboy with his bookbag.

He had then insisted on buying her a ticket for the Heathrow Express. ("Expensive, but worth it.") At Paddington station, he had even asked to take a photo of Mrs. Blossom with the statue of Paddington, somehow intuiting the wish she could never have brought herself to say aloud. She and her grandchildren loved the Paddington movies, and while she felt a little silly, a grown woman standing next to a statue of a bear, she was delighted to have the photo. Allan took quite a few photos, fussing with the lighting, insisting she had no bad angles. "Can I text this one to myself?" he asked at one point, and she nodded bashfully. They were in each other's phones. Even Mrs. Blossom knew that was a milestone of sorts.

For all this hustle and bustle, she remained in a jet-lagged haze that muted her anxiety, the world unusually soft and fuzzy. Twice already she had forgotten to look to the right as she began to step off the curb. Both times, Allan pulled her back, literally saving her life.

And although it was only 11:00 a.m. in London, Allan sweet-talked the hotel into getting her into a room immediately, arranging yet another upgrade—a junior suite for the price of a regular room.

"Oh, there's no need for that, I'm just here for one night—" Mrs. Blossom began.

"I told you, it's on my firm. Now here's the thing," Allan said, handing her a key card. "You will be tempted when you get into the room to fall straight onto that big soft, inviting bed. Don't do it. Power through the day. It's much the best way to get past jet lag. And even if you take the midday train tomorrow, it will be hard to get up if you don't adjust to the time."

"Train? I need to rebook with Air France, then call the cruise company about my change of plans so the driver won't be left waiting for me at the airport there. You told me the concierge could help me do that."

"Yes, but now that I think about it—when you factor in going back to Heathrow tomorrow, how long everything takes there—it's so much easier to go by train. It's right here, at St. Pancras. Only a little over two hours and you arrive in the heart of Paris. It's not quite as convenient since Brexit, but it's still the best way to go in my opinion. We just need to call your travel company and your hotel and explain why you'll be delayed for a day."

"But the train—how, I mean—does it—I mean I know it does, but—" She worried she would sound ignorant if she finished the question.

"Go under the Channel? There's the Chunnel."

"No, I know *that*. But how long is the train underwater?"

"Thirty or forty minutes, I think. Is that a problem?"

It was very much a problem, but Mrs. Blossom didn't know how to tell this kind, handsome stranger about her peculiar brand of claustrophobia. She could endure some small spaces, but she loathed tunnels especially underwater. She had a fear of submarines so pronounced that she had never been able to watch *Das Boot*—and it was one of Mr. Blossom's favorite movies. A train, inside a tunnel, passing beneath a body of water was even worse than a submarine.

She simply would have to find a way to get through the Chunnel part of the trip. *Mind over matter*, she told herself. *Mind over matter*. Part of the reason she had chosen a cruise was because she wanted to push herself outside her comfort zone; the closeness of a ship cabin, even one shared with a good friend, was a test of sorts. But at least she would be on top of the water, not under it.

"Look," Allan said. "Go to your room, take a shower, change if you like, then meet me here in the lobby. I'm going to make sure that you stay up all day. And that you have a wonderful time while doing it."

The room was restful and the bed did call to her, a siren in percale. But Mrs. Blossom did as Allan had told her she must. She showered, delighting in the hotel's soaps and moisturizers. Even before she had been exposed to the unforgiving sun of Arizona, Mrs. Blossom had taken good care of her skin, part of her mother's tutelage. *If you're going to insist on having so much skin, you might as well tend to it properly.*

Shut up, Mother, Mrs. Blossom instructed her cheerfully.

But when she opened her suitcase, she experienced something new and unexpected: a profound dissatisfaction with her wardrobe. Mrs. Blossom liked clothes and had tended toward flowery prints even before her marriage to Harold Blossom. They both enjoyed the silly joke of it, Mrs. Blossom arrayed in blossoms. And since Harold's death, her riotous dresses and blouses had felt like a connection to him. She clung to his favorites, remembering how much he liked her in green/blue hues—"Nice with your eyes." Harold was not a sweet talker, but sweet talkers were overrated in Mrs. Blossom's experience.

Now, surveying the profusion of flowers and colors in her suitcase, she yearned for—*what?* Something different? To be *someone* different? She had always been a relatively contented person, happy in her life and her body. Why would she want to change now?

It had something to do with the way Allan looked at her and treated her. With a sexless affection, as if she were a child, or simple-minded. Appointing himself to be her guardian on this trip. Setting her watch for her, as if she couldn't do that herself. Photographing her with Paddington. His kindness was the type of kindness shown to an incompetent. She wished it was something more.

Oh my. Had that idea really gone through her head? *She wished it was something more.* She couldn't remember ever feeling that way, in all the years since Harold had been gone. Mrs. Blossom believed in soul mates, singular, one per lifetime. To expect more would be greedy, and she was anything but greedy. All her life, she had been cautioned—by her mother, by well-meaning friends, even by strangers—that the worst thing she could do was indulge her appetites. She must never be seen as wanting too much, whether it was food, love, or money.

But certainly there was no harm in a flirtation, not under these circumstances?

She met Allan in the lobby, wearing voluminous pants the color of a perfect pumpkin and a flowery top. He praised her new shoes, orange Allbirds slip-ons. "Pretty," he said, "yet perfect for walking these uneven London streets. Are you up for a lot of walking?"

"I walk five miles a day," she said, waiting for the look of disbelief this usually provoked. Mrs. Blossom had always been active—her first granddaughter had been enormous, and the twins had quite bulbous heads. It had been like carrying around bowling balls. Plus, she had been going to Curves for strength training long before her grandchildren were born. Her mother had suffered from early-onset osteoporosis, bones that looked like Queen Anne's lace in X-rays. But long before her mother's somewhat premature death, Mrs. Blossom had vowed to do whatever it took to be her opposite.

Allan registered no surprise at her declaration. "Take my arm," he said. "These cobblestones can be treacherous." After a second of hesitation, she slipped her hand into the crook of his arm, telling herself that it was no different from walking arm in arm with her friend Elinor. If she clung to him a little more tightly when they crossed the Thames, so be it.

London was disorienting in every sense of the word, but it was a kind of thrilling discombobulation, like being in a movie montage. She barely knew where she was or what was happening, yet she enjoyed everything immensely. Allan took her to visit something called the Eye, a type of Ferris Wheel where they had mimosas at the lounge. He insisted they visit Harrods, which was much too much; her brief desire to change her style was vanquished by the sheer overload of choices. They went to the Tate Modern, where she showed off a bit, chatting to Allan about the twentieth-century abstract expressionists, pleased to have a modicum of expertise in anything, although she had to fake her way through the Philip Guston exhibit. He took her to high tea at the Savoy, cautioning her not to overindulge because he had a surprise for dinner.

True, he was on his phone a lot, but who wasn't these days? In fact, he had two phones, one in each pocket of his trench coat. About every hour or so, one buzzed, soon followed by the other. He checked them, quickly thumbed back his responses, then returned his attention to Mrs. Blossom. "I have one phone on my US plan, another for when I'm traveling in Europe," he told her at one point. "But not everyone can keep it straight."

Dinner turned out to be Gymkhana, an Indian restaurant—a wildly fancy one. They didn't sit down to eat until nine, which normally would be a shock to Mrs. Blossom's system, but it wasn't even dinnertime back in Baltimore. Allan continued his gentle insisting, ordering the tasting menu, including paired wines, which was probably more alcohol than Mrs. Blossom had consumed in the last year. She also worried it would be too much food. People often assumed she had a huge appetite.

But the courses were light and balanced, the wine servings tiny. She didn't feel stuffed or tipsy at all. And Allan was flatteringly focused on her enjoyment.

"Tell me about yourself," he said over the dessert course, a saffron and pistachio dish with a name that made her giggle. She thought she had been talking about herself, but maybe not. Still, what was there to tell? The most interesting thing about her—the source of the money that had paid for this trip—was a story that those closest to her thought she should not share with anyone.

"Why are you being so kind to me?" she asked instead.

"You're the type of person who inspires kindness," he said. "And because—I feel so awful about this—it's my fault you missed your connection."

"You couldn't have known that our plane would be late. Or that I would have such a severe reaction to melatonin."

"That's the thing, the gummy I gave you—it wasn't melatonin."

"Excuse me?"

"It was, well, cannabis. THC." He registered her shock. "All the other gummies in the bottle are melatonin I promise you. It's illegal to travel to the UK with edibles. But I had just the one, nestled among the others, for my personal use. No harm in swallowing it over the Atlantic. I was a little anxious about my meetings this week. However, I decided you needed the gummy more than I did."

Mrs. Blossom was overwhelmed by this revelation, which seemed like something from a Lifetime movie, far worse than anything her friends and family had warned her to be on guard for during this trip. *Hold your purse closely, with the strap crossbody, use a special case for your phone so it can't be cloned, watch for pick-pockets in crowded spaces.* But no one had suggested—her mind, grasping for the right words, could find only the most anachronistic slang—someone might slip her a mickey on the plane.

"You DRUGGED me?"

"You seemed very nervous."

There it was again. Not exactly condescension. But something close. She wanted him to see her as a woman, not as some innocent abroad, in need of caretaking and oversight.

"I'm not incompetent. I can take care of myself."

"Of course you can. I wanted to be helpful because you have lovely manners. I noticed that right away, when I was behind you in line at the ticket counter. I've seen it all day today. You make eye contact, you engage people, you are polite and gracious to everyone. It wasn't an accident that the ticket agent offered you an upgrade."

"But no one ever notices me," she said. "That's why I was such a good private detective."

This surprised him, she could tell. It usually did. "A private detective?" His rich baritone scaled up in wonder.

Shoot, she was gilding the lily a bit. She had worked *for* a private detective years ago in Baltimore, but her primary responsibility had been surveillance, and while she had considered becoming licensed, she had never gotten around to it. She explained as much now, adding: "I'm good at watching people because I'm invisible. Like most women my age."

"I have a hunch," Allan said, "that you're nothing like most women your age. Do you think—would it be possible—for us to stay in touch? We don't live that far from one another. And we are already in each other's phones. In fact, let's make it a date, back in Baltimore. May I take you to dinner later this month? There's a wonderful French bistro on Maryland Avenue that's been written up in *Bon Appétit*."

Mrs. Blossom nodded, suppressing a grin. Oh, she knew all too well that there were men who made such suggestions and never followed through, but there was a specificity to Allan's invitation that seemed sincere. She risked a joke.

"It's the least you can do," she said, "after slipping me that gummy."

April 2

THE CHUNNEL TURNED out to be less formidable than Mrs. Blossom had feared. Her happy, jumbled thoughts were enough to distract her from obsessing over being inside a metal box, inside a tunnel, under a body of water. She was bubbling over with happiness. It was all she could do not to hum out loud.

Oh dear, she *was* humming out loud. And the song was "April in Paris." She had officially lost her mind.

She glanced around the train, wondering if anyone had overheard her. A young man one row back seemed to be staring straight at her. Well, "young man" was a stretch, but younger than she was by at least twenty years. Had he heard her? He looked French to her, with his subtle plaid suit and fashion-forward glasses, tortoiseshell with gold details. Or was he noticing the color in her cheeks? They had been blazing pink, in a state of perpetual embarrassment and excitement since last night, when Allan had asked if they could have a nightcap in her room.

Mrs. Blossom wasn't naive. She knew what such a question usually implied. She just hadn't believed he could be interested in her that way, despite the suggestion of a dinner in Baltimore. But she was open to being wrong and—oh, how glorious—she was.

They had kissed, nothing more, but it was terribly exciting. Saffron- and anise-flavored kisses, deep and soulful, his hands moving over her body but remaining outside her clothes. Mrs. Blossom hadn't been kissed for ten years, and if someone had asked her yesterday morning how she felt about *that*, she would have said it was fine, that it wasn't kissing and sex she missed since Harold had died, but his first-rate company. Someone to eat dinner with, to talk to about the news and family. Someone to watch television or listen to the Orioles on the radio with. She often imagined Harold joking to her that if she had to be a de facto snowbird, couldn't she have ended up in Florida, where the Orioles had spring training, instead of Arizona, home to teams they didn't follow. Conversation, that's what she believed she missed most of all, and she wasn't wrong. She could take care of her sexual needs with the same brisk efficiency she brought to much of her life, setting aside five to ten minutes a few times a week with an excellent appliance that she hadn't dared pack for this trip. (What if her suitcase was searched and she was asked what it was?)

But, as it turned out, she had been missing kisses. Kisses, a man's hands caressing her, the wonderful *inefficiency* of it all. At one point, Allan had kissed her on the right side of the neck, and she had almost swooned, having forgotten this particular pleasure point.

Then, he had done the most romantic thing possible: told her that she must get a good night's sleep. "Do you still have the melatonin?" Adding swiftly, at her look: "I swear to you, all the others are melatonin. I would never have risked bringing THC gummies into the UK, much less exposing *you* to that risk."

"I put them in my dopp kit when I unpacked," she said. "I'll go take one."

She went into the bathroom to change. She wasn't sure if it was the alcohol or all the kisses that had gone to her head. She definitely wouldn't need a pill to sleep tonight. She opened the bottle, looked inside. She was sure Allan wouldn't lie to her, yet the memory of how groggy she had been just fourteen hours ago unnerved her. What if he had included even one extra THC pill among the melatonin, if only by accident? As he had said, they were illegal in the UK, and who knew about France? Some of them looked a bit, well, crustier than the rest. She should probably throw the entire bottle away, but—it had been a gift. From Allan! Besides, if he used her bathroom before leaving, he would see the vial in the wastebasket and that might hurt his feelings.

Also, whatever they were, they clearly helped with sleep. Maybe there was a way she could keep them without risking detection?

She looked at her traveling pill case, in which her daily doses of hormones and calcium were segmented. Nervous about theft while traveling, she had found an ingenious pillbox with a secret compartment, where she kept her most valuable possession, a pair of diamond studs given to her by Harold on their twentieth wedding anniversary.

She had been shocked. "I looked it up—porcelain is the twenti-eth anniversary gift. It's supposed to represent the delicate balance it takes to make it this far. I was going to propose we get a double vanity for the master bath."

"Why wait," Mr. Blossom had said. "You deserve diamonds now."

They hadn't even made it to ruby, the fortieth.. So maybe Harold had been onto something. Or maybe—

She tipped the salmon-colored gummies into the false bottom of her pill case, where they provided a beautiful background for her diamonds, pink courtiers to the shiny perfect couple, which is what everyone believed Mr. and Mrs. Blossom to be, possibly even Mr. Blossom.

Now, what to wear? Her flannel nightgown was matronly, which hadn't bothered her twenty-four hours ago, but oh how she wished she had chosen a simple black or white gown, maybe with a slit up one side or a deeper neckline. It did have pockets, however, so she slid the empty vial into one.

Allan had *then tucked her in* and taken a seat in the armchair near the bed. "I'm going to stay until I'm sure you're asleep," he said. "You have a big day tomorrow. I'd take you to the train station myself if I didn't have meetings."

Really, if it hadn't been for the jet lag and all that Indian food in her stomach, she might have been tempted to have sex with him. But the moment had passed and stopping where they had—well, it put a pin in things, created this shivery sense of anticipation. He had all but made a date with her, back in Baltimore. Would they or wouldn't they? Would he call her today? Should she call him? Strange, but the person she yearned to confide in was her oldest granddaughter, Angie, who was only twelve, but preternaturally worldly. Mrs. Blossom had been mad last year when Angie had created a dating profile for her without her permission, but Angie did seem to understand how things worked now.

Mrs. Blossom liked sex. That was one of the reasons she had married young. She could tell she was someone who could easily go out of control. It was the 1970s, sort of a sexual Harrods; the choices and possibilities overwhelming. Then fate delivered up Harold. And he turned out to be someone with hidden depths and desires, too, at a constant slow simmer. They had been compatible in every way. Of course they had rough patches; you couldn't be married to someone for almost forty years without rough patches.

But he had been an exemplary husband. Her attraction to Allan felt almost like a betrayal.

Now, trapped in the Chunnel, she felt herself blushing at her memories of last night, relatively chaste as it had been. Could this man who was staring at her sense what she had been up to? Gracious, this vacation was not turning out at all as she had expected.

But then, what had she expected? Everything had happened so quickly, back in Arizona. Her son-in-law's announcement—*pronouncement*, presented as a fait accompli—that the family was moving to Tokyo. Mrs. Blossom's decision to return to Baltimore because her family was the only thing tethering her to Phoenix.

And then, out of nowhere, a winning lottery ticket, the cherry on top of the surprise sundae. No, that wasn't quite right, because the ticket was so much bigger than everything else that was happening, more like a—*cantaloupe* on top of a sundae. Her golden ticket. She had, in fact, felt like Charlie Bucket, peeling back the wrapper of his Wonka Bar and seeing that glint of gold that was going to change his life.

Not that Mrs. Blossom played the lottery. The way she saw it, she didn't need to pay someone in order to fantasize about what she would do with millions. She had an imagination; she could indulge in the dream without parting with any money at all. No judgment on those who did play. Not everyone had her talent for fantasy, a talent that had seen her through her often lonely childhood, comforted her in widowhood, and, just that once, gotten her into hot water. Her ability to tell herself lovely little stories that were never going to come true was her minor superpower.

Her new life began on a depressingly hot March day, almost ninety degrees. She had stopped for a fountain Coke at the Circle K closest to her granddaughters' school when she saw a lottery ticket in the parking lot, dancing in the dry, hot breeze, as if desperate to call attention to itself. She hated litter, so she pocketed the ticket and forgot about it.

Then, a week or so later, she read in the paper that a Triple Twist ticket sold at that particular Circle K was worth $8.75 million. She dug the ticket out of her pants pocket and checked the numbers once, twice, three times, ten times. This was the winner, there was no doubt about it.

Oh, how she had agonized. This ticket belonged to someone else; it wasn't her rightful property. She decided to come forward but asked the lottery agency if they would try to find the rightful winner. "How would we do that?" she was asked. "Well, assuming the numbers weren't picked randomly, we could ask someone to tell us what the numbers are and how they chose them."

The person at the lottery agency had a good laugh at that, reminding her that the numbers had already been announced. Mrs. Blossom had the ticket. The money was hers. The state would be happy to keep the prize, if she insisted, but there was no way to find the person who had purchased it. As the Arizona Lottery Commission's own brochure attested, an unsigned lottery ticket should be treated like cash. Mrs. Blossom chose to receive her winnings as a lump sum—a thirty-year annuity seemed a bit optimistic at the age of sixty-eight—and opted to remain anonymous, a choice extended to anyone winning more than $100,000. She had posed for the lottery's website, a giant check blocking her face.

She was grateful for her choices when a woman came forward several weeks later and claimed to have bought the winning ticket. She was about Mrs. Blossom's age and in terrible circumstances, on the verge of eviction from a modest apartment on the city's south side. She spoke tearfully to a television reporter about how she had chosen the numbers, with each one marking a profound personal attachment—mother's birthday, only child's death, the street address of her first home. Mrs. Blossom was touched and on the verge of trying to find a way to give the woman her winnings, when her old boss, Tess Monaghan, intervened: "Let me make a few calls."

Tess contacted a private detective she knew in Arizona, part of a loose consortium of female PIs who communicated via WhatsApp. Within twenty-four hours, the Tucson-based detective had established that the woman was fronting for her nephew, who had, in fact, purchased a lottery ticket at the Circle K where the winning ticket was sold: he had contacted the commission and tried to use the CCTV footage from the store to prove the winning ticket was his, but all it established was that he had bought *a* ticket on the day the winning ticket was sold. Meanwhile, the stories his aunt had told about the ticket didn't check out, something easily proven through public documents. Her mother's birthday, her previous addresses—none of it matched the winning numbers. And there was no dead child at all.

It was true that she was on the verge of eviction, however—because her nephew, who lived with her, wasn't on the lease. He had broken into the coin-operated washer-dryer in the basement, trying to steal quarters, and the landlord was throwing them both out.

"Was I naive to believe that woman?" an embarrassed Mrs. Blossom asked Tess.

"No, because she was on TV, you thought she was vetted," Tess assured her. "The television station was naive to run her story without checking it out. I don't blame them, either—almost every reporter I know has fallen for this kind of sob story. And remember, no one knows that you're the winner, so don't take it personally. You're nobody's fool, but you do tend to think the best of people. Ironically, trust may be the one thing you can no longer afford."

Even after taxes, it was life-changing money for Mrs. Blossom. She bought a new place in Baltimore, at Highfield House no less, a historic mid-century modern building she used to walk by when she lived in a much plainer condo nearby. She gave her daughter money, set up college funds for her granddaughters. If she were careful—and lucky with her health—she would never have to worry about money again. But then, she had never really worried about money before. Practical, responsible Harold had seen to that.

"Watch out for gigolos!" Tess advised when she heard about the trip to France, prompting Mrs. Blossom to giggle. "I'm not kidding. You're an attractive woman, and you have a lot of money. You're planning to travel abroad. READ HENRY JAMES!"

The train burst into daylight. Mrs. Blossom exhaled as if she had been holding her breath for the entire thirty-five minutes underground. She decided to send Allan a polite text, nothing more, thanking him for his kindness in London, adding a photo of herself on the train, as the light was flattering, highlighting the blue of her eyes. Thank you for the Eurostar tip. It worked wonderfully. Should she add a photo to his contact information? Alas, she had failed to take any pictures of him, so she gave him Paddington's face.

There's a French bistro on Maryland Avenue. Let's make a date, later this month. It would be unkind to float that plan and not mean it. But then she remembered that some people lived for that brand of casual cruelty.

Out of the Chunnel, Mrs. Blossom felt as if the rest of the trip took hardly any time at all. She went through immigration with calm efficiency, met the driver that Hart Tours had arranged to take her to Le Bristol. Even with the loss of a day, she would still have time to do all the things she planned to do in Paris before Elinor joined her. Elinor had been to Paris on her second honeymoon, or possibly it was her third. At any rate, she had seen Paris's most famous sights.

"You have arrived on a very special day," the chic young woman at the front desk told Mrs. Blossom. How Mrs. Blossom admired her smooth chignon, the artfully knotted scarf at her neck. Mrs. Blossom would look like a 1970s flight attendant if she attempted such styles.

"Really?" Mrs. Blossom said, feeling as if she must be leading a charmed life. First the chance encounter with Allan, now a special day in Paris.

"Yes," the woman said. "There is a national strike. You will find that transportation throughout the city is limited."

"Oh." Mrs. Blossom was disappointed that the special day was not, in fact, truly special. But she had always planned to walk almost everywhere, so the strike shouldn't affect her. She was intimidated by public transportation in the United States; the thought of attempting it in a foreign country was terrifying.

In her room, she unpacked in full and then, and only then, looked at her phone. No response from Allan. Should she call him? *Non.* Too needy. He had those big meetings, his thoughts were probably on work. She checked the watch charm on her bracelet—how odd, she had thought Paris was an hour ahead of London. Yet the time on her watch matched the time on the digital clock on the bedside table. Her phone agreed, it was 4:00 p.m. here. Oh, wait—Allan had *told* her he was setting her watch to Paris time. Funny, that means she would have been able to make her flight, but he was so frantic and she was so groggy that neither one of them remembered this detail. Thank goodness! The day with Allan in London had been worth starting her trip a day late.

She had reservations at a restaurant called Substance, but she also had been invited to a 5:00 p.m. drinks reception by the hotel manager. If she did that, she would have just enough time for a leisurely stroll up the Champs-Élysées to her dinner.

Leaving the hotel after enjoying a Kir with the manager and a few other guests, she caught a glimpse of a tall, silver-haired man, and for a moment, she thought it might be Allan. She even called out his name, but the man was walking swiftly and quickly disappeared. Oh, goodness, she was being silly. She had kissed someone and now she expected to see him everywhere. Good god, she was much too old to be acting this way. What was the point of *dating* at her age? She had met some men in Arizona who seemed to be courting her, but they were really looking for a caretaker they wouldn't have to pay. There was no point in dating if one wasn't interested in marriage or cohabitation.

Sex, on the other hand—once she was seated in the restaurant, which struck her as hip but not overwhelmingly grand, a cozy jewel box, her thoughts drifted back to last night. Distracted, she was unprepared for the way that the amuse-bouche, which looked like a mushroom, dissolved in her mouth. She cried out in surprise, and people turned toward her, but everyone smiled sweetly, mistaking her surprise for ecstatic enjoyment. That is, everyone turned to look except for one man, seated at the short counter, his face buried in a copy of *Le Monde*, the warm bistro light burnishing his very stylish tortoiseshell-and-gold glasses, the subtle plaid of his suit distinctive even among the fashionable types gathered here.

It was the man from the train.

He was trying to avoid her eyes, she was sure of it. Still, it could be a coincidence, he being in this restaurant. Coincidences happen all the time. She met Mr. Blossom because a dog ran into the street. She had enjoyed a lovely day in London with Allan because she arrived early for her flight. Mrs. Blossom was $8.75 million richer (or had been, before taxes and the purchase of the apartment at Highfield House) because she stopped for a fountain Coke at Circle K.

And maybe it was the culmination of those coincidences that had changed her, made her bolder. She walked over to the man trying to hide behind *Le Monde*, the man from the train, and said: "Weren't you on my train from London today?"

He didn't even bother to raise his eyes from the paper. "Your train?" To her surprise, he was clearly an American. "Do you own the Eurostar?"

Oh, a jokester, someone who thought he could intimidate her by making fun of her. Forty-eight hours ago, this tactic would have worked on her. Not now.

"I was on the one o'clock train out of St. Pancras station to Gare du Nord. You were sitting a row behind me on the other side of the aisle."

His gaze still averted, he opened his mouth, then paused. She sensed, in that pause, that he was deciding whether he could deny what she knew to be true.

"I was on that train today," he said, "but I didn't notice you."

It was possible, of course. As Mrs. Blossom had told Allan, she had been good at surveillance because she was, in effect, invisible. But having done something so out of character as confronting a stranger, she wasn't about to back down. "That's funny because you were staring right at me. You looked at me so hard that I thought I had something in my teeth."

The man smiled. He had shifted his body toward hers and begun making eye contact. They were nice eyes, brown and warm with flecks of gold, the perfect complement to his eyewear. But there also was something calculating in his gaze. "Did you?"

He had the slightest hint of a southern accent. It was charming. That is, Mrs. Blossom felt it was *intended* to be charming, which was something entirely different. She had learned a thing or two about charmers in her life.

"You tell me," she said. An old phrase went through her mind. *Bold as brass.* What did it even mean? "Brassy," whether applied to a woman's personality or hair, was never a compliment. But maybe it should be? After all, it was considered a good thing when a man had brass balls.

"I couldn't see your teeth from where I was sitting, not even when you turned to stare at *me*. You smile with your mouth closed. Has anyone ever told you that? It's barely even a smile."

She shook her head, her brief burst of confidence melting away. She had always been helpless around glib fast-talkers. But it had not escaped her attention how effortlessly, how smoothly, this man contradicted himself. One minute, he was saying he had not seen her; now he was describing her smile and expression, even offering a critique, then claiming it was she who had stared at him.

"Yet you were smiling so much in your own way," the man continued. "You looked as if you were caught up in the most wonderful daydream." He leaned forward, lowered his voice to a conspiratorial whisper. "Your face, it's like a lighted window on a dark night. It's not your mouth that gives you away, but your eyes. Even a stranger can read your thoughts. You need to be careful about that."

Mrs. Blossom tossed her head, a first for her. All her life, she had read books in which girls, women, were forever tossing their heads with great confidence, and she had never understood what that meant. She did now. "Then what am I thinking, right this second?"

"You are thinking *This man should go fuck himself.*"

She blushed. "I would never—"

"OK, maybe not those precise words. But close, am I right?"

The waiter came over. "Perhaps madame and monsieur would like to dine together?"

"Oh no—" Mrs. Blossom began. "Oh, yes," the man interjected, then said something in rapid French. He explained to Mrs. Blossom, "It would be a kindness to the restaurant for us to eat together. The counter is for drop-ins. If I join you at your table for two, they can offer my counter seat to one of the unfortunates without a reservation."

She had no desire to dine with this man, but she couldn't say no, now that he had made the case that it would be the considerate thing to do. Mrs. Blossom was a sucker for the considerate thing to do. Besides, she had felt self-conscious, eating by herself, something she had never done in a fancy restaurant. She felt self-conscious enjoying a quick snack of mozzarella sticks at Arby's.

She returned to her table, aware of her surroundings in the way she had been most of her life—the narrow aisles, the scant margin between the banquette and the table. The man from the train made adjustments without her asking, pulling the table out and to the side, creating enough room for her to slide in gracefully. Maybe he wasn't so bad, after all.

"Danny," he said. "Danny Johnson."

"Muriel Blossom. Of Baltimore."

"Funny, I went to college there, although I live in Atlanta now."

"Hopkins?"

"My parents wish. I went to MICA."

"The art school?"

"Yes. What brings you to Paris?"

"Vacation. You?"

"Same. I did a week in London, went to see all the new musicals on the West End. What did you do in London?"

Musicals, her mind cataloged. Art school. One must not stereotype. Her grandchildren were always jumping on her for making assumptions about people, pigeonholing them, but—*musicals*. Musicals, MICA, and, she couldn't help noticing, the most perfectly groomed eyebrows behind those very fashionable frames.

"Oh—I wasn't really there. I mean I was there, obviously, but it was an unexpected detour of sorts. I missed my connection at Heathrow, so I stayed overnight and took the train."

"But did you not take advantage of your unexpected detour?"

She felt surprisingly protective of that day with Allan—and yet also keen to talk about it, the way one does in the throes of a crush. *Oh, lord, get a grip, Murie! He hasn't even responded to your text.* "I walked, saw the sights. Had a nice Indian dinner."

"Where?" Before she could answer, he laughed and said: "Silly of me. There are good Indian restaurants all over London."

"Oh, of course—" she began, then stopped, embarrassed.

"Of course, what?" He arched an eyebrow. His eyebrows were eerily perfect. He must have them waxed to achieve that shape and symmetry. Goodness—were they *gelled*?

"Nothing," she said.

"You were going to say I must like Indian food because I'm Indian. It's OK. I was born in the United States. In Baltimore, in fact, although my mother and I left there when I was young. My father is Pakistani, my mother is British. I have multiple passports, not a bad thing in these turbulent times."

Well *this* was a conversational minefield. Mrs. Blossom often felt that way as of late. There were so many things one was no longer supposed to say, as her daughter and grandchildren kept explaining to her. She was fine with that; she never wanted to give offense or seem ignorant. She just wasn't sure what should be said in place of the things one used to say. She had narrowly avoided asking Danny Johnson if he was Indian and been spared from making the mistake of asking *What are you then,* because he had graciously provided the information. She was sitting opposite an American-Pakistani-British man and she was absolutely tongue-tied.

"Atlanta," she said at last. "Do you like it? I was there only once with my late husband. We went to this hamburger chain that he loved, a place he knew from his childhood when they used to drive all the way to Columbus, Georgia, to visit family, making the trip in just one day. This burger place was a big deal to him. But I confess, I didn't understand why he loved it."

"The Varsity?" Danny queried. She shook her head. "Krystal?"

"That was it!"

"There are people who are devoted to it," he said, "but it's a mystery to me, too. When I'm home, I head straight to Steak 'n Shake. But this place is almost as good."

He raised a forkful of agnolotti and mushrooms, the fourth course in the tasting menu. There were eight courses in all, but they were tiny, no more than a bite or two.

I'm having dinner with a strange man for the second night in a row, Mrs. Blossom realized, astonished at herself. Not that she had the same kind of spark with this man. He was much too young and—OK, she was just going to say it, in the privacy of her own brain—almost certainly gay. His clothing was impossibly perfect. Crisp white shirt, that plaid suit, a pale green tie with—were those little rocking horses? He seemed particularly interested in clothes in general, studying the other diners, rating their outfits as if he were a judge on a reality show. At one point, he even asked if he could touch the fabric of her top, palpating the sleeve between his fingers like a doctor probing a mysterious bump.

"I get that you're going on one of those river cruises," he said, because she had shared her travel plans by then. "And I understand that what you're wearing is practical for travel, living out of a suitcase in a small cabin. But wrinkle-free isn't a *style*. You should have some beautiful caftans. Not for during the day, but they would be perfect for dinner."

"*Caftans*," she said, not bothering to hide her irritation. "Everyone's always trying to put me in caftans."

"You think I'm making a comment on your size," he said. "I'm not. I'm focused on your *potential*. Caftans, good ones, are gorgeous and never go out of fashion. Also, you should wear much lower necklines, in general. Your decolletage—what I can see of it in that abomination of a shirt—is extraordinary. Your skin, in general—" He did a chef's kiss. "What's your skin care regimen?"

Mrs. Blossom was also tired of hearing about her skin. Fat women are forever hearing about their nice skin.

"Pond's cold cream," she said. "Then Oil of Olay. Sunscreen every day."

"Amazing," he said. "How I wish I had time to take you shopping in Paris. I'm a stylist," he added, picking up on her confusion. He talked so fast, this man, and jumped so quickly from topic to topic. It was like dancing with someone who kept twirling and dipping you—and not in a good way. "I was in Paris for Fashion Week, ran up to London for fun, now I'm back doing personal shopping."

"I thought you said you were on vacation?"

"Well, Paris is always a vacation, *mais non*? Most of my clients, I'm afraid, try to look too young, obsess over trends. I'm forever reining them in. You, Muriel Blossom—you are trying to look older than you are. No—it's even worse. You're trying to look like *nothing*. Your clothes are *anti*fashion. You really need to let loose."

She blushed, remembering just how loose she had let herself be the previous night. But she would never speak about such things to this stranger.

The check came and she insisted on paying for both of their meals, although she almost fainted at the amount. She and Harold had never managed to spend this much at dinner, not even the time they went to the Prime Rib for their thirty-fifth wedding anniversary. She expected Danny to fight her for the check, but he let it go easily, as if he were accustomed to people buying him dinner. Well, he did, by his account, work for wealthy women.

It was dark now, and when Danny said he would walk her to her hotel, Mrs. Blossom found the offer gallant and nonthreatening. He was nothing if not entertaining, darting from topic to topic with his rapid, gossipy chatter. That said, she was looking forward to being alone in her hotel, falling asleep to her memories of Allan.

"Fancy!" he said when they arrived at Le Bristol. "Oh, and so many good shops nearby. Maybe we could figure out a way to work out a visit to some of them."

"I don't need a stylist. Besides, I can't afford one." Except maybe she could? No, she had to be practical. Life was long, if one was lucky, and always uncertain. Never touch your principal had been Harold's ironclad law.

"Hmmmm, what if this stylist offered to work for one perfect almond croissant and a cup of espresso?"

If something is too good to be true, Muriel, then it is. That was her mother's sour voice again, still castigating her across the years. Yet even her old boss, Tess Monaghan, who thought well of Mrs. Blossom, had warned her to be more skeptical of people. The hotel, her insistence on paying for dinner—he might think she was richer than she was.

"I'm not going to buy an entire new wardrobe," she said stiffly.

"I'm happy with what I have. I planned my outfits carefully for this trip and I like them, even if you don't."

"Just one nice dress?" he wheedled. "Tell me you'll think about it. Something for the captain's dinner, assuming they have a captain's dinner on river cruises?" He made the last two words sound disreputable.

She turned to shake his hand outside the hotel's front door, her way of indicating he should not follow her into the lobby. She did not want to prolong *this* encounter with an after-dinner drink, not that it seemed likely.

Danny ignored her outstretched hand, his eyes sliding past her to focus on a group of people milling in the lobby. "Something's up," he said, and he pushed past her into the hotel, his good manners forgotten. Ugh, a rubbernecker, someone who was excited by others' turmoil. Mrs. Blossom had no use for such people.

It never occurred to her that the hubbub could have anything to do with her.

There were two uniformed policemen and one suited man in a huddle, talking to the front desk clerk, and a petite woman in a black dress, whom Mrs. Blossom recognized as the hotel manager. She had introduced Mrs. Blossom to the Bristol's resident cat at the drinks reception earlier today, shared the history of the hotel.

Everyone in the huddle turned toward Mrs. Blossom as if they had been waiting for her. In that split second, a handful of worst-case scenarios filled her mind. *Her daughter, one of the grandchildren. Elinor.*

"Muriel Blossom?" one officer asked.

"Yes." She felt the world go wobbly.

"Do you know a man named Allan Turner?"

She did and yet she didn't. That is—she knew *a* man named Allan Turner, but perhaps they were asking about a different Allan Turner. Besides, what did it mean to know someone? And why would police officers care? It wasn't against the law to spend a day with a pleasant stranger.

"Um—sort of."

"Sort of?" This was the woman, the manager that Mrs. Blossom had met at the drinks reception. Her English was much better than the officer's.

"I met him on the flight from Baltimore to London and we shared a meal in London. He had work there." She couldn't help wondering if Danny, who remained by her side—such a nosy parker—noticed the discrepancy between what she told the police and what she had implied to him.

"And you texted him this afternoon?"

"Yes, from the train today." Thank god, she thought, that her text was generically polite. Still, it made her blush that the police knew about their communication. Also—*how* did the police know this?

"And he remained in London? To the best of your knowledge?"

"To the best of my knowledge." She felt dim, repeating his words. "He had meetings on Monday."

"Do you know his family? Anyone he might be close to?"

Danny leaned in, began speaking in French. The officer retorted, seemingly miffed by whatever point Danny was trying to make. He held up a hand, as if to indicate Danny should stop talking, and turned back to Mrs. Blossom.

"I'm sorry, but I have to deliver bad news. Mr. Turner died this afternoon. Here, in Paris, not that far from you."

"D-d-d-ied—?"

"He fell from the balcony of his hotel room at the Opera Ambassador."

In her grief and shock, she found herself asking the stupidest question possible. "Is that a Marriott hotel? Because he told me that he had a lot of points."

"Perhaps, madame. It was a nonsmoking room and he stepped out on the—I believe you would call it a Juliet balcony—to enjoy a cigar and a little brandy. And he just went . . . over."

She thought of the silver-haired man who seemed to pick up his pace when she called Allan's name. *Had she—? Could she—?* Her feelings were a jumble, and she did not want to react too strongly, given that she had told the police she had barely known him. But there had been a promise there, she was sure of it. She had believed she would see him again, that they would follow up on what they had started. It was, perhaps, a pure fantasy on her part, but it had seemed a harmless one. To have this possibility snuffed out because of a freak accident—

She thought again of the person who had lost the lottery ticket. Had it felt like this? To be so close to something wonderful, only to have it snatched away? She knew Langston Hughes's famous lines about a dream deferred, but this felt like a big beautiful balloon popping. Something gave way inside her. A nice man, a man who had been kind to her, who wanted to see her again—dead.

"And you came to talk to me just because I texted him?"

"We came to talk to you because the last text he sent from his phone was to an unknown number—and it was accompanied by a location marker for this hotel, along with your name and photograph."

"May I see?" Mrs. Blossom asked, her voice squeaking annoyingly.

"I will show you the copy I have on my phone." The police officer held out his screen. It was her selfie, taken on the train. Beneath it was her name, the hotel's address, and a short message:

A very nice lady, she has your eyes.

"What does *that* mean?" Mrs. Blossom asked.

"Maybe he was sending it to his mother?" Danny offered. "You probably reminded him of her." Mrs. Blossom added *catty* to the rolling list in her head. Catty, perfect eyebrows, stylish glasses, musicals, obsessed with clothes. Allan may have been a tad younger than Mrs. Blossom was, but he was *nowhere close* enough to being her son, for goodness' sake.

Besides, Danny couldn't know the age of the dead man.

"I think," the police officer said, "that we should accompany you to your room. Just to make sure no one else is there."

No one was lying in wait in Mrs. Blossom's room. It was exactly as she had left it—her empty suitcase on the luggage rack, her clothes put away neatly in the closet and its built-in chest of drawers.

"You could do better," Danny said, looking at the black dress hanging in the closet, the one she planned to wear on her splurge meal with Elinor on the last night in Paris. He was unabashedly whisking through the hangers, inspecting all her clothes. She wouldn't be surprised if he started pawing through her underwear drawer.

Why are you even here? she wanted to ask.

The policeman did ask. "Why are you here? Who are you?"

"Her son." Danny's lie was swift and smooth, and Mrs. Blossom was too shocked to contradict hm. "I'm not staying here, though.

Mom's got bucks, but I'm traveling on my employer's dime, and they're tight."

The police officer looked from Mrs. Blossom to Danny and back again.

"My father's genes were very dominant," Danny added.

"May I see some identification?"

Danny pulled what appeared to be a driver's license from his wallet.

"Ah, OK—but why are your surnames different?"

"She married Mr. Blossom after my father died. I can see why you're confused. She looks much too young to be my mother."

There he went again, jumping from comparing her to Allan's mother to claiming she looked too young to be *his* mother. Mrs. Blossom was almost flattered. That is, she would have been flattered if she hadn't been terrified by this man having just lied to the authorities, and she had been too tongue-tied to stop him. And now it was too late to set the record straight. It was all too much. This strange man pretending to be her son. Allan, dead, falling from his hotel balcony. In Paris, when he said he had business in London. He had sent her photo and location to someone. What the frick was going on?

It was a long evening. The police allowed her to identify Allan via a photograph of his strangely undamaged face, but seeing him on a gurney was distressing enough. They took her to the station, and Danny followed, because what else would a good son do in this situation? She told them everything. Well, *almost* everything. She told them she had met Allan on the flight to London, that he had arranged for her lodging when she missed her connection, then helped her book the train to Paris. She told them they had done some sightseeing and dined together in London. But she could not, would not, tell them about champagne at the Eye, the Tate, tea at the Savoy, dinner at Gymkhana, the kisses in her hotel room. The kisses, in particular, did not seem relevant—it's not as if Allan had followed her to Paris in a haze of love. (*Had he followed her to Paris in a haze of love? Don't be ridiculous, Muriel.*)

Danny walked her back to the hotel. She didn't want him to, but she also didn't *not* want him to. Her body had finally triumphed over the jet lag, but the events of the day had left her mind muddled.

"Why are you keeping so close to me?" she asked.

"I was worried about you. I was ready to call the US Embassy if things got weird."

"Weird, how?"

"What if they didn't think it was an accident? What if they had accused you of pushing Allan out that window? What would you have done? Whom would you have called?"

"*They* said it was an accident." Mrs. Blossom had led the kind of life that allowed her to still put her trust in police officers. "Besides, why would I kill Allan? Why would anyone kill Allan?"

"I don't know," Danny said. "Have you really told the police—and me—everything you know about him?"

The question spooked her. Yes, the police probably deserved to know more than she had told them. Danny, however, did not.

"I shared everything that matters," she said. "You were the one who put me at risk, lying about being my son. I was so confused I didn't say anything at first, then it seemed dangerous to correct you after letting it go."

"I told you—I wanted to look after you. I couldn't fake being your lawyer. I thought about saying I was your boyfriend—classic story, right, wealthy widow and younger man—but I didn't think you would like that." Mrs. Blossom blushed. He was right about this at least. "So I said I was your son. Look—I don't think you've focused on the most important part. Why would Allan Turner share your photo and location? And with whom?"

Mrs. Blossom didn't think this was important at all. Or, at least, she didn't find it ominous. In fact, it cheered her a little, thinking that Allan had wanted to share her photograph with someone. She wished she could break away from Danny and keep walking on her own, alone with her thoughts—but she actually had no idea where she was going, and her phone had died.

"Oh, I'm sure it was an accident. I'm forever texting people my location by mistake. Once, I thought I was texting my grandkids, and I sent a GIF to my dental practice that had just texted me about an appointment. They were so confused when they got a video of a dancing cat."

"Of course you do dancing cat memes." Danny made a face. "At any rate, I don't think this was a random mishap. He wanted someone to know where you are. Is it possible that Allan put something in your luggage? Have you heard of 'mules'?"

Her indignation was automatic. "Of course I have, but Allan never had access to my suitcase." She realized this was not exactly true. "I mean, yes, he helped me with my bag at the airport. And, well, he did stop by my room after dinner. For a nightcap. And I did have to use the bathroom while he was there." She chose not to tell him that she had fallen asleep while Allan sat in an armchair, watching over her. That was a tender memory. She wasn't going to let this man—really, a stranger, someone who seemed far more suspicious than Allan—destroy it.

Danny inspected her with seeming admiration. "Look at you, Mrs. Blossom. On the prowl."

She blushed. "I am not. *Was* not. He was a perfect gentleman."

He was, she thought. You could be a gentleman while kissing someone.

"If he had put something in my luggage," she said, "I would have noticed it by now. I've unpacked thoroughly because I'm here almost a week."

"By *now*," Danny said. "After the police took you to your room and you inspected your luggage. Who knows if someone was in your room while you were at dinner. The restaurant, where we met—did Allan suggest it? Did he book it for you?"

"No," she said, affronted. "I made that reservation myself, weeks ago, after reading it about it in *Bon Appétit*." She did not, in fact, read *Bon Appétit*, but she had googled her way to its recommendations for dining in Paris.

"Did you mention your plans to Allan?"

She was about to say no, then she realized she had. In the overwhelming splendor of Gymkhana, she had wanted to convey to Allan that she was no rube. She had told him about Le Bristol, and all her dining reservations, even some of her more adventurous sightseeing plans—a visit to the current exhibit at the Louis Vuitton Foundation, a day trip that she had planned on her own. She had wanted to impress him.

"*Maybe*," she allowed. "But it's not like I opened my Filofax and showed him the time I had booked."

"Was he ever alone with your Filofax? Do you carry it in your purse? Could he have sneaked a peek at it?"

"You ask more questions than the police. Are you really a stylist?"

Danny laughed. "I an excellent stylist and all good stylists are busybodies. I ask my clients a thousand questions in order to create the stories they want to tell."

"Stories? Don't you just pick out clothes?"

For once, Danny looked to be offended. "Clothes are narratives, our first chapters. Before we open our mouths, we have told people a dozen things about ourselves. Let me take you shopping tomorrow and prove to you I am who I say I am."

"I told you—I have all the clothes I need."

"*Need*, perhaps, but not the clothes you deserve. Your look is so Ann Taylor."

"It is not," she said. As if Mrs. Blossom could fit into Ann Taylor—the clothes there went only to a size eighteen.

"The point is," Danny said, "you should be dressing like *Elizabeth* Taylor. You're all breast from clavicle to waist. Let's work with that."

"Let's not," Mrs. Blossom said. "Besides, why would I believe anything you say, when you just lied to the police a dozen times over?"

"Because," Danny said, "I'm always right in matters of taste and I can be delightful company, given a chance. I only lied to the police because I wanted to be able to help you. You don't speak the language, you don't know the legal system here."

"Hmmpfh," Mrs. Blossom said, unconvinced. She stumbled on the curb and Danny grabbed her elbow, steadying her.

"I want to start over, you and me. We've had a shaky beginning, but I'm a good person to know. You'll see. And I have a feeling that you're a good person to know, too."

They had finally reached Le Bristol. He held out his hand. She accepted the offer of a handshake, noting that his manicure was better than hers. This was a man who cared about appearances.

Which, in Mrs. Blossom's experience, meant a person who had something to hide.

"I THOUGHT WE were going to a department store," Mrs. Blossom said, trying to disguise the fact that she was out of breath.

They had been walking for what seemed like miles since they set out after breakfast. (Separate ones. Mrs. Blossom's meal was included with her room rate and she wouldn't dream of missing it. Such lovely scrambled eggs with salmon.) Mrs. Blossom happened to have amazing stamina, and she was wearing her reliable Allbirds, but the neighborhood Danny was leading her through at a fast clip did not look at all like what she imagined a Parisian shopping district should be.

"I gave it some thought overnight," Danny said. "While I love Galeries Lafayette, it will have limited selections in your size. Then I remembered I know someone—she used to be at Marina Rinaldi, but she's gone out on her own, and she specializes in plus-size couture. She's agreed to see us in her atelier."

Mrs. Blossom wanted to profess indignation at his high-handedness. *How dare he change the plan without consulting her? What if she didn't like the designer he had chosen? Who or what was Marina Rinaldi?* But Danny's reasoning was sound: She seldom found a good selection in department stores. Then again, how quickly could someone make a couture outfit? Even on *Project Runway*, they needed at least forty-eight hours.

The "atelier"—such a lovely word, she filed it away to use airily when describing this adventure to her family—was on the third floor, which the French insisted on calling the second. Still, Mrs. Blossom chose to take the stairs when she saw how small the old-fashioned elevator was. She was worried the space would be uncomfortably cramped for two people.

There was no name on the door, only a number, but the studio behind the door looked like the home of a serious professional. Bolts of fabric were stored according to color and pattern, while other materials were kept in rows and rows of clear bins. And while the only window faced on an interior courtyard, the light was quite good, so that Mrs. Blossom could see the place was as clean as it was neat. The same could be said about Danny's friend, who wore a simple white blouse and black slacks that she had clearly tailored to fit her perfectly.

Mrs. Blossom expected a designer specializing in plus-size clothing to be someone her size, because who else would be interested in making plus-size clothes? But the woman to whom Danny introduced her, Cece, was tiny—maybe five feet, her weight not even in the triple digits.

The personality, however, was enormous.

Cece immediately put Mrs. Blossom on a pedestal and circled her, talking out loud, describing her as if she couldn't hear.

"Really lovely skin, you were right about that, Danny, and such good posture. Do you always wear your hair that way?"

That way was a chin-length bob, Mrs. Blossom's style for—oh goodness—thirty years. "What other way would I wear it?"

"I mean, pick a lane, as you say."

"I never say *that*," said Mrs. Blossom.

Cece shrugged. It was, to Mrs. Blossom's way of thinking, an extremely Gallic shrug. "When I see a woman with this haircut, what I see is someone saying, *I'm old, don't look at me, I've given up, as far as I'm concerned, hair is just there to keep my scalp warm.* It's a nonchoice. You have the bone structure to go very short—if you let me, I would chop it all off right now."

Mrs. Blossom instinctively put her hands to her head, which made Cece laugh.

"Don't worry, I will not cut it off. And it's not like I could make it grow just by shouting at it."

Mrs. Blossom wasn't so sure about that.

Cece reached up and took a tendril in her hand, not bothering to ask for permission, which normally would have annoyed Mrs. Blossom. But there was something about this woman that inspired trust.

"There's some wave here, though, if you would grow it out a little, use some product," Cece muttered. "Not beachy waves, exactly, I hate that term, but something soft and flattering. Also, if you grew it out, you could do a chignon and that's always a chic option. You know, even hair this short can achieve an updo—"

Danny was not scared to interrupt this runaway train of a woman. "Cece—we came here for a dress, not a makeover."

"I can't send her off with one of my dresses if she doesn't know how to pull it off."

Mrs. Blossom felt she needed to assert for herself. "I'm standing right here," she said. "I have opinions about what I should wear. I might not"— she didn't want to be rude, but apparently she was the only one in the room who worried about that—"I might not be able to find anything here that suits me."

"Oh, you will," Cece said. "But, Danny, promise me, you will make her buy shoes, beautiful ones, to go with the dress. Meanwhile—" She left the room and came back with a wig so platinum it was almost white.

"Oh, thank you, but I'm not a wig person—"

"Well, now you are," Cece said. "That's a good quality wig. You'll want a cap to wear with it. It's yours. You can send it back to me once you grow your hair out."

Mrs. Blossom turned and faced her own reflection. *I look ridiculous*, she thought. And then—*wait a minute—maybe I look good?* She didn't spend a lot of time studying her face in mirrors. She wasn't a teenager, after all; she had things to do. And by the time one is in one's sixties, there's no question that one has lived more years than one has left. Mirrors were another reminder of one's mortality. Photographs, too, which she also avoided.

Not with Allan, a wistful voice in her head reminded her. She had let him take all he wanted. Why hadn't she thought to take a single photograph of him?

But there were things, good things, she had forgotten about this old friend looking back at her. The blue of her eyes, made more startling by the platinum wig. She had almost no frown lines because she didn't frown that much. She was a happy person. That is—she had thought of herself as happy, but maybe it was more correct to say that she was a *contented* person and that had always been good enough. Until that Saturday in London—good lord, it was only two nights ago—when she had glimpsed, or thought she had glimpsed, the possibility of something more for the first time in ten years. Now that tiny hope had been extinguished. Worse, Danny's rude theories about Allan's death had made her wonder if he was interested in her at all. She had stayed up late last night, examining ever cranny and crevice in her luggage, searching the pockets of her clothes, and coming up empty. So she wasn't a mule, unless—what if *Allan* had been in her room? Had he retrieved something while she was at dinner? Was he the man she saw while leaving Le Bristol yesterday? Then why hadn't he turned around when she called his name?

"OK, strip," Cece said. "Everything off. I'm sure you'll need underwear completely different from what you're wearing. Don't worry, I keep an inventory of new things, it won't be used. And it won't be anything that nips at you, or tries to hold anything in. No *shapewear*." She made the last word sound like an obscenity. "Just beautiful, comfortable things that don't produce lines."

"*What?*" She was supposed to get naked? In front of someone she had met five minutes ago?

"Don't worry, I won't let Danny stay for this part. In fact, make yourself useful and go get us espressos, Danny. Mrs. Blossom will need energy for this, although I'm pretty sure I know exactly which dress will look best. It will probably require a few small alterations, but the color is perfect. And I have a robe for you to wear while I'm hemming."

By the time Danny returned with the coffees, Mrs. Blossom was wearing, yes, a caftan. But *what* a caftan. It had broad vertical stripes, a plunging V-neckline, and a slit almost to midthigh, but only on the left side, which somehow seemed classier than two slits. The sleeves were a solid plum color with bands of gold at the wrist.

Cece also had removed the wig and showed Mrs. Blossom how to coax her hair into a reasonable facsimile of an updo. "It's OK that you have some tendrils at the neck," Cece assured her. "It just makes you look sexier."

Danny gave a long, low whistle. Not a wolf whistle, not a Tex Avery *aHOOga*. This was a respectful whistle, if such a thing were still possible.

Still, Cece was not through. Mrs. Blossom had a feeling that Cece was never going to be through with her. "You should wear *huge* hoops with this. Preferably in gold, but fake is fine. Shiny is what matters. Or, you could wear diamond studs if you have them—"

"I do," Mrs. Blossom said, excited that she owned something, anything, of which Cece might approve.

"—but then you want an *enormous* cuff. They have amazing ones in resin. I would love to see you in a strappy high heel, but I suppose that's too much to ask. There are really comfortable slides and wedges; you'd be surprised, you can get the height you want and still be able to walk quite comfortably. I'll write all this down for Danny, not to worry."

"What do you mean?"

"I won't let that beautiful dress go out of here with you unless you promise to accessorize it properly. I'm on to you, Mrs. Blossom. You will 'mouse' it up. You're not used to all eyes being on you. In this dress, they will be."

"No," she said. "No dress can do that. Not for me, not at my age."

Cece shrugged. "Well, if that's what you believe, that's what will be true. Still—this is my creation, and I expect it to be respected. Danny, I am counting on you to make sure she has what she needs."

Danny nodded, sipping his espresso, his eyes bright with admiration. For a moment, Mrs. Blossom wondered if this whole expedition was a way to take her mind off Allan. Then she remembered that Danny didn't know that Allan was anything more than an acquaintance to her.

Danny kept his promise to Cece, and more. By midafternoon, Mrs. Blossom had a pair of new shoes (bright fuchsia wedges that uncannily matched one of the stripes in the caftan, which had required only hemming and slight changes to the darts in the bodice), a vintage cuff in rose gold, and a giant bangle in black resin. He also had persuaded her to buy hoop earrings—"Costume," he said, "are fine if you're not allergic." Finally, he had even persuaded her to "invest" in a scarf and a pair of sunglasses that seemed outrageously overpriced. "But you will wear them every day," Danny said. "It's no different from having a daily Starbucks."

"I make my own coffee," Mrs. Blossom said.

"I bet you do," Danny said. "In a Mr. Coffee. No French press or fancy espresso machines for Muriel Blossom."

"A Proctor Silex," she said. "I've had it for more than twenty years."

"Time for an upgrade, no? Spring for a Nespresso machine at the very least."

"*No*," she said, more sharply than intended. She had, according to her calculations, made Harold more than fifteen thousand cups of coffee in that bright red Proctor Silex. She had made more than three thousand pots of coffee since Harold had died, yet she felt a closeness to her husband every day when she pushed the button to start brewing. She used his favorite mug. It wasn't anything special, a large white cup with three blue stripes circling the top. But for the twenty or so minutes she held it in her hand, she relived those thousands of breakfasts, silent but happy meals spent with the *Beacon-Light*—sports for him, the front page and the living section for her. She had never taken her husband for granted, not exactly, but she also had never imagined he would be gone before she turned sixty. So much had been left undone, unsaid.

"Speaking of coffee—aren't you hungry? We shopped through lunch."

"A bite would be nice. I do feel as if I wasted the day."

"*Wasted*? You have put together a chic outfit and bought enough accessories to amp up the rest of your wardrobe. That's a very good use of a day."

"But I'm in *Paris*."

"Yes, the perfect place to pick a new outfit."

"But I meant to go to the Louvre today and then—"

"If you say the Eiffel Tower, I'll cry."

"Why? I'm a tourist, this is my first time here. Why wouldn't I do the tourist-y things? Didn't you, the first time you came here?"

Danny laughed. "Fair enough, although I was twelve. Now let's get falafel."

"*Falafel*? In France?"

"Trust me, you'll love it."

Danny walked swiftly, but it wasn't his pace that Mrs. Blossom found challenging, more the etiquette of trying to navigate the crowded sidewalks in the Marais District. It was a relief when he turned down a broad, cobblestoned pedestrian path, although there were still throngs of people. Within a few blocks, he joined a queue of almost twenty people outside a forest-green storefront with bright yellow trim.

"We're lucky to be here sort of off-hours," he said. "The line's not too bad. You prefer takeaway, yes?"

She glanced through the windows. The restaurant was small, with fragile-looking chairs. "Yes," she said. "Takeaway."

A man moved down the line, jotting down orders to speed up the process at the register. Danny ordered for them both, the falafel special, adding two cans of Coca-Cola. He must think her quite the typical American, Mrs. Blossom thought. But when they got to the window and were asked if they wanted their sandwiches spicy or mild, Danny didn't hesitate to ask for two spicy ones, which pleased her. She might be timid about many things, but food was not among them.

They settled with their overstuffed pitas on benches in a nearby playground. So far, April in Paris was on the chilly side. Peeling back the paper on her sandwich, Mrs. Blossom realized she was famished. The sandwiches reminded her of a Baltimore restaurant she had loved, Cypriana, which was within walking distance of her new apartment. *Oh, yes, Danny Johnson, I know my way around a falafel.*

"Did you get enough?" Danny asked. Pigeons had gathered at their feet, only to be disappointed by the two fastidious eaters who didn't drop so much as a crumb.

"I don't eat *that* much," Mrs. Blossom said.

"Hey, I was just trying to make sure you were OK. I know I've run you a little ragged today. And, well, you've been through a lot. The police, this dead man you barely knew—"

He paused, almost as if he expected Mrs. Blossom to contradict him. The weird thing was, she wanted to. She wanted to tell someone, anyone, about the amazing twenty-four hours she had spent with Allan. She wanted to rehash his comment about the French restaurant on Maryland Avenue, ask if it sounded like a real date or an empty gesture that he had no intention of following through on. She had been looking forward to regaling her friend Elinor with the story. She had imagined them walking together along the Seine, arm in arm. She wouldn't bring it up right away. They would exhaust the usual topics—her grandkids, Elinor's gardening, health, aches and pains, favorite television shows, widowhood—and then Mrs. Blossom would begin, *"Actually the most amazing thing happened to me on the trip over—"*

The problem was, the story she had anticipated telling didn't end with a man falling to his death from his hotel balcony while trying to enjoy a cigar. An accident, the police had said, and she didn't see why she should doubt them. Stranger things had happened. Stranger things happened every day.

"When did you know—" she began, then stopped, realizing there was no polite way to ask what she wanted to ask. But she had a hunch that one of her grandchildren was moving toward what Mrs. Blossom thought of as a "more nuanced" sexual identity and she was curious about the journey ahead.

"Yes?"

"Um, that you liked . . . fashion?"

"I was five," he said. "My parents were going to a wedding, and I saw my father in a sherwani for the first time. God, he was so elegant. My best and almost my last memory of him. My parents broke up when I was six."

"I'm sorry."

"It happens. Anyway, that and the montage in *The Devil Wears Prada*, which I could watch every day for the rest of my life. Clothes are powerful. They tell stories. They tell the story of who we think we are—or, more precisely, who we want others to think we are. Before you open your mouth, your appearance has already conveyed so much, whether you want it to or not. Oh, we pay lip service to the idea that we don't judge books by their covers, but of course we do, literally and figuratively. I think people like myself learn that earlier than most."

People like myself—she wondered if he was referring to his ethnicity or sexuality. But one must not ask. Besides, she wasn't sure she agreed.

"Oh, come on," she said. "Clothes are utilitarian. Sometimes a dress is just a dress."

He laughed. "As in sometimes a cigar is just a cigar? OK, fine. But even the absence of a story is a story, if you think about it."

"What story were my clothes telling, when you saw me on the train?"

"You were saying you don't want people to look at you."

"I wear bright colors," she protested. "And prints. I'm not trying to fade into the woodwork."

"Yes, exactly. You want people to notice the colors, the patterns, but not *you*, the woman inside the clothes. You've talked about being invisible, as if it's something that happened to you, passively. Did it ever occur to you that, as Cece suggested, you are trying not to be seen?"

"No, you're wrong. This isn't something I willed for myself. People simply don't see me. You'll understand when you're older. It was an asset in my job."

"What was that?"

She decided to be more truthful with Danny than she had been with Allan. After all, she had no need to impress Danny.

"Soon after my husband died, I met a private investigator and ended up helping out in her office, mainly with surveillance. I was quite good at it. I even thought about getting licensed, but then my daughter started having babies and I moved to Phoenix to help, living in the casita on their property so she could go back to work. Anyway, who cares if anyone notices me?"

"I care," he said.

"Why?"

"You remind me of my mom."

Of course. It was all she could do not to sigh.

"Let me guess. She was" Mrs. Blossom paused, considering and rejecting several words—"my size."

He shook his head. "No, she was extremely thin. But she could never be thin enough, not for herself. She was forever dieting. She was anorexic, but no one dared to say that out loud until it was too late. It was as if she didn't want to take up any space at all. And now she doesn't. She died from heart failure, probably caused by her eating disorder."

He looked straight ahead, avoiding her gaze, keeping his eyes wide open, like a child trying not to cry.

"I'm sorry, Danny. How long has it been?"

"Three years. She didn't live to see—I'm sorry. I didn't mean for our day to take such a dark turn, quite the opposite. Let's get you and your precious cargo back to the hotel. Promise me you'll wear the sunglasses and the scarf every day. They go with everything. And people are nicer to you when they think you're chic."

"That's ridiculous. And *offensive,* frankly. Everyone deserves kindness."

He shrugged. "Lots of true things are offensive. Doesn't make them any less true. Here, I'll show you how to tie the scarf over your hair, you'll see. This updo that Cece concocted—it really is ingenious. And flattering. But you will have more options if you let it get a little longer."

It was almost five when Danny left her at Le Bristol. She caught a glimpse of herself in the lobby's mirrors. She did look nice, she had to admit. Almost glamorous. Her lips were full, the shape of her mouth almost a perfect Cupid's bow. Maybe she should consider a brighter shade of lipstick? Not a fire engine red, but a deeper pink hue?

She let herself into her room, eager for a nap—only to find that every single item of clothing had been removed from the closet and piled on her bed.

Mrs. Blossom, like anyone who has watched a lot of television and movies, had seen her share of tossed rooms. The carelessly strewn clothing, drawers wrested from dressers, curtains torn from their hooks. She knew what a ransacked room looked like.

This was not one of those rooms.

The destruction here was tidy, methodical. You couldn't even call it destruction; it was more of a de*con*struction, a word that had been applied to the worst sandwich she ever eaten in her life. Bread on one side, tidy piles of meat on the other, miniature jars of condiments, bowls of pickles and lettuce. If she wanted to make her own sandwich, she could do it in her kitchen for a fraction of the cost.

Now here, in a Paris hotel room, she also was confronting rows and rows of tidy piles. Every item of clothing she had packed had been removed from the suitcase, closet, and drawers, turned inside out, and then laid across the bed, organized by item. Tops, bottoms, dresses, underwear. (It embarrassed her, a little, to think of some stranger handling her bras and panties.)

The insoles from her shoes had been removed. Every compartment in her suitcase had been searched, the pockets turned inside out. The modest contents of her jewelry pouch had been arrayed on the bedside table.

In the bathroom, the miniature bottles in Harold's old leather dopp kit had been emptied into the sink, then propped upside down on a bathroom towel to catch any last drips. The seven slots on the top of her pillbox stood open in full salute, the pills undisturbed. She checked on her diamond earrings: they were safe in their secret compartment.

Whom should she call? The front desk? The police? And what would she be reporting? Not a thing was missing, except for her lotions and shampoos, which angered her. She had spent an entire evening pouring fluids into these little marked bottles, using a funnel, all to ensure that she would comply with the airline rules for carry-ons.

She imagined her call: *"Hello, police, I wish to report the theft of three ounces of L'Oréal shampoo and conditioner. Also a small jar of Pond's cold cream."*

She wondered if she could even find Pond's cold cream in Paris.

Should she call Danny? *No.* Danny was the one who had kept her out all day. Danny, now that she thought about it, had been on and off his phone constantly in the atelier. He would have been able to tell someone where she was, and when she would be returning. Or he could have just shared his location, which would have been the same as sharing hers.

One thing seemed certain: whoever had gone through her things had not been worried about being interrupted. In fact, they might have had time to put things back, but chose not to. She still would have noticed the emptied travel containers, of course, but she could have blamed that on an overly meticulous maid. No, whoever had done this simply didn't care if Mrs. Blossom knew. They might even be putting her on notice.

Only what were they looking *for*? And was it connected to Allan, who had shared her location with some unknown person? If she called the police, she probably would have to tell them more details about her day with Allan and it would look weird that she hadn't told them before. They might even detain her, which could derail the whole trip, which would be unfair to Elinor, to come all this way and miss the cruise, or have to go on it alone, because stupid Mrs. Blossom had flirted with a man who had the bad luck to go and fall from his hotel balcony while having a brandy and a cigar.

Even if it wasn't bad luck—no one was interested in *her*. They had searched her room while she was out. If they had found something that had eluded her, good for them. Either way, their curiosity should be sated.

She realized she was pulling at her lower lip, a sure sign that she was anxious. It was a habit from childhood, babyhood even. When nervous or upset, she had held her little square of blanket to her face—"bank" as it was known. But, instead of sucking her thumb, as most children did, she plucked at her lip the way someone might pluck the same string on a guitar over and over again. "Bank" had disappeared long ago; Mrs. Blossom suspected her mother might have hidden it, exasperated that her grade-school daughter was still sleeping with it at night. But her mother couldn't stop her from plucking at her bottom lip.

Someone had been in her room, for reasons unknown. A man had fallen—an accident, according to the police—and died.

But—wouldn't she be safer on the ship, where only guests and crew would have access? And if she canceled, or tried to concoct a new plan, how could she justify the expense?

Yes, better to tell no one. She was here for only three more nights. She would use the security lock.. She would be alert while out and about. She remembered Allan's comforting idea that no problem was unique, so therefore a solution existed. Mrs. Blossom took it a bit further: there was not only a solution, but also an explanation, and it was almost certainly banal. Really, it was almost egotistical of her to imagine she was the center of some sinister plot.

She put her clothes away and filled her miniature bottles with the shampoo, conditioner, and moisturizer provided by the hotel. They were probably superior to what she had bought at CVS anyway.

Mrs. Blossom was resolute. Her dream trip was not going to be spoiled by these odd occurrences, which really were not that sinister, except for the part about Allan being dead. It was discomfiting that some stranger had her selfie, but also probably coincidental: Allan had said she was *nice*. She was going to see the Louvre, darn it, and the Eiffel Tower. She'd eat a croissant while wearing a beret if that's what she chose to do. She was just a nice woman from Baltimore who was treating herself to a vacation. That wasn't a crime, last time she had checked.

SOMETHING AT THE *Eiffel Tower . . . something something . . .*
CIA agent . . . secret formula . . . double agent pees himself? . . .

It was her last day alone in Paris and a blissfully unself-conscious
Mrs. Blossom was taking in the view of the city from the top level
of the Eiffel Tower, an old song pinging around in her head. She
needed a second to remember the song's name. It felt like a very
long second. As one ages, every moment of forgetfulness fills one
with dread.

Then it all came roaring back. The song had been called "Mission à Paris," the band was Gruppo Sportivo, they wore goggles
and swim caps on the album cover. She could see herself at the
record store on Sulgrave Avenue, browsing the used bins. Though
only twenty-three or twenty-four at the time, she believed herself
an old, married woman. Only five years ago, she had been dancing
at places like the Marble Bar. She hadn't even needed a fake ID,
because eighteen was the legal drinking age in her day.

In her day. Who said that except an old person? OK, fine, she
was an old person.

And *in her day*, Mrs. Blossom had eclectic taste in music,
embracing punk and New Wave while still in high school. She
tried to remember the names of the bands she had loved. Jules

and the Polar Bears. Tuff Darts. Television—she had been so sad when Tom Verlaine died. Mrs. Blossom didn't feel old enough to see her teen idols dying. Although she hadn't thought of musicians as idols, much less heartthrobs. She read *Creem* and *New Musical Express*, not *16 Magazine* and *Tiger Beat*. It had been the music, not the men, that interested her.

Then she had gotten married at age twenty. To a twenty-three-year-old who was perfect in every way, except—he didn't really care that much about music, didn't like concerts, and definitely did not understand why his young bride still wanted to go to dark little clubs and throw her body around as if she were in the throes of an exorcism. So, per the Bible's advice, Mrs. Blossom put away childish things. She even sold most of her record collection, only to slowly re-create it in her thirties, slinking around Normal's in Charles Village as if she was up to no good. Eventually, she wasn't.

Stop it, Muriel. Everyone's entitled to make mistakes.

Then the music changed—at least, that's how she saw it—and she switched her allegiance from clubs to museums, taking art history courses in Hopkins's continuing ed program. She'd visit the local museums, although Mr. Blossom hadn't cared for those, either. Still, it was a respectable way for a middle-age woman to spend her time. And she didn't regret broadening her knowledge of art, but did life have to be an either-or? Couldn't she have music and art? And travel and good food and—*just say it, Muriel*—love?

Thanks to her lottery ticket, she could buy herself music, art, travel, and food. Love, ah well, the Beatles told us long ago that it could not be bought. It was hilarious that Tess had warned her about fortune hunters. In Mrs. Blossom's admittedly very limited experience, men in her age bracket wanted caretakers, but they were nervous around women who had more money. As for men not her age—no, she just couldn't!

Who cared? Here she was in Paris, and she had done everything she had promised herself she would do, seen everything on her list, even after losing one day to London (Allan!) and another to the shopping trip with Danny. She also had done most of it by herself, no small feat. She was living the high life, figuratively and, for the moment, literally.

But she was not going to end her solo time in Paris at the Eiffel Tower. Even Mrs. Blossom, happy tourist that she was, thought that would be a little, well, banal. She had saved what she believed would be the highlight of the week for her last few hours alone, to be followed by a massage back at the hotel. But—she checked the dangling watch on her charm bracelet—given that it would take her almost an hour to walk to the Bois de Boulogne, she probably needed to hustle to arrive in time for her ticketed entry, the last slot of the day.

Back in Arizona, when she had started planning her trip, Paris had not been the obvious choice. London had been her first thought, in part because it was the one European city that could be reached via a nonstop flight from Baltimore. She also had considered Ireland. It had been intimidating to contemplate visiting places where she didn't speak the language.

Then she had learned that a special exhibition would be open in Paris during the time frame for her trip—the works of Claude Monet and Joan Mitchell, exhibited side by side. That was all she needed to know, even if she had only discovered the work of Joan Mitchell quite recently, while on a trip to Baltimore.

That long hot day was seared into her memory. She had just seen the apartment that would become her new home. An old friend of sorts had reached out to her and suggested lunch at the restaurant at the Baltimore Museum of Art. Then the friend, true to form, had been a no-show.

Embarrassed to dine alone in such a nice restaurant—another weakness she had been working on this week in Paris, her anxiety about solo dining—she had decided to tour the museum's latest exhibit instead, a Joan Mitchell retrospective. She had never heard of Mitchell, and yet, within minutes of coming face-to-face with her work, she found herself teary-eyed from joy and awe. The paintings were bold, enormous; this was a woman who clearly was not afraid to take up space. And so much color, so many evocations of flowers! Mrs. Blossom had wandered through the rooms transfixed, feeling as if this work had been created explicitly for her.

The news of the Paris exhibit helped her make up her mind. She had even arranged a day trip to Vétheuil, once home to both Monet and Mitchell, although obviously not at the same time. She wanted to see the countryside where these two different yet similar artists, the male impressionist and the female expressionist, had created stunning work, although Monet's time in that particular river town was admittedly a blip in his life.

Mrs. Blossom had gone dutifully to museums all her life, first as a schoolchild and then as an adult who believed in self-improvement. She had always enjoyed the BMA, with its collection of Matisses and Picassos. But there was something different about the Mitchell show, which arrived at such a fraught moment in her life, a time when she was looking forward and backward. It had been almost a decade since Harold's death, seven years since her daughter had moved to Arizona, Mrs. Blossom following without even being asked. She had considered her presence a gift to her family, and she believed her daughter and her granddaughters felt the same way. She wasn't as sure about her son-in-law.

When he announced he had accepted a transfer to Tokyo, her unfiltered response was: "But I'm not sure I want to live in Japan."

Her son-in-law, whom she did like, she really did, said: "I have to admit, that wasn't one of the things that factored into the decision, Muriel."

Her daughter, perhaps sensing her hurt feelings, had rushed in: "What Trout"—that was an abbreviation of his last name, and he had never outgrown it, alas—"what Trout means is that the girls are older now, and you're entitled to a life of your own."

A life of her own. Mrs. Blossom recalled the phrase as she entered the Bois de Boulogne, the site of the museum. What did that even mean? Aren't we always living lives of our own? Or do mothers never live lives of their own? Anyway, she found the lottery ticket only a few weeks after that fraught conversation, and everyone seemed to think it was fortuitous, a harbinger of her new life.

It didn't seem to occur to anyone that she had been fine with the old one.

Fine with the old one. There was her subconscious again, challenging her perception of herself as a happy person, reminding her that there was a difference between "good" and "good enough," that *fine* was not the same as *happy.* If she wanted to be happy, she was going to have to work at it, which seemed like the ultimate oxymoron, working at happiness.

It also was embarrassing, in Mrs. Blossom's opinion, to be even the tiniest bit unhappy when one had—what was it called, the basic building blocks of a good life? Oh, Maslow's hierarchy. She had never lacked for food, water, shelter, and for a huge portion of her life, more than half, she had been loved. What else had been on that pyramid, which she first encountered in a community college class, another one of her forays into self-improvement? Once again, her memory failed her, and once again, this stressed her out. She knew it was her frontal cortex seizing up, and that the information would come back to her when she was relaxed, but she was forever on guard for signs that her memory lapses were something more than ordinary glitches.

Once she was inside the Louis Vuitton Foundation, the Monet/ Mitchell exhibition simultaneously soothed her and moved her. She sneaked a tissue from her purse and pretended to blow her nose, but she was really trying to pat dry a few errant tears, which seemed more embarrassing than a big honking blow. She noticed a man glancing at her, and who could blame him? What kind of sentimental fool cries in public? At an art exhibit?

Sated by art, she began the long walk back to the hotel. She decided to stop by the Galeries Lafayette, the department store that Danny had thought would intimidate her. He wasn't wrong; it was overwhelming, filled with crowds that jostled her. But it didn't seem that much grander than Baltimore's original Hutzler's back in its heyday—about the same time as Mrs. Blossom was eighteen and, arguably, in *her* heyday. The sizes did skew small. Not that she saw much that tempted her, although she did buy two more resin bangles.

Eventually she found her way to the shoe department, where her size six feet were always welcome. *I'm not asking the price of anything on this trip*, she reminded herself. As a consequence, she walked out of the store with a pair of $500 suede Isabel Marant ankle boots. She had noticed how many Frenchwomen—she assumed they were Frenchwomen—paired ankle boots with pants and even skirts. Maybe they would even work with her caftan or her black dress. And they were relatively comfortable, although not exactly Allbirds.

Allbirds. Allan had liked her shoes. She understood that she didn't really know him, that she couldn't have actual feelings for him. She was not mourning a flesh-and-blood person, but a possibility, a possibility that had seemed like an impossibility for so long, and now felt impossible again. Who could love her? Only Harold Blossom. Hadn't she learned that the hard way? She was lucky to find one great love in her life. It was greedy, maybe even sinful, to want more. Some women never got even one.

She caught a glimpse of a woman in a stylish scarf and sunglasses in the window of a bakery. The scarf and the sunglasses were similar to hers. Wait—it was her! In the updo that Cece had taught her how to coax from her shortish hair. She lingered, pretending to study the various breads and croissants on display, but she was really looking at herself.

As was a man, across the street. He, too, was reflected in the glass, but he was focused on Mrs. Blossom, not his own reflection, staring at her back with such fierce concentration that it really did seem as if he could burn a hole through her coat's fabric.

It was the man who had noticed her crying at the exhibit. But she had been walking for more than an hour since then, in an extremely haphazard fashion, ducking into various stores, shopping for boots. It seemed far too much of a coincidence for this man to be standing across the street, watching her.

Was it the same man? His clothes—a beige trench coat, a hat— were practically a uniform for Frenchmen. But, no, she was sure: this was the man at the exhibition; he had followed her here, and now he was pretending to be studying his phone. Mrs. Blossom had used the same trick when she used to follow people, although she also liked to use an actual map as a prop. People were always anxious to ignore an older woman with a map. God forbid, she might come up to you and ask a question! It was counterintuitive, but sometimes making a spectacle of one's self was the best way to deflect suspicion.

Mrs. Blossom, so skilled in the art of surveillance, had never been surveilled. Not to her knowledge, at least, which, of course, was the hallmark of *good* surveillance. She was sure in her bones that this man was following her. What was the best way to shake a tail? It was a novel problem because no one had ever managed to elude her.

She started by walking rapidly and randomly, making abrupt turns, sailing in and out of stores. But he was relatively good at what he was doing. Not as good as she had been, at her best, but good enough. Perhaps he didn't care that she had spotted him? But that seemed even more sinister, like the methodical deconstruction of her hotel room.

She decided to head toward the Seine, although the hotel was in the opposite direction. For a few blocks, the streets were strangely empty, then suddenly she rounded a corner and there were masses of people for blocks and blocks. *What the*—she remembered the concierge's euphemistic wording about the "special day" back when she arrived. It had been a week of special days, with French transit workers striking and demonstrating over the proposed increase in the pension age. It seemed relatively polite for a protest, but the crowd was large and tight, and she wasn't sure if it would be considered rude to try to move through it to reach the busy boulevard along the Seine. She could backtrack, of course, but that would make it easier for her tail, whereas—

Whereas—it was clear what she had to do. It just happened to be her own personal nightmare.

Mrs. Blossom didn't like crowds. Moreover, she didn't enjoy the way others treated her in crowds, as if her size made her especially burdensome. And this was a crowd of people whose language she couldn't speak, whose culture was unfamiliar. Maybe there was a different etiquette for crowds in France than there was in the United States, like there was for holding one's knife and fork.

She glanced over her shoulder. The man was getting closer.

She took a deep breath and plunged in. It was slow going, like trying to swim through mud. But that meant it was slow going for her tracker, too. She ducked her head, removed her scarf and glasses, put them in her purse. With her head down, the distinctive scarf gone, she would be harder to spot. Thank goodness her coat was black.

Large people know a lot about shrinking. They are forced to do it all the time. Mrs. Blossom could never be small, but she knew ways to seem smaller. She collapsed in on herself, rolling up like a potato bug, which had been her father's name for pill bugs. Only a potato bug who could keep walking even as she scrunched and compressed her body. Bit by bit, she made it through the crowd, murmuring "*pardonnez-moi, pardonnez-moi*" all the while. When she finally reached a spot where she wasn't surrounded by people, she felt like Jonah bursting from the whale. She all but ran for a block or two until she saw the Seine ahead. She caught her breath and walked alongside the river until she spotted the Place de la Concorde. She had overshot the hotel, but that was OK.

The hotel! Her massage! If she was lucky, she'd make it just in time. The appointment had seemed an indulgence when she booked it, but now she was truly in need, her shoulders a bundle of knots.

Why would someone follow her? She had been warned about pickpockets in Paris, but an ordinary pickpocket would not have stuck with his quarry so doggedly. Besides, what would he have gotten from her? A wallet, a pair of reading glasses, a map of Paris, and some breath mints.

Something at the Eiffel Tower . . . something something . . . secret formula. Her trip at moments seemed as jumbled and silly as that old song she had once danced to. All very well to laugh about a Parisian spy mission when one is young and jumping around a Baltimore bar, but it wasn't quite as funny when it was actually happening to you.

"**MURIEL, YOU LOOK** marvelous," Elinor said between dainty yawns. Mrs. Blossom had worried that it was too much, asking Elinor to overcome her jet lag for this multicourse dinner at Epicure, the hotel's three-starred Michelin restaurant. But Elinor was always game for luxury if a bit leery of a tasting menu of eight courses.

"A man helped me pick out the dress. And the earrings," Mrs. Blossom confessed.

"Oh, really?" Elinor leaned forward and rested her elbows on the table, cupping her chin in her hands. Back in Baltimore, two mothers were rolling in their graves. "*Now* things are truly getting interesting."

Mrs. Blossom blushed. The two had been friends for more than sixty years, although they had been forced to learn early how to maintain that friendship over distances and differences. They had met in first grade, but Elinor's father had been transferred to Lexington, Kentucky, the summer before fourth grade. They had reunited in seventh grade and managed to stay together through junior high, only to be separated again when Mrs. Blossom's parents sent her to Notre Dame Prep, despite being extremely lapsed Catholics. (She suspected they were really terrified about the possibility of forced busing.) Elinor had ended up at Park School, a private school favored by many of Baltimore's Jewish families.

Mrs. Blossom had stayed in Baltimore for college, enrolling at the University of Baltimore, while Elinor had attended Randolph-Macon, where she had met the first of her three husbands, who had taken her back to Kentucky, only Louisville this time. Luckily, the two friends were both old-fashioned letter writers, although the times eventually caught up with them. They switched to emails in the late 1990s, then texts.

Sometimes, they even spoke on the phone, playing catch-up as Mrs. Blossom walked and Elinor gardened.

Throughout all those years, from first grade until now, Elinor had always been what used to be called boy crazy, making two ill-considered marriages in a row. She had finally found the love of her life at sixty only to lose him to cancer two years ago. She claimed she was already on the hunt for Husband Number Four—and she probably was. Elinor, unlike Mrs. Blossom, had signed up for dating apps, tried speed dating, and even considered a match-maker's services. When Mrs. Blossom had asked her to come along on this once-in-a-lifetime trip, all expenses paid courtesy of her miracle lottery ticket, Elinor's immediate response was: "Why not? It sounds like a good way to meet men."

Elinor's focus on companionship was part of the reason she disdained museums. "Terrible places to meet eligible men," she always said. "The straight ones who are there have been dragged there by wives or girlfriends." Elinor also had a theory that the racetrack was the best place to meet potential suitors, but maybe that was a byproduct of living in Louisville; Mrs. Blossom could not imagine that Baltimore's Pimlico racetrack produced much in the way of prospects.

"Go on," Elinor said. "Tell me about your new love interest."

"It's not like that at all," Mrs. Blossom said. "This man is a lot younger than I am."

Elinor literally clapped her hands in delight. "More interesting, still. Some of my best adventures have been with younger men. They're not for marrying, of course, but they're quite fun."

"Elinor—I'm pretty sure he's gay."

"How do you know?"

"Well—" How *did* she know? Her little laundry list of reasons— groomed eyebrows, an interest in musicals and clothes—seemed flimsy. Flimsy and bigoted. "He took me *shopping*."

"And you've never looked sexier."

"Elinor!"

"I'd love for a man to take me *shopping*."

Mrs. Blossom had already decided not to tell her friend that she had come close to finding a real love interest of sorts. The story had such a bummer of an ending, and the strange events of the past few days—her methodically searched room, the man who had followed her—might unnerve Elinor. Better not to mention any of it, she had decided.

They had met in the hotel lobby about noon because Mrs. Blossom persuaded Elinor, as Allan—Allan!—had persuaded Mrs. Blossom to power through the day after a shower and a change of clothes. The two friends had gone to the famous cemetery Montparnasse, where Elinor wanted to find the grave of a minor peer, someone related to one of the Real Housewives. Mrs. Blossom was a little confused about that, because she watched only the competitive reality shows, not the ones that claimed to be about "real" life.

They had a light lunch in a perfectly ordinary café, walked until their legs began to protest, then taxied the rest of the way to the hotel, where Mrs. Blossom allowed Elinor a twenty-minute catnap.

So they were quite satisfied and self-satisfied as they finished this dinner, a meal so exquisite that it made Mrs. Blossom feel as if she had never eaten before. Mac-and-cheese with truffle! Who knew? Plus, the food just kept coming, course after course. At one point, Elinor stifled an unladylike squeal of alarm at the sight of a plate of little cakes and *tossed water on her portion.* (She later admitted she had learned that trick from another Real Housewife.) "I need to fit into my clothes!"

Mrs. Blossom offered apologetically to the waiter: "I'm sorry, I think we've hit the wall."

The phrase seemed to surprise him, and he asked her to repeat it, puzzling over the words. Once he understood the concept, he chuckled and said: "We will tell you, madame, when you have 'hit' this wall."

"It was fun," Mrs. Blossom said, "finding that Real Housewife grave. Well, her husband's ancestor's grave. Even if I have no idea who she is. I felt like I was on a treasure hunt."

"You shouldn't be such a snob, Muriel. Those shows are funnier than most sitcoms."

"Sitcoms are fine for me—my granddaughters are always introducing me to new ones—and sometimes they end up loving the ones I watched back in the day. You know, I was reading an article the other day that says the Golden Girls were actually younger than we are now."

"Oh, I don't think so, Muriel."

"I'm talking about the actresses. The oldest one—not the one playing the mother—was fifty-five—fifty-five!—when it began. And only sixty-two when it ended. We're—"

"I know how old I am, Muriel." Elinor was one of those people who treated her age as a curse that must never be spoken aloud. "We're in Paris, enjoying an outstanding meal, and about to embark on a cruise. If this is old age, I wish I had gotten here sooner. Maybe next year we'll do that trip where the Four Seasons flies you around the world in a private jet."

Mrs. Blossom smiled. "I didn't win *that* much in the lottery, Elinor. Once I go back to Baltimore, a big night out is going to be the pit beef place on Pulaski Highway."

"Oh, Muriel," Elinor said. "I'm sure you can afford an occasional all-lump crabcake from Faidley's at Lexington Market, the one they serve on gold foil. I'm going to make you enjoy having money. See if I don't."

They decided to take a short walk along the Seine after dinner, a tiny bit unsteady from the wine that had been served with each course. But even if they hadn't been wobbly, Elinor still would have stuck her tiny hand in the crook of Mrs. Blossom's elbow. They had always walked this way. A cruel girl had once said the two friends looked like the numeral 10 walking down the street, one so thin and one so round. Elinor had stuck out her tongue and said: "No, we are a twenty, because we're both perfect tens."

They saw beautiful young couples on the passing ships, holding hands, embracing.

Mrs. Blossom asked: "Do you really want to marry again, Elinor?"

"Oh, absolutely. I'm not like you, Muriel. I get lonely."

"Elinor, I've been lonely ever since Harold died. Why do you think I took that night course and ended up working for a private investigator? Why do you think I moved to Arizona to be near my daughter and grandchildren? I was trying to fill my days. I'm nervous about being alone back in Baltimore—but it's be alone there, or be alone in Arizona, which never really grew on me."

"Your former boss has a baby now, right?"

"A toddler and a ten-year-old. I have offered to help her out with childcare. They're sweet kids. But they have real grandmothers, one in town and one down in Virginia, not too far away. They won't think of me as family. Nor should they, I guess."

"You'll figure out a way to spend the days," Elinor said. "You have such a vivid imagination. Remember how we used to run around in Herring Run Park, building lean-tos and pretending we were koala bears?"

Mrs. Blossom had forgotten. It was nice to be reminded that she had been free and spontaneous as a child. Could she ever be that way again? She had been a little impulsive this week, deviating from her schedule here and there, trying not to be too rigid. But once they got on the boat, things would be very regimented, with almost no choices to make. A full itinerary every day, meals at set times.

She couldn't wait. *Freedom* might be another word for nothing left to lose, but, in Mrs. Blossom's opinion, it was *exhausting*.

It was not yet 10:00 p.m., but Elinor was, as she put it, "knackered"—Elinor, in addition to her affection for "real" housewives, watched a lot of British shows on PBS—and Mrs. Blossom was satisfied that her friend's inner clock was on its way to being reset.

An hour later, she was about to drift off to sleep when there was a tap at her door.

"Who is it?" she called from bed, not wanting to get up.

"Madame is checking out tomorrow?" A man's voice.

"Yes."

"I just wanted to let you know that you could leave your bags in the hall when they are ready. No matter how early—or how late. I can take them now if they're packed."

She crept to the door and looked through the fish-eye. The man was wearing the distinctive uniform of the Bristol's bellmen. Still, she was skeptical. So many odd things had already happened.

"I can take care of my own bags," she said. "There's only the one and it's a carry-on."

"Of course, madame. My apologies, madame."

She pressed her ear against the door, waiting to see if the bellman would knock on other doors. No, she was the only one being offered this special service. Interesting.

She counted to thirty, slipped her coat on over her nightgown, and put on the wedges Danny had persuaded her to buy. They were easy to get on fast, even easier than her Allbirds. She crept down the hallway, pausing at a corner. The bellman had rung for the elevator. She inventoried the view from the back: thick blond hair, sunburned skin above the collar. The uniform wasn't quite right, she noticed. She couldn't pinpoint the precise discrepancy, but it was an approximation of what the bellmen here wore, not the real thing.

She was only on the second floor—the one they called the first—so she decided to head down the stairs; if it was just a flight, she had a chance of beating the elevator, which was a little slow. Feeling ridiculous, she positioned herself in an alcove by the lobby. Several minutes passed, and she began to suspect the man was long gone. But, no, here he came heading out into the night, his cloak now over his arm.

She followed him at a careful distance, reminding herself that he didn't necessarily know what she looked like because she had never opened the door. Then again—a photo of her had been sent to someone's phone.

It was quite dark, but there were enough people out that Mrs. Blossom could stay relatively close to her quarry without standing out. He turned often, but that was just a trick of the Parisian streets; he wasn't trying to lose her. He had no idea he had anyone to lose. After about ten minutes, he arrived at a café where he took a seat at a table outside despite the night's chill. Soon, he was joined by another man.

It was the man who had followed her from the Mitchell exhibition. Or at least one dressed the same way—hat, trench coat. And the face looked familiar.

Then, when Mrs. Blossom didn't think her stomach could drop any further, a third man arrived.

Danny.

She knew she should leave. An old woman could linger unnoticed only so long in the shadows, especially if she was wearing a nightgown under her coat. Besides, she couldn't hear much of anything from where she stood, wasn't even sure if they were speaking French or English. French, she decided, based on the shapes of their mouths as they spoke. The other two men were full of exaggerated Gallic movements—shrugs, shaking fists, shaking heads. Their voices never rose to the point where others in the café turned to look at them, but they were clearly agitated, especially Danny. He seemed to be dressing them down, and for all their protests, they were taking it.

One word rose above the chatter, or maybe it was simply that it was the same as in English: *valise*.

She walked back to the hotel, wishing she could vary her route, but afraid she would get lost if she deviated from the path she knew. She stopped at the front desk, having forgotten her key when she sallied forth. Luckily, they had photocopied her passport upon arrival, so she didn't have to prove she was Muriel Blossom to convince them to let her back into her room. Le Bristol didn't use key cards, but real keys, heavy and substantial. Did that make a lock easier to pick?

She asked the bellman who accompanied her, a real one this time: "Do you ever collect suitcases from outside the rooms the night before departure?"

"Oh, no, madame. First, even in a hotel as secure as Le Bristol, there would always be the risk of theft. And every airline asks if the valises have been under the traveler's control. How could they guarantee that if they left them outside their rooms? Obviously, we gather them at a guest's request and sometimes store them. But we would never ask people to leave them outside their rooms where anyone might tamper with them."

She nodded and thanked the man for his troubles, tipping him a euro. She had studied travel books carefully: You were supposed to tip for extra services in Europe. That reminded her to leave a few euros for housekeeping as well.

Back in bed, incapable of sleep, she considered how automatically travelers affirmed that they had been in control of their luggage the entire time—and how often they were not. What if one checked a bag with a hotel's bellman? Or allowed a tour group to collect it? There were many instances in which a person couldn't vouch for who had access to their bags.

She thought about Allan, offering to carry her bag at the airport. It had seemed an act of gallantry—and she still believed it was. She would have noticed if he had put something in her suitcase.

But he had access to her bag, in her room that night. She had fallen asleep while he was still there. He had left a lovely note. Had he left anything else? Someone had searched her luggage here in Paris, but they clearly hadn't found what they wanted or why else had someone followed her yesterday? Why did a fake bellman try to smooth talk her into putting out her suitcase tonight?

And what did Danny have to do with all of this? She became so paranoid that she got up and examined the purchases they had made together. She had read news stories about clothing that was somehow soaked in drugs, cocaine, and MDMA. But that would have made the clothing significantly heavier. Had Cece sewn something into the hem of her caftan?

Her head was spinning, and she wished she could talk about her anxious thoughts with someone. Maybe Elinor? But it was late, and her friend had endured a long day. Mrs. Blossom was now extremely eager to leave Paris, but although they would board the ship tomorrow, they would remain docked in the north of the city for two days. Had she mentioned the itinerary to Danny? She had, but only generally.

He had teased her about it, she recalled. Disparaged the Eiffel Tower and the Louvre, turned up his nose at the staidness of a cruise.

But maybe the teasing had been a smokescreen, allowing him to gather intelligence on her.

She knew this much—Danny was connected to every odd thing that had happened to her in Paris so far. He had been with her the day her room had been searched. He knew the man who had tried to accost her on the street yesterday. He knew the fake bellman who had tried to persuade her to put her bags out tonight. He had been on her train. He had been at the restaurant where she had dined that first night.

He had been with her when she found out Allan was dead.

She got out of bed and made sure the safety latch was on. Not that it mattered. She wasn't going to sleep tonight, not really.

April 7

MRS. BLOSSOM OPENED bleary eyes to the sound of a key in the lock, a woman's voice calling out "Madame? Madame?" She had finally fallen asleep about dawn and now it was—she glanced at her phone—gracious, almost ten! She never slept this late. Checkout was at noon, she needed to pack and check her bag, and she wanted to have breakfast before service ended.

She tried to explain all of this to the confused maid who had been thwarted by the security latch on the door, but the woman simply smiled and indicated she would return later.

Luckily, Mrs. Blossom, prepared as any Boy Scout, had packed most of her things the night before and laid out the clothes she wanted to wear today. She made it to breakfast by the skin of her teeth. Why were scrambled eggs so good in France? But then, she knew the answer was probably butter or cream, maybe both. Butter and cream made everything better.

She glanced at the hostess's roster as she left the dining room—Elinor had not been down to eat. But her friend had never been much for breakfast, and she was probably still jet-lagged—and overfed from the night before. They had planned to meet in the lobby at noon, check their bags, then walk to Notre Dame. They would then have lunch at a traditional bistro near the hotel, re-claim their luggage, and take a taxi to the boat.

She was dressed in one of her Danny-dissed outfits, as she thought of it now. Could she still feel comfortable wearing the things he had picked out for her? Actually, she probably could. They were pretty, and given that they were new, they couldn't possibly be the reason that her room had been searched. And she had satisfied herself last night that nothing had been hidden in the hems or the seams.

Noon came and went without Elinor showing up in the lobby. Then twelve fifteen, twelve thirty—Elinor wasn't the most prompt person in the world, but this was late even by her standards. Mrs. Blossom, who had been sitting in a comfortable armchair, went to the front desk and asked them to ring her friend.

"Mrs. Schaperstein checked out this morning, madame."

"What?" Elinor could be a bit of a flibbertigibbet. Had she got-ten confused and thought they were leaving for the boat *before* they went to Notre Dame?

"It was about nine or so; she closed her account via the video checkout in her room."

Mrs. Blossom walked away from the desk and used her cell to call Elinor. It went to voicemail. And while her text was delivered, it wasn't read. She knew that for a fact because Elinor had never learned how to turn off the "read receipts" on her phone.

OK, she said to herself. *Deep breaths, Muriel.* Maybe Elinor had been unable to sleep and gotten up earlier than usual. Elinor had probably gone shopping and lost track of the time. Where would she go? Elinor liked clothes and jewelry and handbags—*handbags*. Elinor would never buy a Birkin, but a trip to the nearby Hermès store would be as exciting to her as Mrs. Blossom's trip to the Louis Vuitton Foundation had been for her. And the store was only a short walk from the hotel. Mrs. Blossom charged down the Rue du Faubourg, not caring if she bumped into people as she walked, her usual self-consciousness undone by her concern over Elinor.

But Elinor had not been to Hermès—the sales associates, who were kind and compassionate, not at all snooty, were sure of it, passing Mrs. Blossom's phone among themselves and studying the best recent photo she had of Elinor. Mrs. Blossom went through the same drill at Chanel. She was about to start ducking into every store along Faubourg Saint-Honoré when she realized how inefficient this system was. She checked her watch—she still had several hours before they were to board the ship. She tried calling Elinor. Again, straight to voicemail.

Mrs. Blossom reminded herself of her new rule: whatever was happening, there was not only a likely explanation, but a banal one. Still, it was hard to cling to that idea when so many strange things had happened this week. A man was dead. Elinor had checked out early. What was going on? She had given Elinor explicit instructions last night—check out and leave your bag with the front desk, then Notre Dame, then a cab to the boat after Mrs. Blossom called to ascertain its docking location. She couldn't have gone straight to the boat because only Mrs. Blossom had the boat's contact number. There was no getting around it: her friend was missing.

How did one find a missing person? Mrs. Blossom was old enough to remember a world without mobile phones, without answering machines even, where people could not update you when their plans went awry. She remembered one terrible evening when

Harold was three hours late getting home from work. There had been an accident on the JFX that had closed the roadway down and he had sat in his car, incapable of doing anything. She had been angry with him, unreasonably so. *"What was I supposed to do, Mur, send word via carrier pigeon?"* She conceded her anger was irrational, but she had imagined so many terrible outcomes in those three hours. Back then, she would rather imagine the worst and be pleasantly surprised, than assume everything was going to be fine only to learn it would not be. Hope, Emily Dickinson be damned, could be a dangerous thing, soaring only to fall flat. Better always to keep your expectations tamped down. Harold, considerate to the end, literally, had the kindness to die so quickly and definitively that Mrs. Blossom knew he could not be saved no matter how swiftly 911 responded. She had sat with him, holding his lifeless hand, devastated, yet grateful to be spared false hope.

Good lord, was Mrs. Blossom cursed? Harold, dead at the age of sixty-one, without any warning. Allan, falling from a hotel balcony. And now Elinor, missing. No, she scolded herself. She was being self-centered, creating linkages that didn't exist. Perhaps Elinor had thought they were to meet *at* Notre Dame and was now scouring Paris for Mrs. Blossom? She checked her phone, looked at her email. Nothing. Well, nothing from Elinor, but there were twenty-plus missives nudging her to buy things she didn't want and didn't need.

She looked up the address of the US Embassy in her phone. It was quite nearby. Should she go there? *Could* one go there? Did one just knock on the door and say—"Excuse me, my friend has gone missing in Paris, can you help me?"

Anyway, if Elinor had gone to Notre Dame, she had probably despaired of Mrs. Blossom showing up by now. Were the two friends searching for each other? Was Elinor as upset and anxious as Mrs. Blossom was right now?

She decided to return to Le Bristol. The plan had been to leave from there by late afternoon. All she could do was hope Elinor would show up at some point. And if she didn't—well, Mrs. Blossom wasn't going to think about that, not yet.

And sure enough, someone was waiting for her at Le Bristol. The only problem was that it wasn't Elinor.

It was Danny.

It was *always* Danny, as Mrs. Blossom had already realized. Whenever something odd or strange happened to her, Danny suddenly appeared out of nowhere. On the train, in a restaurant, taking her shopping while her room was searched, meeting with the fake bellman who had tried to take her bag. The man who had followed her through the streets of Paris. Danny was the thread that connected these things.

What, she asked herself, *if he was connected to Allan as well?*

"Where is Elinor?" she asked, assuming she would have to go through his usual rigamarole of contradictory lies. *Who's Elinor? I don't know Elinor. Oh, that Elinor!*

Danny surprised her by answering directly: "Having the lovely spa day that you planned for her."

"I didn't plan a spa day for her."

"Well, I gave you the credit for it. In fact, I wouldn't mind if you paid me back. L'Institute is not cheap, and I had to go into my own pocket."

"Who are you?" she asked.

"Danny Johnson. Would you like to see some ID?"

"I would, in fact."

He took out his wallet and handed her his driver's license, which was from Georgia—complete with a large peach as the background. There he was, Danny—Danny, not Daniel, she noted, simply Danny—Johnson, a resident of Cumberland Road in Atlanta, Georgia, six feet tall and 160 pounds, forty-two years old.

"Why should I believe you when you tell me that Elinor is at a spa?"

"Why shouldn't you believe me?"

"Because you lie all the time! Because whenever something odd happens to me, I turn around—and there you are."

The lobby of Le Bristol was not that large and although both Danny and Mrs. Blossom had kept their voices low, their body language was beginning to attract attention. They were obviously two people at odds with one another.

"We need to find a place to talk," Danny said. "Someplace private, away from here."

"I don't think so," she said. She listened to enough podcasts to know the rule about never following someone to a second location.

"There are things you should know before you leave on your cruise today."

She was torn. He said he knew where Elinor was. She was scared to let him out of her sight.

"There's a park not too far from here," Mrs. Blossom said. "I'll sit there with you and listen to what you have to say. But if I feel threatened in any way, I'll start screaming my head off."

"*Threaten* you," Danny said. "I've only spent every day since I met you trying to keep you safe."

The park Mrs. Blossom chose was a small playground, a neighborhood place full of locals; she had passed it several times while on her walks through the city. She felt that *genuine* Parisians would notice if Danny did anything odd or aggressive, whereas tourists in the larger, more famous parks might assume it was some kind of Punch and Judy show.

"You must think," she began in a quiet controlled tone that those who knew her would recognize as Mrs. Blossom at her angriest, "that I am a very stupid woman."

"No, not at all," Danny said. "But you are an innocent, in the best sense of the word. Trusting *and* trustworthy. If Allan had done what he was expected to do, I would never have intruded on your trip."

If Allan had done what he was expected to do—was Danny now going to rob her of the pleasant memories she had from her day in London?

"What exactly was Allan supposed to do?"

"He was going to meet with a Pakistani billionaire and hand him a missing antiquity. He expected to be paid five million dollars for his trouble. But, in fact, he was going to be detained and possibly charged with the theft of the object, a statue taken from Chitrali in the mid-twentieth century. And everything was going according to plan—until he met you."

"What are you suggesting? That I'm a thief or merely an unwitting coconspirator?"

He laughed, as if this was the funniest thing he had ever heard, which made Mrs. Blossom even angrier. "If I were a thief," she said, "I'd be a good one."

"I suspect you would," he said. "Now try to see this from my side of things. I spent weeks organizing this London meeting. And, as of March thirty-first, when you, Allan Turner—and I by the way—boarded the same British Airways flight in Baltimore, everything was unfolding as anticipated. Allan was en route to London, presumably with the statue. Two days later, he was dead in Paris—your planned destination, not his—and the police are adamant that there was no statue in his hotel room."

"Danny, I was *there*. The police told us no such thing," Mrs. Blossom said.

"Yes, well, the police are slightly more forthcoming when the FBI gets in touch with them and provides new information."

"How do you know that?"

"Because I'm an agent with the FBI's stolen art division," Danny said.

Mrs. Blossom needed a second to absorb that. She knew that the FBI did, in fact, pursue stolen art. The news had been full of scandals at multiple museums, wealthy benefactors pleading ignorance of their objects' provenance, others unmasked as out-and-out criminals. But wasn't the FBI a domestic agency? Why had they lured Allan to London if he had the statue in Baltimore?

And what did any of this have to do with Elinor? Should she ask to see his ID?

Danny registered her skepticism.

"By setting up a meeting with Allan in London, I gave myself two chances to get the statue. The meeting was Plan B, the fallback. Plan A was customs—we informed officials that we believed Allan Turner was traveling with a stolen antiquity and asked them to stop him and search his bags. But Allan didn't have the statue in his checked bag or his carry-on."

Mrs. Blossom remembered how long she waited in arrivals for Allan to come through—but also, how he swung his old-fashioned suitcase by the handle, as if it were light as air.

"But, OK, we still had a second shot, with the meeting. Except he canceled that after spending a day with you—"

"How do you know he spent the day with me?"

Danny's smile was almost a leer. "You two kept up quite the pace. The Tate, tea at the Savoy, drinks at the Eye—it was exhausting. When you went to dinner at Gymkhana, I finally had to bow out. Much too expensive for a government employee, and I couldn't put it on my expense account. Besides, I knew you were both at the St. Pancras Hotel. I planted myself in the lobby early the next morning and waited to see what would happen."

She didn't like the idea that Danny had been following them the entire day. For one thing, it wounded her professional pride—she should have picked up such a lengthy surveillance. But it also felt violative. Part of the glory of that day had been the sense that they were in this bubble, all to themselves. She hadn't noticed anyone but Allan.

"It's not a crime to spend a day with a man."

"No, it's not. And yet he headed to Paris the next morning—*your* destination, but ahead of you. He left the hotel minutes after he texted my fake billionaire that he couldn't make it on Monday, then headed to the train station. He surprised me by boarding the train at the last possible minute, and I couldn't get a ticket in time. Then, just as I'm about to give up—here comes the woman he spent the day with, arriving two hours ahead of her scheduled trip."

"It's less stressful to get places early," Mrs. Blossom said, feeling defensive again about her cautious habits.

"Anyway, you were my only lead. I hoped you would help me find Allan. And, in a sense, you did. But now he's dead and the statue's missing."

"Danny, I obviously don't have a statue in my luggage—I always know where my luggage is because I use a tracking system called a CUBE. I can open up the app on my phone right now and show you where my luggage has been since my trip began. No one's bothered me this week—except you and your people."

"It's not a *huge* statue," Danny began, then laughed at himself when he saw Mrs. Blossom's expression. "OK, it's true. There's no way you've been lugging a statue around. But what if someone hid it in your suitcase and took it out before you realized it?"

"Excuse me?"

"Is it possible that Allan put it in your luggage on the trip over, then removed it later?"

Mrs. Blossom thought of Allan, settling into the armchair in her room at the St. Pancras Hotel, insistent that he watch over her until she fell asleep. Could there—had he—but, no, that seemed impossible.

"How much does the statue weigh?"

"Fifteen to twenty pounds."

"I would have noticed if my luggage's weight increased by fifty percent." Even as she said it, she was recalling that she had wheeled her luggage through the airport and onto the Heathrow Express, but Allan had gallantly insisted on lifting it in and out of the overhead rack on the train, in and out of the taxi's trunk. Would she have clocked the additional weight while rolling her bag? She had been such a strange combination of groggy and keyed up.

"Theoretically—only theoretically—yes, he had the opportunity to access my luggage before we landed in London and, well, maybe later." There was no way she was going to tell Danny that Allan had been in her hotel room, waiting for her to go to sleep. "But if that's the case, then he must have got it back at some point. Maybe he hid it somewhere in Paris before the accident. Maybe he sold it to someone else. At any rate, it has nothing to do with me. If I was ever in proximity to that statue, I'm definitely not now. What is it, by the way? Why is it so valuable?"

Danny fixed his eyes on her the way Mrs. Blossom had stared down her daughter when she was sure the girl was telling a lie or withholding important information. An old hand at this game, she had no trouble holding his gaze. Mrs. Blossom was, by nature, a very truthful person. But on the rare occasions she had needed to be dishonest, she was heartbreakingly good at it.

"The statue is a Quqnoz—very much like a phoenix, a mythical bird that rises from the ashes. It's priceless to the Pakistani government, but I'm not sure it really has that much value on the black market, which has tightened in the past few years. Most of its value is in the materials—there are sapphire details on the head and tail. We had offered four million dollars for the statue. Allan managed to get us up to five million, which we agreed to because it was all theoretical, after all."

"He could have found another buyer," she reiterated.

"Possibly, but Allan's not exactly plugged in to the underground art world. He's a lawyer, specializing in estate planning. My people reached out to him, through an intermediary. He was really a glorified errand boy."

"For all you know, Allan believed he had a legitimate claim to the statue—and the right to sell it."

She couldn't help clinging to the idea that the man she had met was a decent person. He was the one who insisted they should have dinner together back in Maryland. He had even mentioned a specific place—that French restaurant in an improbable location near the train station. *You can tell me if it meets Parisian standards*, he had joked. *I've never been to Paris.*

Are you OK being friends with someone who's not as worldly as you?

Flattery. Mrs. Blossom had a memory of her mother, chiding her about the pleasure she had taken in a compliment from a boy at church. She had been taught from a young age that flattery was dangerous, that anyone who complimented her must want something. The implication being that no one could ever want *her*.

Actually, her mother's words had been far crueler: "Anyone who tells you that you're pretty is just trying to butter you up, to get something out of you. The sooner you learn that, the better off you'll be."

Mrs. Blossom had loved her mother, she really had. But Muriel Senior had been an aggressively thin woman, dismayed that her daughter's metabolism would not bend to her will. She had tried to diet young Muriel into an acceptable form, but it was impossible. Mrs. Blossom dutifully followed the diets her mother imposed on her—yet the scale didn't move, not in the long-term. Oh, for a week or two, the latest variation of rabbit food would yield results. Then it would stop, and her mother would accuse her of cheating. She—she said unkind things. She painted a dire future for her daughter. Who could love her if she refused to be thin?

And then one day, in a freak coincidence, Not-Yet-Mrs. Blossom met Harold Blossom and realized that the world was a 31 Flavors of Bodies. (Not that she had been allowed to go to 31 Flavors very often.) Yes, sure, not everyone loved Oregon Blackberry. But those who loved it, *really* loved it.

That was all one needed, Mrs. Blossom realized: one ardent Oregon Blackberry fan. In the almost forty years she and Harold had been together, she had awakened every day to a man who adored her. She knew from other women (Elinor, for one) that this was not to be taken for granted. Every morning, for thirty-eight years and 237 days—of course she had counted—Harold's loving gaze was waiting for her. They had never spent a single day apart.

And now they had been apart for more than 3,650 days.

"What happens now?"

Danny said, "I need you to tell me everything you and Allan did during dinner, and then after. And everything he said."

"Everything?" her voice squeaked.

Danny's dimples, always present, deepened. "You may draw a veil over the more tender moments. I'm mainly interested in knowing if there was anywhere you went that I don't know about, or if Allan left you alone anywhere you went—the Tate, Harrod's—anywhere."

Mrs. Blossom felt a blush more powerful than any hot flash she had ever known. It seemed to stretch from her hairline to her toes.

"I also would like to go through your bag one more time. Just to be sure. That's why my friend the bellman escorted Elinor to the spa—we thought there was a long shot that she might have unwittingly brought the statue to Paris, that Allan's plan was far more complicated than we knew. No such luck."

"I don't understand," she said, "why you need to look through my bag again? Your people were pretty thorough on Monday."

"On Monday? The day we went shopping?"

"Yes, they were very neat, your people. How did they get in, though? Did the fake bellman persuade the housekeeper to give him access?"

Danny seemed genuinely panic-stricken. "No, no—that was *not* me."

"I know it wasn't *you*—"

"It wasn't any of us. No one I'm working with entered your room on Monday. Now I'm even more concerned, Mrs. Blossom. What if the people who killed Allan—"

"Wait—do the police now believe he was *murdered*?" Too much information was coming at her at once. Missing Elinor, stolen statue, a possible murder. But the police had said there had been only one glass of brandy, only one cigar. How could Allan have been killed if he were alone on his balcony?

"The case is open for now. Still—that text he sent. Who knows who the recipient was—or their intentions. Allan put someone on your tail, if only to divert suspicion from himself."

"Whoever they are, whatever they want—they know now I don't have any statue. I couldn't be safer at this point. I board the ship today and it leaves Paris the night after next. I'd like to see them follow a boat up the Seine."

"The itinerary is easily found online, and it would be a simple matter to drive the route. Faster, in fact, than the boat. They could be waiting in every port."

Mrs. Blossom felt light-headed. "This is ridiculous. You are looking for a statue. They searched my room. I have gone through all my belongings and found nothing, absolutely nothing that I did not put there. I CLEARLY DO NOT HAVE A STATUE IN MY LUGGAGE."

Danny looked thoughtful. "As I said, it's not a *huge* statue."

Mrs. Blossom wanted to laugh, she wanted to cry, she wanted to go back in time and refuse that upgrade at the British Airways ticket counter, she wanted to go forward in time and get on the boat with Elinor and leave all this mishegoss behind. (Mr. Blossom had been Jewish. She had picked up a thing or two.)

"I am getting on my boat this afternoon," she said. "I am going on my trip. If I find this Quizno, I'll call you."

"Oh, I'll definitely be in touch," Danny said. "I have to keep tabs on you, make sure you're safe."

"With all due respect, I'll feel safer when you're not around."

PART II

Welcome aboard the MS *Solitaire*, your home for the next eight days and seven nights! Once you are settled in your cabin, please come up to L'Étoile lounge for the welcome reception and safety briefing. Dinner in the main dining room, Le Soleil, is available from 18:30 to 20:30 hours, and our casual bistro, Cedric's, will be open until 22:00 hours.

Some important facts to know about your new home: When you check in, the front desk will take your photo, which will be paired to the unique bar code on your room key. Whenever you leave the ship, you must check out, and you must check in upon return. Again, your key is matched to your photo, so keep track of your specific key.

Generally, you will enter and exit the ship through the sliding double doors on the same level as the front desk and the lounge. This also is the Platinum Deck, where you will find the sixteen staterooms beginning with the number "3." The Gold Deck has twenty staterooms and the Silver Deck has twelve, along with the gym and a small spa. When at capacity, the MS *Solitaire* holds ninety-eight guests and eighty-four staff, but we are not at capacity on this trip. We have provided all guests with a full passenger list.

Per the itinerary, we actually have two days in Paris before we set sail. There are land excursions planned for every day, but none of them are obligatory. We will tell you the departure time and whether you need to bring your voxes—the closed-audio system that our guides use. If you want to participate in an excursion, all we ask is that you show up on time. If you prefer to sit on the sun deck and drink wine, that's fine, too. But don't be late—we always leave promptly at the appointed time. While the MS *Solitaire* has been designed and decorated with a nod to art deco traditions, this is your vacation and we want you to be comfortable. Fancy dress is not required. We do ask that people wear shoes at all times (except in the Roof Deck hot tub, of course) and to be mindful of their attire when visiting cathedrals. Other than that, anything goes.

A reminder: Smoking is prohibited in the cabins and other indoor areas, but permitted on deck. However, please be considerate of other passengers.

"OH, IT'S SO lovely, Muriel!" Elinor said, looking at the cozy cabin that was to be their home for the next eight days.

At three hundred square feet, it was the largest room available on the MS *Solitaire*, although part of the extra space was the balcony, a perk available only to those on the Platinum Deck. It was the most expensive cabin level; Mrs. Blossom's family had urged her to spare no expense on this trip. Besides, even with a friend as old (and tiny) as Elinor, Mrs. Blossom had worried about the logistics of sharing a cabin. The smallest bedroom in her new apartment was larger than this space.

Thankfully, the floor-to-ceiling French doors that led to their balcony gave it an expansive feel. And the bed—actually two twins, pushed together—looked enormous, the equivalent of a king. Mrs. Blossom realized it would be the first time since Harold died that she would be sharing a bed with anyone, except for the rare occasions a grandchild had fallen asleep with her while she was babysitting. She wondered if she had any bad habits of which she was unaware—restless limbs, loud snores.

She should have thrown caution to the wind and had sex with Allan.

The thought shocked her, in part because of the hackneyed phrase *thrown caution to the wind*—Mrs. Blossom tried to avoid clichés—but also because it flew in the face—darn, there she went again—of all the knowledge she had acquired in the past twenty-four hours. How could she still be harboring what-might-have-been thoughts about Allan, a suspected thief? But she hadn't known about the statue that night in London. What if the St. Pancras Hotel was her last chance, *ever*, at romance? OK, fine, sex. Mrs. Blossom had ruled out love as a possibility for her when Harold died. She believed that was the best way to respect his memory. People said "Oh, Harold would want you to be happy," which was absolutely factual. Others said, "Oh, Harold would want you to fall in love again." She was less sure this was true.

"I'm afraid to report I started talking in my sleep a few years ago," said Elinor. Her thoughts must have been running along similar tracks. "But I don't ever say anything interesting, according to Richard." Richard had been Elinor's most recent husband. "I just list unrelated nouns, as if I'm making a strange shopping list."

"Who knows what I do in my sleep," Mrs. Blossom responded with a laugh. "Come, let's explore the ship before orientation."

They walked arm in arm on the upper deck. The exterior of the ship had been designed to look a little like a nineteenth-century steamboat, while the interiors were art deco. This seemed an odd combination to Mrs. Blossom, but she supposed the era of steamboat travel overlapped with art deco. She just didn't understand why a European vessel wanted to look like a Mississippi riverboat. She had chosen Hart Tours specifically because their boats were pretty but not overly grand. An ostentatious ship would have made her ill at ease.

"How was your spa date?" Mrs. Blossom asked. They had not had a chance to speak of it in the rush to get in the cab and arrive at the ship.

"Lovely. I doubt Notre Dame could have topped it, so I'm glad you called an audible on that play. But why didn't you treat yourself as well?"

Once again, Mrs. Blossom had to make a decision on the spot. She could tell Elinor everything, which might upset her and spoil the trip. Or she could tell her nothing, which was the same as lying. She decided to try a middle path.

"I had a massage earlier in the week." That was true. "And I had to, um, take a meeting with someone." Also true. "I know this is going to sound odd, but—I met a man, on the flight from Baltimore to London. I missed the connecting flight, we ended up spending a day in London together. It even got a little, um, romantic."

"Muriel!" Elinor's tone made it sound as if Mrs. Blossom had won a second, larger lottery.

"But then, um, authorities in Paris told me he is suspected of having a stolen statue. A bird, a very old one. So he wasn't who I thought he was." All true. There was no point in telling Elinor that he was dead.

"A bird? Was it the Maltese Falcon?"

"If only!" Mrs. Blossom allowed herself a wan giggle at Elinor's joke.

"So you booked a spa date for me this morning because—" Elinor was clearly puzzled, and who could blame her?

"Because the authorities wanted to ask me a few more questions." Danny was with the FBI; that made him an authority. "They were hoping I might provide some leads, but I know nothing about it. He certainly didn't mention any statue to me."

"Very thrilling stuff," Elinor said. "Do they have him in custody?"

"They don't really have grounds." Again, no lies detected. "Anyway, it's all behind us now. Smooth sailing ahead."

The Parisian skies took Mrs. Blossom's words as a dare and burst open with a little tantrum of a rainstorm.

"April in Paris, my ass," Elinor said. "Let's go to the bar and have an aperitif before orientation."

"I think they call it an *apero* here," said Mrs. Blossom. "And an apple juice is fine for me."

"It is *not*. I'm going to have a Kir, and I insist you join me. It's not that long before the briefing starts. We can get our drinks and settle into the lounge."

They went inside the bar, the ship's one unabashedly luxurious and maximalist space. The wood appeared to be mahogany, the velvety fabrics were in shades of dark green and burgundy. It was like a gentlemen's club in London, or, more accurately, the way Mrs. Blossom imagined such clubs would look, having never seen one. The difference here was that there was so much glorious light spilling in through the windows, even with a rainstorm in progress. At least twenty other travelers were there, enjoying drinks and snacks, speaking as if they had known each other forever. There were at least two big family groups, with what appeared to be three generations. Mrs. Blossom had offered her family the opportunity to take this trip, but Trout had said the girls couldn't miss school.

In one corner, two men were hunched over a backgammon board, laughing and taunting one another with each roll of the dice.

"I feel as if I'm being taken," one man said. He had pink cheeks and an even pinker sweater. To Mrs. Blossom's eyes, he was the epitome of a certain kind of old-school Baltimore preppie, a type to which she had always been drawn. It wasn't that he was handsome and it wasn't that he was *not* handsome. More that he had a quiet, low-key charisma, a steady flame behind those oh-so-blue eyes.

Harold, Mrs. Blossom thought. *He reminds me of Harold.* Not so much in his features, although he had a similar bear-ish build. He had the aura of someone who made the world seem a little warmer, a little safer. Almost fifty years ago, she had literally run into Harold's arms without even knowing his name. She would never be that bold again.

"Oh you are," a familiar voice responded. "I'm very good at this game. Luckily for you, I agreed to small stakes."

Danny. The other player, with his back turned to her, was Danny.

She frowned, waiting for him to turn and notice her. How dare he? *How dare he?* This was supposed to be her magical trip. She was leaving all that strangeness behind. No more being followed, no one sneaking into her room and searching her luggage, pouring her toiletries down the sink. (That still irked her, the loss of her carefully allotted portions of shampoo and conditioner.)

He turned, saw her staring at him—and he *winked*. Was this a game to him, no more serious than the white and black discs on the backgammon board? Shouldn't an FBI agent be a little more circumspect? Didn't he owe her at the very least the courtesy of informing her that he was going to join her cruise? He had said it would be easy enough to follow her from port to port, so why couldn't he do that?

She stalked over to him.

"What are you doing here?" she demanded of Danny. The other player seemed taken aback by her directness, but she didn't care. Where had good manners gotten her so far?

"Muriel!" he said. "Like you, I am embarking on this cruise up the Seine and back. I am especially looking forward to Giverny. I think I'll skip the excursion to the Normandy beaches, though. As the song goes, I'm not going to study war no more."

Once again, his glibness, his shamelessness when caught in a lie—and he had lied by omission about his plans—threw her off-balance. She was nonplussed. She was plus-size nonplussed.

Her only rejoinder was a stammering: "How did you get a booking so late?"

"To be honest, I inquired earlier this week after hearing you describe your trip and put a room on hold. It sounded so alluring. They had several empty cabins; it's not the most popular time to take such a cruise."

Mrs. Blossom knew this was true—it was part of the reason why she had chosen an early April sailing—but she inferred condescension. She was prone to inferring condescension. She was a rube who planned a trip way in advance, while Danny was able to waltz onto the same ship at the last minute.

His backgammon opponent cleared his throat, waiting to be introduced. Danny obliged.

"This is Muriel Blossom, lately of Arizona, now of Baltimore," Danny said. "And this is—"

"Paul," the man said in a soft, velvety voice. It was almost as if he was restraining his rich baritone, lest it overwhelm a person with its power and resonance. The hand he extended also was soft, but in a good way—not indifferent to work, but well cared for. Nails cut straight across, no rough spots—and no rings. No rings on either hand. Not usually something Mrs. Blossom noticed and not always meaningful, not in a man. She realized she didn't even know if Allan had worn a ring.

"Paul Paterakis."

"Oh," she said. "That's a name of some significance in Baltimore. Paterakis, I mean, not Paul. Although we do have a St. Paul Street. They have all the bread. I mean—the literal bread, they own a huge bakery, but I guess they have bread in the other sense, too—" Good lord, she was blathering.

"I'm from Ardmore, Pennsylvania. I'm afraid I have no connection to the Baltimore Paterakis family, much less its bread, although I do enjoy eating it in all forms."

Mrs. Blossom was vaguely familiar with Ardmore—it was on the Main Line outside Philadelphia, a place for well-to-do people. Then she remembered—she was on a rather expensive cruise. She was surrounded by well-to-do people. Well-to-do people were the norm here and she was now one of them. She was going to have to keep reminding herself of that.

"Mr. Paterakis—"

"Please call me Paul."

"Would you mind if I could have just a second here with my friend—" She glanced at Danny, wondering if he was using his real name on board or an alias. Lord help her, he *winked again*. "It's somewhat personal."

"Well, given the drubbing I'm taking, maybe his dice will cool down while the two of you chat. I'll go get a drink from the bar. May I bring you anything?"

"No, we're fine," Danny said. The gall of him, speaking for her. Of course, Elinor was already fetching Mrs. Blossom a drink. But Danny didn't know that. He had no right to wave away Mr. Paterakis's kind offer.

She took the chair that Mr. Paterakis—*Paul*—had been sitting in. There was a whiff of cologne, or maybe it was aftershave. Subtle, old-fashioned, spicy, the kind she liked.

"Why didn't you tell me you planned to follow me?" Wasting no time on niceties or preambles. Danny was entitled to neither.

"I'm not at liberty to tell you everything. Frankly, it's safer for you if you don't know too much."

Oh, yes, everyone was so safe with Danny around. A statue had been stolen, a man was dead, her room had been searched.

"You work for the US government and I'm a taxpayer so, in a sense, you work for me."

Danny laughed in what appeared to be genuine delight. "I like the way you think, Mrs. Blossom, but you'll have to trust me for now. I know my job. I know what I'm doing."

Did he? But Paul was returning from the bar with his drink— what appeared to be an iced tea. She did like a teetotaler. Harold drank only ritualistically—beers at the ballpark, wine at celebratory dinners.

"Iced tea," she asked. "Or something fancier?"

"Just plain iced tea, with lemon. Doctor's a little worried about my blood sugar, so I cut back where I can. But I still love wine with dinner, a brandy afterward."

"Well, I'll leave the two of you to your game," she said.

"Who is that?" asked Elinor when she joined her at the bar.

"Oh, he's the stylist I told you about, the one who picked out my new clothes. Did I forget to mention he's on our trip? That's how we met."

She wasn't sure why she lied to her old friend. She had already told her about Allan and the missing statue. But she didn't want to blow Danny's cover.

"Oh, he's a cutie, for sure, but I was talking about the other man, the Pink Panther. I do love a man who wears pink. It shows that he's confident."

"Pink Panther—is that going to be his code name?"

"Why not?"

Elinor and Mrs. Blossom had done this all their lives, created nicknames for males who caught their interest. As shy grade-schoolers, it had been their way to discuss certain boys without revealing their intentions. They had learned at a young age that it was dangerous to let the world know too much about what they desired.

"His name is Paul Paterakis."

"One of *the* Paterakises?" Elinor arched an eyebrow.

"No, he's from Ardmore, Pennsylvania."

"Still, obviously Greek. Look at that hair. Isn't it wonderful how Greek men never lose their hair?"

"Try telling that to Telly Savalas."

Elinor ignored her. "The important thing is—is he married?"

"Elinor!"

"Just looking out for you, my old friend. We can check the passenger list, back in our room. A little flirtation wouldn't do you any harm."

I had a little flirtation, Mrs. Blossom wanted to say. *And someone ended up beyond harmed.* But, no, she was committed to Elinor having a carefree week. All unpleasant topics past and present, up to and including men falling from hotel balconies, were to be avoided.

"The welcome reception is about to start," she said. "But I guess there will be time afterward to go back to the cabin and change for dinner."

When Mrs. Blossom and Elinor entered Le Soleil dining room, she realized instantly that they were overdressed. Overdressed and a little on the early side; most of the diners at this hour were the multigenerational families with young children. The adults in these groups tended toward what Mrs. Blossom would describe as high-end gym clothes—undoubtedly expensive, but perfectly suitable if one wanted to take a jog between courses. Their sneakers probably cost almost as much as her new boots.

The two women were seated at a table for four—there were no tables for two; Mrs. Blossom was beginning to sense that Hart Tours was big on enforced fraternization—with a lovely view of what Mrs. Blossom was fairly certain was the Right Bank. *Could she live in Paris?* Ever since the discovery of the lottery ticket, she kept testing out several futures/cities in her mind. Tokyo? No, she had not been invited. New York City? The subway scared her, even though the idea of living without a car was appealing. In the end, she had settled on home, boring old Baltimore. God, she was hopeless.

"Is this seat taken?" Danny slid into one of the chairs at their table before they could reply. It was easier not to object, as that might have prompted questions from Elinor, who knew Mrs. Blossom's only ironclad rule for her daughter and granddaughters was never to exclude anyone. Mrs. Blossom made an introduction, leaning hard on the word *stylist*, so Danny would know that she hadn't told Elinor his true identity. Lord, it was hard keeping track of even the most benign small mistruths. How did compulsive liars do it?

Danny, no surprise, had many opinions about the right things to order from the menu. "Unless you have allergies or simply hate the protein offered, the chef's recommendation is the way to go. And while there are a lot of American-friendly dishes, those are for children—or people who eat like children."

The waiter, who introduced himself as Esteban, was jovial and charming, teasing Danny about his good luck in having "two such beautiful dates." Elinor ate it up sideways with a spoon, but Mrs.

Blossom was unnerved. Maybe extra tips were expected, despite Hart Tours's insistence that its prices were all-inclusive. She hated being unsure of the etiquette in any situation, but she was especially concerned when it came to money. Danny ordered for all three of them—just showing off his French in Mrs. Blossom's opinion, but Elinor was charmed by this as well. Elinor, like Browning's last duchess, was too easily impressed.

And that was before a tall, dark-haired man appeared at their table.

"I'm Marco," he said. "May I join you?"

He was not quite their age, but probably close, and undeniably attractive, with a deep tan and hazel eyes. He wore a navy blazer and a white polo shirt with pressed khakis, along with tasseled loafers that probably were the equivalent of a mortgage check.

Elinor caught Mrs. Blossom's eye and mouthed: "Marco Polo." Really, they could have been thirteen again.

"Please do," Elinor said, and he took the open chair between Elinor and Mrs. Blossom. Danny, noting the way the two women looked at their new companion, sighed openly.

He wasn't Ken-doll handsome, this Marco, but he was arresting, with a distinctive nose, which looked as if it had been broken a time or two, and high cheekbones. He had thick gray-black curls and black brows, but they weren't the furry caterpillars so many older men allowed to march across their faces. Mrs. Blossom wondered if they were dyed. At any rate, they provided a nice contrast to his deep-set eyes.

Those eyes were focused on Elinor almost from the moment he sat down. Oh dear, how had Mrs. Blossom not considered this? Elinor was so pretty and delicate; men had always been drawn to her. She had assumed Elinor was joking about shipboard romances and finding a fourth husband. But if this man proved persistent—was

Mrs. Blossom going to be third-wheeling it, as her granddaughters liked to say, on her own trip?

Then again, if it had been Paul who had asked to sit with them—well, maybe Elinor would be worrying about being the third wheel. But the gentleman from Ardmore, Pennsylvania, had not yet entered the dining room. Mrs. Blossom knew this because she had been stealing looks at the door since they sat down.

Brief biographies and hometowns were exchanged; Elinor kicked Mrs. Blossom under the table when she said they had been friends for sixty years; was she really trying to pass for someone in her fifties? Marco—actually "Marko with a *k*," he clarified—described himself as a nomad with no fixed address.

"That sounds quite glamorous," Elinor said.

"But surely," Mrs. Blossom said, "you're from somewhere? You didn't ride up on the beach on a clamshell."

He looked confused. Not a fan of mythology or Botticelli, then. "I grew up in Washington, DC, but I've been bouncing from place to place for the past ten years."

"And are you traveling alone?" Elinor asked.

"Oh, no," Marko said, but before Elinor's eyes could so much as flicker in disappointment, he added: "I'm with my sister. She always promised that we would make it to Normandy, but we've put it off so long that this cruise was the only sensible way to do it. She can't do a lot of walking, so she enjoys the boat while I do the day trips. Speaking of which—tomorrow—if either of you is interested in the Orsay—"

Danny said: "I'm taking the women shopping. To the vintage stores in the Marais."

Another day of shopping was *not* what Mrs. Blossom would have chosen—she had been thinking about the small outsider art museum near Montmartre—but she understood that Danny had sized up the situation and was trying to help her. She felt at once grateful—and pitiable.

"Yes," she said. "And more of that falafel? I had meant to tell you about the plan earlier, Elinor. Danny knows all the best second-hand shops. In fact, Danny was the one who told me about the spa where I sent you."

She could almost read her old friend's mind. Elinor was, lord help her, a bit of a Rules girl. She played hard to get, at least in the early innings. (She had confided once that it was a risky strategy with older men, because the laws of supply and demand made them lazy and complacent.)

"Well, if Muriel has made plans, I am all in," she said at last. "She's done awfully well by me so far this trip." She stretched, which allowed her to show off her well-muscled arms. Elinor had been doing Pilates for literal decades. "I had the most divine massage this morning. The masseuse unknotted knots I didn't even know I had."

Marko stared at Elinor's biceps in frank admiration. "That's fine. We all have a week to get to know each other. If not Paris tomorrow, then perhaps Versailles the following day?"

"I think that could work," Elinor said.

Mrs. Blossom finally saw Paul—the Pink Panther—enter the dining room. Would he have been their dining companion if he had arrived at dinner thirty minutes earlier? Would he have paid attention to Elinor, as all men seemed to do? Or would he have focused on Mrs. Blossom, speaking in that low buttery rumble that just begged a person to lean in closer?

Well, as Marko had just said—they all had a week to get to know each other.

"**DANNY IS SO** *lovely*," Elinor said, dropping to the bed the minute they were back in the stateroom the next afternoon, removing her shoes to rub her feet. She had not worn the most practical shoes for walking Parisian streets despite Mrs. Blossom's careful instructions. Not the worst, but not the best. "He would be a wonderful gay best friend. Can we still say that?"

"I don't know," Mrs. Blossom said. "And I don't know for sure that he's gay. Or that I want him for a best friend. I have a best friend."

Said pointedly, or as pointedly as Mrs. Blossom ever said anything. She wanted Elinor to remember who had invited her on this trip—and who would be there for her when this trip was over.

But the day, while not at all what Mrs. Blossom would have planned, had been fun. Largely thanks to Danny, she had to admit.

After breakfast on board—an elaborate buffet unlike any Mrs. Blossom had ever seen, although, to be fair, most of the buffets she had seen had been at places like the Golden Corral and the occasional Mother's Day brunch—they had taken a taxi back to the Marais, which was shockingly close, not even twenty minutes. Mrs. Blossom kept thinking she had left Paris, despite seeing the Eiffel Tower through the dining room's windows.

Danny did know his way around the vintage shops. (Had he actually been a stylist before he was an FBI agent?) Mrs. Blossom experienced a small pang at the first place they visited, assuming he would be more interested in helping Elinor. After all, Elinor loved to shop, and she was so much easier to find clothes for, given that she was still a size four. A hard-won size four, who drank her coffee black and seldom ate bread, but still—a size four.

Yet Danny had seemed more intent on interesting Mrs. Blossom in scarves, bracelets, shoes, handbags. He had tried hard to persuade her to buy a pair of flowing black chiffon pants—"These would work so well with your, um, bright tops," he had said—but Mrs. Blossom had been adamant. No more clothes. She had enough.

She was, however, beguiled into acquiring two more scarves. Not Hermès or any other notable designer, simply pretty scarves, one a field of bright red poppies against a black backdrop, the other reminiscent of a Mondrian. Now, as she pulled them from the reusable bag she carried for shopping, she saw that Danny had somehow slipped the black pants in with them. When? How? Good lord, had he *shoplifted* them? No, he was an FBI agent; his job was to uphold the law. This was a gesture, a nice one.

So why did it feel so creepy?

"He likes you," Elinor cooed from the bed as Mrs. Blossom held up the pants to her waist and examined herself in the mirror. "Maybe he isn't gay."

"Don't be silly. Whatever his sexual, um, inclinations—he's young enough to be my son. Or yours."

"Well, 'our' son didn't buy *me* anything," Elinor said. "Although he was divinely helpful. The way he bartered in French. It was thrilling. There's no way we would have gotten the same prices with our Baltimore high school French."

"I hope," Mrs. Blossom said, "you have more sensible shoes for some of the excursions coming up. You can't wear heels to Normandy!"

"Why not? It's not as if I'll be storming the beaches." Elinor laughed at Mrs. Blossom's disapproving gaze. "I do have walking shoes, but can I help it if I like how my calves look in a bit of a heel? Now would you mind terribly if I took a nap before dinner? I haven't quite licked the jet lag."

Mrs. Blossom decided to sit on the upper deck, although the air carried a sharp chill. She had been there about five minutes when another woman, possibly about her age, although it was hard to discern, given her huge sunglasses and scarf-wrapped head, seated herself next to her.

"Hello, neighbor," the woman said cheerfully.

"Neighbor?"

"Well, neighbor of a sort. I'm directly below you. I confess, I covet your room."

Mrs. Blossom was not used to having things that others coveted, especially not a woman such as this, whose clothing and jewelry implied *real* wealth, to-the-manor-born wealth. For the most part, she seemed to be following the dictum that real wealth whispers, but there was a pink ring—a diamond?—on her left hand that probably cost more than Mrs. Blossom's first house. She wore flowing wool trousers reminiscent of Katharine Hepburn in her heyday, a coat that made Mrs. Blossom think "vicuña," although she wasn't exactly sure what vicuña was.

Yet the woman, with her long limbs and imposing posture, also seemed so, well, jolly and down-to-earth. This surprised Mrs. Blossom, too, because in her experience thin women weren't generally jolly, and this woman was extremely thin. A strong breeze could have easily knocked her over. But she had a bouncy, happy energy, despite her stiff-legged walk and cane.

"I don't think the rooms are *that* different. Most of the extra size is taken up by the balcony."

"Exactly. That's the feature I wanted. A little balcony where I could sip wine and watch the sunset instead of having to come up here. I insist that you invite me for a drink before the cruise is over."

The woman's tone was at once teasing and sincere. Mrs. Blossom could imagine her as a little girl, working her wiles on an indulgent father.

"I didn't bring any alcohol on board," said the ever-literal Mrs. Blossom.

The woman laughed. "I think we can rustle up some wine if we exert the tiniest bit of effort." She extended her hand. "I'm Patience Siemen, although I urge you to call me Pat. Not one of *the* Siemens, there's no *s*. Just think, one extra little letter and I would be worth *billions*."

"Muriel Blossom," she said, taking Pat Siemen's hand, which was even softer than Paul Paterakis's. *This*, she thought, *is a rich person's hand*. A hand that had never washed a dish or carried anything heavier than her own purse, a hand that was slathered in cream every night. Expensive cream, not CeraVe or any of the drugstore brands that Mrs. Blossom used. If Pat Siemen didn't have billions, she almost certainly had tens of millions.

"Where are you from?" Pat asked.

"Baltimore."

"Oh, I know my way around that old port city. Remember the *New Yorker* cartoon, the man on a lounge somewhere tropical, saying into his phone—I don't remember the exact wording, but the joke is that it's not as nice as Baltimore."

Mrs. Blossom did know the cartoon and thought it was funny—but only when cited by locals. Still, *old port city* sounded affectionate. She had never heard anyone refer to her hometown that way.

"I'm sorry," Pat said, perhaps noting Mrs. Blossom's expression. "I guess I thought I had standing to tease a little. I lived in Chevy Chase as a child, but I've spent the last thirty years here, there, and everywhere. I just can't seem to settle down."

Chevy Chase—so just outside Washington. Mrs. Blossom, like most Baltimoreans, had a bit of a chip on her shoulder when it came to the nation's capital. But the woman *had* apologized.

"What do you—" Mrs. Blossom felt a little stymied, trying to make conversation on a cruise. "Do?"

"Absolutely nothing." She leaned forward as if sharing a dark secret. "But I do it exceptionally well." She laughed in delight at her own wit. After a beat, Mrs. Blossom did, too.

"You're retired, then?"

"No, I've never held a job at all, not a real one. I don't feel great admitting that, but it's the truth, I might as well own it. You?"

Technically, Mrs. Blossom had never had a "real" job, either, except for her brief stint at the detective agency.

"I had some odd jobs before I became a mother, but after my daughter was born, I stayed home. Do you have children?"

"No, no, when I say I've never worked, I'm including life as a mother, which I believe to be one of the hardest jobs of all. I wouldn't have minded having a child, but it just wasn't in the cards for me. Are you traveling alone?"

She was so frank and direct, almost childlike. But she seemed genuinely interested in Mrs. Blossom.

"Yes and no. I decided to take this trip after my daughter moved to Japan." She felt that detail made her family sound worldly. "I've been widowed for a while, and my oldest friend is traveling with me, but I did a week in Paris on my own. Even though my husband died ten years ago, I've never taken a trip by myself, for myself. A few small things with my daughter and grandchildren. The Grand Canyon. Disneyland. Things like that."

Pat Siemen nodded with seeming approval.

"Once you catch the travel bug, you'll never want to stop. I didn't like cruises when I was younger, but they suit me now." Pat stood up with not a little effort. It was clear the cane, a handsome one with a malachite handle, wasn't for show. Still, her posture was perfect, something else that Mrs. Blossom believed to be the hallmark of the very rich. "It's colder than I realized. I think I'll go back to my cabin."

"Will I see you at dinner?" She wanted to get to know this woman better.

"Oh, I'll probably take dinner in my room. I know this is going to sound silly with all the wonderful food on this cruise, but the club sandwich from the little bistro at the rear of the ship, Cedric's, is divine. I have the palate of an eight-year-old, perhaps because I wasn't allowed to eat like a kid when I *was* a kid. I love sandwiches and macaroni and cheese and ice cream, but always in a cone."

"Yes, ice cream is always best in a cone—but what kind of cone do you choose?" She felt strangely invested in Pat's answer.

"A sugar cone. Only a sugar cone. Never cup, never waffle."

"Same!" Mrs. Blossom said.

"Well, look at us, kindred spirits. Do you know that term? Did you read the Anne of Green Gables books growing up?"

"I *loved* them. But which one of us is Anne and which is Diana?" Mrs. Blossom asked, assuming she was the Diana. She had the dimpled hands, if not the violet eyes. Besides, she was a classic beta, born to be the adoring second fiddle to more charismatic people like Pat.

"There's no reason we can't both be Annes," Pat said. "I think everyone should be the main character in their own life, after all."

She was probably being kind, but that was only another reason to like her. Mrs. Blossom valued kindness above all other things. Besides, being her own main character was an alluring idea. She had noticed, as of late, the use of the term "the main character" on various forms of social media, although it seemed to carry a negative connotation. But she never felt like the main character, real or virtual.

Back in her cabin, she was determined not to be overdressed again at dinner. But then she wondered—was it so wrong to dress up for things? Look at the beautiful clothes Pat Siemen wore just to eat in her own room.

On impulse, she tried on the black chiffon pants, and they fit beautifully, thanks to the elasticized waist. She paired them with one of her more muted tops—a long-sleeved tunic with black flowers on a white background. After studying a YouTube tutorial on her phone, she knotted one of the new scarves at her neck. Things didn't have to match precisely, after all. She added a black resin cuff, slid her feet into her new boots.

"Muriel!" Elinor said, emerging pink-cheeked and dewy from the bathroom. "You look *lovely*."

She beamed. Elinor's compliments were never suspect.

Danny, however—could she trust anything he said or did? True, it had been sweet of him to hatch a plan that kept Marko at bay, at least for today. But why had he bought Mrs. Blossom these pants? Why did he need to be on the ship at all? Was she really at risk?

She looked around the stateroom, but there was nothing to suggest that anyone had been there. Still, just to be sure, she slid open the false bottom of her pillbox. Her diamonds were there, safe and sound among the gummies. Would it be odd to put the pillbox in the safe? Well, who would know? She placed it in the small lockbox in the closet and chose a code that was easy to remember: 5003, the number of the first home she and Harold had shared.

Dinner was a rerun of the night before—Danny seating himself at their table without asking, Marko Polo politely requesting the seat next to Elinor, the Pink Panther entering late, glancing over at Mrs. Blossom—at least, she *thought* he glanced her way—then joining two younger couples who seemed to have befriended him.

Conversation remained fairly superficial. Mrs. Blossom blamed Danny for that, as he deflected personal questions and prattled about generic topics like movies and food, all the better to keep his story straight, she supposed. Mrs. Blossom was happy that she had kept his real identity secret from Elinor because the old adage was true: three could keep a secret if two were dead. Given how cozy Elinor was getting with Marko, it wouldn't have been long before she blabbed. Eventually everyone on board would know an FBI agent was among them, looking for—

Looking for *what*, exactly? Obviously, the bird wasn't on the boat. Was Mrs. Blossom like one of those traps in an old cartoon, where a delectable bit of food was placed under a box propped on a stick? Was she Danny's *lure*, just a big old stupid hunk of cheese?

The evening entertainment was the ship's piano player, crooning standards in heavily accented English. Mrs. Blossom stayed until she saw Elinor touch Marko's forearm. *That old trick.* But it worked, as all women know.

"I'm feeling a little odd," she said. "Probably too much wine with dinner. I think I'll go outside to clear my head."

She sat on one of the lounge chairs, looking south toward the Eiffel Tower. She couldn't be mad at Elinor, not really. If the situation had been reversed, if she were the one pursued by an attractive man—

But the situation had never been reversed, not once over the course of their long friendship. To be fair, Mrs. Blossom had been married for almost forty of those years, but men still flirted with married women. Just—not her, not usually. She knew it wasn't about their respective sizes, not really. Elinor put herself *out there*. Mrs. Blossom seldom did, and when she did, it ended badly. (Was there any ending worse than a man falling from his balcony forty-eight hours after he met you? Possibly.)

Someone else came out on deck, moving in a way that seemed furtive. Ah, it was a man, sneaking a smoke, a cigar. The flame from his lighter illuminated his face—it was the Pink Panther! But when he realized that someone else was on the deck with him, he gave a comical little cry and snuffed out the cigar.

"You don't have to put it out," she said, although she disliked cigars. "This is one of the few places one can smoke on board. They said so explicitly in our welcome letter."

"Still seems rude, when someone else is around, especially when that person is downwind," he said. "But I wanted to smoke a cigar while looking at the Eiffel Tower and holding a snifter of brandy. I'm a hopeless cliché, I guess." The tower, just south of them, was postcard perfect, as were the twinkling lights of the city.

"I think Paris brings out the hopeless clichés in all of us," Mrs. Blossom said. "That might even be the point of Paris—to do and see all the usual things." She warmed to her topic, crafting the argument she wished she had been quick-witted enough to make when Danny had disparaged her touristy plans. "I, for one, would feel awfully sheepish if I came to Paris and didn't see the *Mona Lisa*, or go to the top of the Eiffel Tower. I don't think that we get points, on our deathbeds, for avoiding popular things."

He laughed. "Wouldn't it be funny if we got to the pearly gates— speaking of clichés!—and St. Peter said, 'I'm sorry, Mr. Paterakis, but you once went to New York and spent the weekend watching the Rockettes and craning your neck to see the skyscrapers. Straight to Purgatory for you."

"What happens if I go to Philly and get a cheesesteak?"

"I'm pretty sure that's a venial sin, although it depends on whether you choose Pat's or Geno's."

"What's the right choice?"

"Dalessandro's."

Oh, she was having *fun*. Such a light, silly conversation, yet somehow more substantive than the one at dinner. She wanted to prolong the encounter, but she wasn't sure how.

"Where's your friend?" the Pink Panther asked. (*Paul*, she reminded herself. Besides, he was wearing a kelly-green sweater tonight. She sneaked a look at his ankles—bare, in Top-Siders. Really, his nickname should be the Pink Preppie.)

"She's in the bar, listening to the piano player." Or maybe groping Marko in some hidden corner of the ship. Once Elinor started to move, she moved fast. A woman didn't marry three times in thirty-five years by taking her time.

"No, I was speaking of the young man, my backgammon opponent."

"Oh, he's more of an acquaintance, someone I met in Paris."

"I wondered. He's a slick one, for sure."

Interesting. Maybe Paul had good instincts about people. If so, she wondered what he was picking up about her.

"As I said, I don't really know him well. Are you going to Versailles tomorrow?"

"Yes, you?"

Dammit, she wasn't. She had a solo trip set for tomorrow, a personal quest that she believed would be one of her trip's highlights, but now she was full of regret. "I've planned a special trip on my own." She added quickly: "I am looking forward to Giverny, the next day, the tour of Monet's gardens. The tulips should be in bloom."

"I confess, I don't know much about gardens *or* art. I always get Monet and Manet confused."

"Ah, there's a trick to that," Mrs. Blossom said. "Manet paints men, Monet paints outdoors."

He pointed his extinguished cigar at her. "You are a very helpful woman, Mrs.—I'm sorry, I've forgotten your name. I'm terrible with names."

"Muriel," she said, "Please call me Muriel."

April 9

"**NO BIKE RIDE** for you this morning?"

Danny had found Mrs. Blossom alone in Cedric's, enjoying a late breakfast by her standards—it was almost nine. Her interest had been piqued by Pat Siemen's praise for the bistro. She also liked being able to make her own coffee here; it had been embarrassing to ask for multiple refills at breakfast yesterday. The French idea of a cup of coffee was so small! She wasn't even sure it was a cup, maybe six ounces at the most.

"Don't be rude," she said, after swallowing a bite of almond croissant.

"How is that rude?"

"Me, on a bike, with all those super-fit families in their high-end sweats. I'm sure you think that's hilarious."

"Oh my god, I wasn't making fun of you." Danny seemed genuinely concerned that he had hurt her feelings. "I've spent enough time with you by now to recognize how formidable your stamina is. We walked almost eight miles yesterday and you never once complained or seemed tired—which is more than I can say for Elinor. You're a beast. That's a compliment these days, in case you didn't know."

"Bikes around cars make me nervous. Anyway, it's moot. If you read the morning bulletin, there were no available spots on the bike trip."

"I never read the morning bulletin. Or the evening one for that matter. The only thing I want on my pillow is a chocolate. But surely you'll do Versailles?"

"Elinor's going. I have my own plans." She pointedly did not delineate them. They had been surprised at Hart headquarters, resistant even, when she had explained her need of a private car for this one day. They tried to dissuade her from going rogue, as she thought of it. *There's really not much to see there, certainly nothing like Giverny.* But she had been adamant, and they had ended up booking a driver, although they had reminded her multiple times that she must reboard by five thirty as the ship was sailing that night. "Are *you* going to Versailles?"

"Been there, done that. No offense, but this is not my dream vacation."

She had had enough.

"When people say 'no offense,'" Mrs. Blossom said, "they are simply announcing their intention to offend. Just as in when they start off, 'I hate to tell you,' they actually, in fact, *love* telling you. Or—'I hope you don't mind—' They just don't care if you mind. I didn't book this tour for you, a worldly young man who travels to Europe all the time. I booked it for me, a sixty-eight-year-old woman who's never been outside the United States."

"I'm sorry, I seem to keep putting my foot in it this morning." He seemed sincerely apologetic. "That *was* rude of me. But what are you going to do if you don't go to Versailles?"

"I have arranged for a guide to take me to Vétheuil." She hoped she was saying it right.

"Vétheuil?" Danny pronounced it as she had, a relief. "Really? What's there?"

"There was an artist, Joan Mitchell—"

"Didn't you just go to her show in Paris?"

How would Danny know that? Ah, right—the man who followed her that day would have reported back to him.

"Yes. She was sort of my gateway to abstract expressionism; Pollock, Motherwell had always left me a little cold, but her paintings—they invited me in, and then I learned about all the female artists no one had bothered to tell me about in my continuing education courses. Helen Frankenthaler, Grace Hartigan, Lee Krasner. Alice Mason. Mitchell is my favorite, maybe because she felt like 'my' discovery. I admire her art and her life story. She had this amazing, well, certitude about everything. For example, when she was quite young, she said: 'I will never paint another realistic figure.' And she never did! Also, she was a very good ice-skater."

Danny laughed, and Mrs. Blossom realized that it was quite the anticlimactic non sequitur. But it had stuck with her, that bit of trivia. To be able to paint *and* ice-skate competitively. To have any talent whatsoever, for anything. She had accepted long ago that she was singularly without talent. She had never been good at anything in particular, except loving Harold. And she couldn't even claim to have been perfect at that.

"Anyway, she left the United States and moved to Vétheuil, bought a house near the place where Monet lived before Giverny. She worked there from the 1960s on and did some of her best work in the 1980s, when she was in her fifties. Now that I've seen their paintings side by side, I want to see their houses, which are practically side by side. Hers overlooks his."

"Are they open for tours?"

She shook her head. "Monet's house is a bed-and-breakfast now, and the owner has been kind enough to invite me to stop by. I'm not sure about the Mitchell property. I don't think I'll be able to do anything but walk around it."

"Sounds interesting. I'll go with you."

Mrs. Blossom was taken aback. "I was looking forward to the solitude. As much as I love Elinor, I'm not used to sharing a room with someone after all this time."

Actually, she wouldn't have minded company; Elinor was the one who had decided, even before Marko came into view, that she would rather see Versailles. And now it would just be Elinor and Marko walking through the palace gardens together, which might accelerate their shipboard romance to the point of making Mrs. Blossom feel very three's-a-crowd. If only she had been faster on her feet last night, talking to Paul. She should have persuaded him to skip Versailles and come with her, maybe even intimated that she had so much more to teach him than the difference between Manet and Monet.

No, the problem wasn't company. The problem was *Danny*. She didn't trust him. She had tried googling every variation of "stolen Pakistani statue," and nothing had really come up, although there appeared to be a few articles behind the paywall at the *Beacon-Light*.

"I have a guide."

"So you said," Danny said. "Is it a *guide* or a driver? Does he charge by the person?"

"OK, he's a driver. Hart Tours helped me arrange it. They said in all the years they've been doing this itinerary, no one has ever asked to visit Vétheuil."

She was proud of this. Mrs. Blossom was not a person who was used to hearing: "*No one ever asked for that before.*" She always ordered off the menu, followed the rules, requested no substitutions.

"It would be only prudent for me to accompany you," Danny said. "Just in case."

Mrs. Blossom was torn. It would be helpful to have Danny and his perfect French on this somewhat open-ended adventure. Was she safer with or without him? She should be safer, right? He was an FBI agent—right?

"You may accompany me," she said. "The car will gather us from the dock at noon."

The trip to Vétheuil was more than an hour by car, and the village itself was nothing special, which was for the best, as they had only an hour or two before they had to return to the MS *Solitaire*. But the yellow bed-and-breakfast was, as the online reviews had promised, a perfect prelude to Giverny. The owner was as gracious and informative as advertised, but her expertise was Monet, not Mitchell, and it was the latter that was the true draw for Mrs. Blossom. The bed-and-breakfast owner did point out Mitchell's house, which was directly behind them, set in a chalk cliff, with balconies that would have allowed Mitchell to literally look down on Monet. Mitchell had rather disliked living on a street named for Monet.

"You should knock on the door, see if they'll let you in," Danny said as they stood outside from what seemed a respectful distance. But Mrs. Blossom could never do such a thing.

"She had—or pretended to have—great disdain for him," Mrs. Blossom told Danny. "She even mispronounced his name when a *New York Times* reporter visited, rhymed it with *bonnet*. But I think that was for show. In person, she could be cranky—the word *truculent* was used—but her work is so beautiful and joyous. When I look at it, I believe that Mitchell had to know true happiness."

"Have you? Known true happiness?"

"Of course," she said automatically, then wondered if this were factual. During her marriage, yes, sure. The early years, then the joy, after years of trying, of becoming a mother. She also had been extremely content during those last few years with Harold; she just hadn't known they were the last few years.

"How did you come to be such a passionate fan of Mitchell?"

But Mrs. Blossom could not, would not tell that story, because it was intertwined with a part of her life she never discussed. She said instead: "I can't believe I'm hungry again. Can we find some food before we meet the driver? He's picking us up at three, to be on the safe side. I was warned the traffic might be heavy, heading back into Paris."

They walked for about fifteen minutes before they found a café that looked appealing. Nothing extraordinary, but so far even the most pedestrian places in France had yielded wonderful meals. Mrs. Blossom chose a croque monsieur and a hot chocolate, while Danny had lamb stew. Its wonderful fragrance gave her real diner's remorse. Danny might be irritating, but he always knew the best things to order.

"I feel sheepish, being ignorant about Mitchell," Danny said. "I did go to art school, after all."

So that part of the story was true.

"Her reputation has taken off in recent years, but if Joan Mitchell had been a man, she probably would have been much, much more famous earlier in her career," Mrs. Blossom said. "I mean, she was well-known, by the end of her life, her paintings were in all the major museums, but she should have been as celebrated as Pollock and Rothko. Most of the female abstract expressionists were a bit over-shadowed. Imagine being Helen Frankenthaler, married to Robert Motherwell."

"Fame isn't a constitutional right, Warhol and his fifteen minutes of fame be damned," Danny said.

"You know, he probably didn't say that, nor was he the first to say it," Mrs. Blossom said, proud to know this little nugget. "And whatever he did say, it's been so twisted over the years as to become meaningless."

"The point is, fame eludes the vast majority of people," Danny said. "Even white men, even in this day and age. It's a scarce commodity. The ground has shifted, there are new ways to be famous, but it's almost as if there's a cap on how many people can be celebrities at any one time—and how long they can stay that way. Ask a Gen-Zer who, for example, Jack Benny was."

"But, surely, it's disproportionate? You're not saying that women and, um, others had the same opportunities as white men?"

"*Others*? You mean people like me, people of color?"

She took an enormous bite of her sandwich and chewed it as slowly as possible. Her cheeks felt fiery from embarrassment. She probably looked like a squirrel, with her mouth so full of food. A squirrel wearing blush, who was panicky about saying the wrong thing.

"It's OK, Mrs. Blossom. I'm aware that I'm not white. There's a game I play sometimes where I try to think of how many famous actors—famous in the Western cinema, not Bollywood and its environs—might play me in my biopic. How many can you name?"

Her brain froze. "The one—he did sort of nerdy roles, but then he made his own movie, and then he was a superhero?"

He laughed. "That could be Kumail Nanjiani or Dev Patel. But, OK, that's a start."

She was stymied, unsure of the rules of this game. Must the actor be Pakistani? Must he be Danny's age? Would it be rude to say "Ben Kingsley"? There had been a very cute actor on *Young Sheldon* that one time. She decided to turn Danny's question on him.

"Well, how many actresses could you name to play me? I mean actresses who are my size."

"There's the one—she's a little young to portray you—"

"*Thanks.*"

"But so beautiful, with that shiny hair. And funny. I can't think of her name, but it's right on the tip of my tongue—"

"I'm not beautiful and I'm not known for being funny."

"You make me laugh all the time, sometimes even on purpose. Also, you should stop running down your looks. You're quite attractive. Oh, wait, I have another one—Olivia Colman. You totally give off Olivia Colman vibes."

"She's *skinny.*"

"Why are you so obsessed with your size?"

"Because the world is obsessed with my size!"

Mrs. Blossom's words burst forward with a vehemence that surprised her. But she couldn't stop herself. She realized she didn't want to stop herself.

"Because strangers offer me diet tips and suggest that I think about having the salad with dressing on the side. Because people say 'Good for you!' and give me a thumbs-up in the gym. Because, since I was in grade school, people have told me what a pretty face I have, and talked about my dainty hands and feet, as if I didn't know what *that* was code for. Because when we went to see *Fantasia* on a class field trip, everyone looked at me when the hippos danced."

Danny looked confused. "What is it code for? Dainty hands and feet?"

"Since my hands and feet are small, people seem to think it means all of me could be small, if I just tried. I did try when I was a teenager. If I hadn't, my mother probably would have locked me in a room and fed me bread and water for the rest of my life. I ate as she told me to eat, but I never lost weight. God, when Harold proposed, I couldn't get out of my parents' house fast enough. We were married three months after we met—and we were very happy, despite her dire predictions."

"Marry in haste . . ." Danny said. "I hate to take her side, but she had a point."

"My marriage was *wonderful*."

"Always?"

"Always," she lied.

Their bill settled, Danny tried to call the driver, but he found it difficult to get cell reception inside the thick stone walls of the café.

What happened next unfolded so swiftly that Mrs. Blossom was never sure of the exact sequence of events, how it all began. She was only certain of the ignominious ending.

A touch, a kind of jostle from behind. She jumped as she always did at any unexpected touch. But her pique was forgotten in the suddenness of a hand reaching for her purse, tugging at it so hard that she was pulled from her seat and onto the floor of the café. She wore her purse crossbody style, but the strap snapped from its mooring as she rolled on the floor. Still, she held on to it as if her life depended on it. For all she knew it did. As the man—she assumed it was a man because the person seemed strong, but she never saw her attacker's face—tried to wrestle it from her, she instinctively rolled on top of her purse, cradling it the way one might shield a child from a vicious dog. The would-be robber tugged again. People in the café had begun shouting, presumably at the person wrestling with her, and a waiter came running to intercede. But it was only when Danny returned, screaming in French and English, that the would-be purse snatcher abandoned his attempt and fled.

"What the—" She was breathing heavily, strangely embarrassed, as if she had caused the unseemly ruckus. Plus, it was humiliating to be splayed on the floor with her dress hiked up to her thighs.

"Let's go," Danny said. He said something in French to the gawping locals; the words meant nothing to Mrs. Blossom, but the tone was reassuring. He then piloted Mrs. Blossom out the door, where their driver was waiting.

"I—I need a moment." She didn't want to get in the car. She didn't want to be in an enclosed space. She didn't want to be in an enclosed space *with Danny*. Why was that? Danny had saved her, hadn't he?

Or had he set her up? He had stepped outside to make a call just before it happened. Whenever trouble came for Mrs. Blossom, it was always Danny adjacent.

The café had an outdoor table that was providentially empty. She took a chair, trying to get control of her breath, but also her thoughts. Something had been bothering for two days, something small, but nagging. It was like a tiny pebble in one's shoe that kept coming back no matter how many times the shoe was upended and shaken. Danny claimed he was protecting her. So why did bad things keep happening when he was around?

"Show me your credentials," she said at last.

"What?"

"Your FBI ID. I assume you have some sort of ID."

"Well, not *on* me. I keep it in the room safe. I can show you later, though."

"Danny—I'm not going to forget when we get back to the boat. I don't believe you're an FBI agent. If you are, you're going to have to prove it to me. If you don't prove it to me, I'm going to start making calls. You may think I'm just a gullible old lady, but I know people who know how to track down information. I'm going to find out if there's a Danny Johnson in the FBI's stolen art unit, see if I don't."

He didn't speak for a moment. Glib Danny was stumped.

"OK, then, I'm not *exactly* an FBI agent."

"Not exactly?"

"I'm a freelance investigator. I've been hired by an insurance company to recover the missing statue. You see, they paid its owner four million dollars after it was allegedly destroyed in a fire, but we recently learned that the bird was stolen *before* the fire."

"Burned or stolen, what's the difference? The owner still suffered a loss."

"The museum wasn't insured for theft, only fire—that's a more common arrangement than you might think, a cost savings for smaller museums. A fire was set, the owner was paid for the entire contents, but the single most valuable item in the collection might not have been there at all. Suspicious, don't you think?"

"But wherever the statue is, it belongs to Pakistan in the end."

Danny couldn't meet her eyes. "Well, Pakistan isn't paying my bills. The insurance company and government officials can work out provenance later. My job is to find the bird and deliver it to my clients."

Danny the FBI agent, trying to do whatever was necessary to re-patriate a stolen antiquity was someone Mrs. Blossom could respect, however grudgingly. Danny the mercenary was a different story. She couldn't imagine her former boss, Tess, taking on a job like this.

"And I'm your lead? You think that if you stick close to me, you're going to find out what Allan did with the statue?"

He gazed skyward at a jet passing by. "I was genuinely interested in learning about this artist you dig so much—"

"Danny—"

"OK, fine. You know something, even if you don't know what you know or how you know it. You're involved in this. I just can't figure out how." He paused. "Or how unwittingly."

Oh, this was rich: Danny was accusing her of being dishonest. The best defense, etc., etc.

"Danny, did you have anything to do with that man attacking me right now?"

"Of course not." He looked insulted. "If I wanted to search your purse, all I had to do was wait for you to go to the bathroom."

"I always take my purse when I go to the bathroom. It has my billfold in it."

Danny laughed, as if this was supremely witty, but it was simply factual. And normal. Mrs. Blossom did not know another woman in the world who didn't take her purse to the bathroom.

"Let's go back to the ship," Mrs. Blossom said. "And, once there, I'd appreciate it if you'd leave me alone. In fact, I insist on it. Keep your distance from me as much as possible, or I'll—" She tried to think of a plausible threat. "I'll tell the captain that you have illegal drugs."

"I'm not the risk. Someone just tried to steal your purse. Someone attacked you. You clearly need someone to watch out for you."

"Not you." Her mind was made up.

In the car, they sat in an uncompanionable silence. Danny stared at his phone, scrolling through what appeared to be his email. Mrs. Blossom inventoried the contents of her purse, making sure everything was there. Everything was.

More than everything was there.

In the zippered pocket that she seldom used because of its small size, there was a device she recognized because she had one in her luggage. The Cube, as it was called, was a little more expensive than an AirTag, but she had chosen it because it had a fully functional GPS that worked even when cell towers were blocked. Even with a carry-on, it had seemed a good bet.

And she had mentioned it to Danny in the park the other day. Perhaps he thought he could get away with hiding one in her purse, that if she found it, she would think she had placed it there by mistake, muddle-headed old woman that she was. He could have slipped it in there minutes ago, as he helped her gather her things from the floor of the café.

He must really believe that she was going to lead him to this statue. If she confronted him now—no, he would make more excuses, tell more tall tales, deny his involvement. Keep it where it was for the time being. See if Danny kept popping up unexpectedly. Once she was sure that it was Danny who was following her, she would find a new home for the tracker.

She had other questions, too. And she knew exactly who could help her answer them quickly.

"Jesus Christ, I despise fucking paywalls," Tess Monaghan said.

"You really shouldn't talk like that around your children," Mrs. Blossom said, looking through the cabin's French doors, wondering how much time she had before Elinor returned from Versailles.

"OK, one, their language is so much worse than mine. You should hear the stuff that comes out of Carla Scout's mouth, it would curl your hair, and now the baby is repeating everything she says. Two, they're not here right now. Crow took them to the movies. God, it galls me to pay the *Beacon-Light* for anything. But, for you, Mrs. Blossom, I will fork over what it takes to read these articles."

They were on FaceTime, Mrs. Blossom and her former boss, although it was often hard to think of Tess as anyone's boss. She was younger than Mrs. Blossom's daughter and sometimes seemed younger still, despite being a mother to two daughters of her own, Carla Scout and Liza Jane.

Part of her youthful affect was her hair, which she wore in a defiant antistyle, a long braid down her back. Her clothes tended toward workout gear—not athleisure, just basic sweats, or jeans with baggy sweaters. Mrs. Blossom couldn't help wondering what kind of makeover Danny would propose for Tess. And, oh how she longed to hear what Tess would have to say back to him. Tess blurted out her thoughts with a toddler's impulsiveness, albeit with a much better vocabulary, one often studded with literary allusions and arcane facts about Baltimore. Her mind worked in a way that made sense to her, but almost no one else could follow her line of thought except her husband, the aforementioned Crow. He also seemed to be resisting adulthood, although he was a very good father, in Mrs. Blossom's estimation, much more hands-on than her son-in-law or Mr. Blossom. But men of Harold's generation were among the first to be expected to "parent" at all, so of course they were inexpert at it.

Tess also was a good parent—but so different from Mrs. Blossom. Less fearful, indifferent to germs. She did try to instill some manners in her children, yet she didn't seem to mind when they fell short.

"OK, OK, OK, OK, I think I'm up to speed, and because I paid for access, I can email you gift links to all the articles. But here's what happened with this statue in a nutshell. In late 2009, a year after the financial markets cratered, Constance Saylor, who had inherited a huge fortune from her father, ended up in a financial freefall. She didn't just invest in shitty bonds—"

"Tess—"

"I told you the kids aren't here. She also started a winery on her estate in Butler. I'm sorry to say this about my native state, but most

Maryland wine is swill. She had one major asset, a museum in her barn. Literally, a former barn. But this happened to be around the same time the IRS began questioning whether the museum met the various litmus tests for running a genuine nonprofit. You see, the Saylor collection apparently was open only one Sunday a month, from one to five. And it required reservations. The IRS couldn't, by law, confirm to the newspaper that it was investigating the museum, but her lawyer inadvertently let it slip."

"Does it name the lawyer?"

"Yes, Allan Turner." Mrs. Blossom was disappointed but not surprised. "He said in an interview that he was confident Constance Saylor's museum would maintain its nonprofit status. Six weeks later—poof, up in smoke!"

Mrs. Blossom was sitting at the desk in her cabin. She wondered if anyone had ever worked at this spindly-legged thing. It seemed unlikely. Maybe someone had written a letter home on the MS *Solitaire*'s letterhead paper, but surely no one on a cruise such as this needed a desk.

"What caused the fire?"

"Arson," Tess said. "There was an attempt to make it look accidental—the fire started in an attic crawl space where flammable solvents were kept—but it was an amateurish job. Her handyman did it. Apparently she had stiffed him on salary and— STOP!"

Tess's three dogs had burst into the room—a retired racing greyhound, an Italian greyhound, and a Doberman. The two greyhounds were even more poorly behaved than Tess's children, but the Doberman was a dignified saint, in Mrs. Blossom's opinion. And, perhaps not coincidentally, the only canine who had come into Tess Monaghan's life fully trained.

"Does it say anything about a statue of a bird?"

"Not in the initial coverage. The museum was ruled an entire loss, Constance Saylor collected a pile of insurance money, sold the place in Butler at a bargain price and left town. Her nonprofit puttered along for a few years, but it had no funds and eventually shuttered."

"In the articles you're skimming—is there anything about the insurance company trying to reopen the investigation?"

"No, no—" Great, another lie from Danny. "Wait—there's no single article about an investigation, but there is mention of it in an obituary for Constance Saylor. She drowned in a boating accident in Lake Lugano in 2019, but the *Beacon-Light* didn't learn of her death until last year because she had been living overseas and had no living relatives. It's not really an obit, more of a reminiscence about a 'colorful character.' You know, that Saturday feature that looks back at the city's history."

Mrs. Blossom did know. It was by far her favorite thing in the paper.

"Anyway, this piece mentions that the insurance company did try to reopen the case, but was stymied by the fact that Saylor had died, leaving virtually no money or assets. And she had no family, so there was no one to hold accountable."

"What about the handyman? Was he really working on his own, or was it a job-for-hire?"

"Were you always this cynical, Mrs. Blossom? I rather like it. Anyway, I had the same thought. So my old friend at PD, Martin Tull, put me in touch with the original arson investigator. He said they offered the guy so many opportunities to flip on his employer, deal after deal, but he never folded, never changed his story. He said he burned down the museum because he was mad at his boss, who had stopped paying his wages about four weeks earlier. They did a deep forensic accounting and couldn't find any evidence of a payoff. She was hemorrhaging money, stiffing all her workers—her gardener, her pool cleaning service. But here's where it gets interesting—"

Mrs. Blossom thought things were already pretty interesting.

"The handyman was paroled from prison last fall. Just two months ago, he died in a gas explosion in his home. It was ruled an accident—malfunctioning gas heater, he lights up a smoke, kaboom. But the guy had a storage unit on the south side of the city. Police inventoried the contents and guess what they found?"

"A bird statue?"

"Absolutely nothing!" Tess said. "I mean, there was some furniture, boxes of books. Things he put in storage when he went to prison. But that was it. I have to admit, I was beginning to think this statue didn't even exist, but I went way back into the archives and found a piece about Constance Saylor from the early 1970s, and there's a photograph. Black-and-white, not great quality, but you can see a statue of a bird on a table near her elbow."

"Would you send that me?"

"Sure. I don't know how many gift links I get, but I can always grab a screenshot. Again—the quality is lousy. But it doesn't look like a four-million-dollar statue to me. More like something you could buy at HomeGoods."

"Tess, a man was killed. Someone searched my room, someone tried to steal my purse today, and someone has put a GPS tracker in my purse. Surely, something important is at stake here. Maybe"—she didn't want to complete her thought—"maybe something worth killing for."

It was lunchtime in Baltimore and Tess had what looked to be a huge deli sandwich on her desk. She picked up a pickle and bit it as if she were trying to snap somebody's spine.

"Did it ever occur to you that what's happening to you has nothing to do with a stolen statue? Correlation is not causation. This could be about something else entirely."

Correlation is not causation. Mrs. Blossom heard Harold's gently chiding voice. It was a mistake she was prone to make, especially in her social interactions with others. If someone were abrupt or unkind to her, she always assumed she had provoked the behavior. Harold was forever reminding her that people were rude for all sorts of reasons. Now Tess was telling her there might be another explanation for these strange occurrences. Come to think of it, Danny was the one—the *only* one—who insisted that she was connected to the missing statue, that she was a supporting player in a larger drama.

"What else could it be, though?" she asked Tess.

"Your lottery ticket."

Mrs. Blossom shook her head. "That makes no sense. I cashed in the ticket and my identity was never revealed. The people who tried to claim it was theirs are not likely to be in Europe, stalking me, even if they did figure out who I am."

"I'm not saying that someone's looking for the *ticket.* I agree, that makes no sense. But someone might have figured out that you're a newly wealthy lady and wants to get close to you."

"Why would a fortune hunter try to mug me?"

"Excellent point." Tess took another ferocious bite of pickle. "Maybe in order to save you? Sort of like that scene in *The Fantasticks*? 'A Little Rape.' Is that the name of the song? It's something like that. Do you think they can even perform that song anymore? It's wild, now that I think about it, one of the longest-running musicals could have a song that—we performed it in my middle school and—"

"Tess—" Her former boss sometimes needed gentle prodding to get back to the subject at hand.

"I confess, Mrs. Blossom, I simply can't make sense of any of this."

"Will you do one more thing for me?"

"Anything for you, Mrs. Blossom."

"If I give you a name, can you run a background check on someone?"

"Sure."

"Danny Johnson."

Tess smacked her forehead melodramatically. "Please, could you give me a harder one?"

"Well, I do know he's from Atlanta and he's forty-two. And he graduated from MICA." Assuming he had told the truth about that.

"Oh, in that case, easy-peasy."

"Tess, there's no need to be sarcastic."

"But I'm so *good* at it. Anyway, I'll have better luck if you can get me a photo of him. Then I can try a reverse Google Image search, see what comes back."

Mrs. Blossom wondered how she could get a photo of Danny when she had told him to stay away from her. But knowing Danny and his indifference to her wishes, it wouldn't be long before he started pestering her again.

"Meanwhile, I'll send you everything I found, even the old piece on Saylor and her sort-of obituary, which mentions the fire, but not the bird. Pretty sad to die and have no one in your hometown notice for five years."

"Sad to die so young, too."

"Young, she had just turned sixty-five—oops, sorry. Who knew I could fit my foot in my mouth along with a gigantic pickle?"

"That's okay," Mrs. Blossom said. "I know I'm not young, Tess. It's silly to me that some people in their sixties still try to claim the mantle of middle age, or say things like 'sixty is the new forty.' Trust me, it's not."

"You've got something better than youth—you're finally living life on your own terms. I'm proud of you for taking this trip. I know how far out of your comfort zone you've ventured. And I'm stoked that you'll be here in Baltimore now. The kids—well, Carla Scout, LJ doesn't really know you yet—are looking forward to having Auntie B around."

Almost as if on cue, the family, like the dogs before them, burst into the room. Both girls were an uncanny mix of their parents—dark hair, light eyes, father's high cheekbones, mother's full mouth. They also were loud and full of laughter. They looked like a delightful family, and Mrs. Blossom was eager to spend time with them.

But they were not *her* family and never could be. Her family was—good lord, how far was Japan from Baltimore? Whatever the distance, she would travel it gladly, assuming she was invited. But even if she was invited—*of course she would be invited*—she wouldn't see them more than once or twice a year.

She would never forget the moment Trout had unveiled the news about his job change, the transfer. No, it was the moment *before* she couldn't forget. The family had been at their favorite Mexican restaurant. It wasn't anything fancy, just a reliable spot near the house, beloved for its familiarity, its competence, the very lack of surprises. A plastic basket of chips, good-enough salsas— one brown, one green—bouncy mariachi music on the PA. Her granddaughters wheedling for sodas, her daughter sighing into her frozen margarita. Everything was as it had always been—and then Trout cleared his throat, made his announcement, really a *pronouncement*, as her daughter had already been clued in. A much better job in his company, with a significant raise. Tokyo! An apartment in a high-rise! The Land of Hello Kitty! Of course the girls were excited, and even her daughter, who had been sitting on this secret for several days, was full of giddy anticipation. Mrs. Blossom had waited to see if anyone would ask "But what about Grammie Bee?"

No one had asked.

It was almost 5:00 p.m., about time for the other cruisers to return from Versailles. But, for now, the MS *Solitaire* felt luxuriously empty and quiet.

Mrs. Blossom went to the upper deck, to the chaise she thought of as "her spot" only three days into the trip. Most of her ideas about traveling on a cruise had been formed by a book she had read as a child, about a college-age girl going to Europe just before World War I. That and the film *Titanic*. Both had indicated a level of luxury that seemed impossible to imagine now—porters ready to tuck steamer blankets around you, ferrying warm drinks and snacks as needed. But that would have made her uncomfortable, being waited on hand and foot. She could fetch a hot chocolate from Cedric's and bring it here, but she didn't want to move. She ached a little from being knocked to the ground. Her dignity was even more bruised. How ridiculous she must have looked, rolling around on the floor.

Her downstairs "neighbor," Pat, soon joined her. She was resplendent, no other word would do for her wide-legged pants, turtleneck, and blazer. Part of it was the tailoring, Mrs. Blossom supposed, but even her inexpert eye could gauge the quality of the fabrics. And while she, personally, would never want to be this bony—it's nice, as one ages, to have padding in case of falls—Pat's frame did lend itself to billowing pants and belted jackets, a look Mrs. Blossom could never pull off.

"You didn't go to Versailles?" she asked Pat.

She shook her head. "The walking would have been too much for me. Besides, I find palaces depressing—royals often have terrible taste."

"Do you think it's objectively terrible, or do you just think times have changed?" Mrs. Blossom had been buying things for her new apartment, and she had noticed she was drawn to the kind of mid-century designs that her mother had favored—and that she had found old-fashioned and embarrassing as a child. Now she wished she hadn't sold all her mother's furniture when she died.

"Fair enough," Pat said. "And, of course, it's all about materials, what's precious in any given time. Do you watch those home renovation shows?"

Mrs. Blossom *doted* on home renovation shows. "From time to time."

"Well, it's just a racket, right? The economy needs us to buy things, so they create these false 'trends' in home decor and make it sound as if you risk your social standing if you have an 'outdated' kitchen. Who can change their kitchen every ten years? It's an endless cycle, makes me think of Wordsworth."

"Wordsworth?"

Pat began to recite: "'*The world is too much with us; late and soon, / Getting and spending, we lay waste our powers.*' Spend your money on experiences. All the so-called happiness experts agree that experiences bring us more enduring happiness than almost anything we can buy."

"Like this cruise," Mrs. Blossom said. She felt elevated, knowing that a woman who wore her wealth with such casual elegance had chosen the same cruise she had. *So there, Danny.* (There she went again, saying "So there" in her head to someone. One day, she really should say it out loud.)

"Yes," Pat said. "Like this cruise. Don't get me wrong—there are some material possessions that can make a person happy." She extended her arm and admired her pink ring.

"Real diamonds!" Mrs. Blossom said in a breathy Marilyn Monroe voice. "They must be worth their weight in gold."

To her delight, Pat laughed. "That's one of my favorite films, too," she said. "But even with this ring—it's actually the *story* of the ring, the man who gave it to me, that makes it precious."

Mrs. Blossom fiddled with the fortune cookie on her charm bracelet, thinking about her own diamond earrings—so tiny and insignificant next to Pat's ring, yet dear to her. "Is it a story that you can share or one you need to hold close?"

Pat's face was grave. "How remarkably sensitive you are, Mrs. Blossom, to know that some stories can't be shared readily. They get worn out, in a sense, if we allow ourselves to tell them too often. Do you remember the experience, when you're young, of having a crush on someone and wanting to say his name whenever possible? Then you get older and you just want to hold those names, those memories, close—yes, that's the perfect way to say it, you nailed it. I imagine you have a few of those stories yourself."

Mrs. Blossom did.

From their perch on the upper deck, they could see the tour bus for the Versailles trip crossing the bridge and making the turn into the parking lot near the dock.

"Ah, the masses return," Pat said. "And soon we will set sail. You will want to be up here for that, it will be very festive. Alas, I have to avoid crowds. I worry about getting jostled."

She glanced up at the sky, which was still quite bright, with a few scudding clouds. "I forget how late the sun sets in Paris in April, how quickly the days expand. It wasn't that long ago that it was dark by this time. By the way, I'm still going to hold you to having me for a sunset drink on your balcony before the trip is through." She cracked her knuckles, rubbed her hands together. "I wouldn't want to do this trip in summer, the crowds are too thick, but this damp chill is hard on my joints. Then again, if it weren't for swollen knuckles, my ring would probably fall off, and *that* would be a catastrophe."

She winked at Mrs. Blossom and made her slow but steady way to the stairs. Whatever the story behind her ring, Mrs. Blossom hoped it was a happy one. Her own precious memories were a little more complicated. She ran her finger over the fortune cookie's clasp. Should she open it, should she read Harold's final message to her?

No, she still wasn't ready.

Elinor's feet did not appear to hurt today, although she had worn her impractical kitten heels again. In fact, she appeared to be walking on air when she came back to the cabin and threw herself on the bed like a teenage girl. Mrs. Blossom knew immediately what had made her friend giddy, and it wasn't the tapestries of Versailles, or even the gift shop. It was Marko. Too bad. Misery loves company.

Misery loves company. Had she really just thought that? Was she miserable? Had she expected Elinor to hunker down with her in the wallow of widowhood, to shoulder a solitary life as she had? On some level, yes, that was exactly what she expected, she supposed. But she wasn't miserable. Was she? Mrs. Blossom was happy, or at least trying to be. She thought of Pat Siemen, who had happiness all figured out. Experiences, she had said, were what made people happy, not money.

Then again—love was an experience.

"Did you have fun? He's a nice-looking man," she told her friend. "If a little on the taciturn side."

"Oh, I talk enough for two," Elinor said. "It's just so exciting to meet a man I don't have to train. Glorious manners, impeccable clothes, no bad habits that I've detected."

She got up and fluffed her hair in the mirror, putting on and taking off different pairs of earrings. Primping, Mrs. Blossom realized.

"Do you, um, require some privacy tonight? At dinner?"

"No, I think we should continue with our regular foursome. Maybe later I'll take a walk with him on the upper deck. Or maybe we'll just go back to his cabin and have sex."

"*Elinor.*"

"What? He's a nice-looking man and it's only an eight-day cruise. Shipboard romances are a storied tradition. If one can't have a fling on a ship making its way up the Seine—" She regarded Mrs. Blossom thoughtfully. "I really should give him to you. You haven't even dated since Harold died."

"Because I don't want to."

"Oh, I know that. Men have always liked you."

That's not how Mrs. Blossom remembered it. *She* had liked men—well, boys, given that she married at age twenty. She had liked them too much, even more than Elinor, although she had been less open about her desire. Marriage to Harold, whom she truly loved, had also been a safe harbor, a way to ensure that her passion wouldn't get her in trouble. It had worked, more or less. When he died, she had no desire to go back *out there*, as people spoke of it, as if life for a single person was some dangerous and formidable territory.

To Mrs. Blossom, it was.

"I'm going to change for dinner," Elinor said. "And at dinner, I'm going to ignore Marko Polo and focus my attention on you. Because, one, I love you and I want to hear about your day. And two, it will drive him *crazy*."

"Elinor, aren't we too old to still be playing silly games like that?"

"No."

They did have a lovely dinner together and it did, in fact, seem to stir up Marko Polo's interest. (Marko, his name was Marko. It was clearly wrong of them to objectify him with a nickname based on what he had worn just once, yet he was now stuck in Mrs. Blossom's head as Marko Polo.) Danny was a no-show; Mrs. Blossom was glad that he was obeying her injunction to stay away from her. Pat also continued her boycott of the dining room, which was a shame, as Mrs. Blossom wanted to introduce her new friend to Elinor.

She also hoped that the empty chair might lure PP—even in her own mind, she was discreet about her crushes—over to them. But he also was a no-show tonight.

She had a decaf espresso, then left Elinor to flirt with Marko in L'Étoile, where the piano player was crooning jazz standards older than Mrs. Blossom. She found herself hoping Elinor would get up to some sort of mischief. It would be fun to live vicariously through her friend. She told herself she didn't have any use for a relationship, or even a fling.

Who are you kidding, Muriel Blossom? She had googled Allan Turner on the train to Paris, found his address in the suburbs, even calculated how long a drive it was from her new condo to his place in Columbia. And now she was yearning for a man after an exchange whose most intimate moment had been a cheesesteak recommendation.

She got into bed, determined *not* to wait up for Elinor. She assumed she would fall asleep quickly, after the events of the day, which seemed increasingly surreal to her. *Had a man really tried to steal her purse? Was it just a coincidence? What about the GPS tracker, how long had it been in her purse?*

But, as it happened more and more these days, she could not sleep. She knew what *not* to do, but she did it, anyway. She got out her phone, connected to the ship's internet, and read the stories that Google News swore were "for her." Oh, somehow she had missed the news about the Joan Mitchell Foundation suing Louis Vuitton over the unauthorized use of her paintings in advertisements. Yes, Mitchell would have hated that, Mrs. Blossom was sure of it.

She played Wordle, although she hated Wordle. She checked Facebook and then did the thing she really should not have done, something she had not done for many months, maybe even a year: she went to *his* page.

Michael Calista. He said his surname was from the Greek, meaning "beautiful," but that his family was Italian. He said *she* should have been named Calista because she was so very beautiful.

He said a lot of things, Michael Calista.

It was the year Mrs. Blossom had turned forty. She hadn't thought of herself as having a midlife crisis. She still wouldn't characterize it that way. But it had been a difficult time. Her daughter had just turned twelve and was increasingly absent, caught up with a new circle of friends at school. On the phone all the time, hanging out at the mall. She didn't need her mother as much. And Harold, perhaps having a slightly delayed midlife crisis, had become distracted and irritable, working longer hours than ever, worried that he was at risk of his younger colleagues passing him by. For a while, Mrs. Blossom even suspected *him* of having an affair.

That still didn't justify what she did with Michael Calista, a man she met at, of all places, a snowball stand, where he was inexplicably ordering soft-serve. Really, the way she met men— running into the street after a wounded dog, ordering a strawberry snowball with marshmallow topping. Go figure that Allan, whom she had met in such a promising, adult way, would turn out to be the truly bad apple in the bushel.

Not that Michael Calista had been any great shakes. Oh, how he had wooed her. Seduced her, there was no other word for it. No man had ever campaigned for her the way Michael Calista had. No man had ever had to. She had all but literally thrown herself in Mr. Blossom's arms the day they met, then refused to leave his side.

Michael Calista spent months pursuing her. It began with email, which was still novel at the time. Boy, that made her feel ancient, remembering how the sight of electronic mail was once a joyous thing. It was all so innocent, at first. Lots of jokes about ice cream. A double entendre about "soft-serve." Suggestions of museum visits after he learned that she was taking an art history course in Johns Hopkins continuing education program. The Cone Collection at the BMA. (More ice cream jokes.) The Walters. The Jacob Lawrence paintings in DC. Sitting in the Rothko "chapel" at the Phillips Collection, feeling overwhelmed by the beauty of the room, with its four perfect Rothkos.

Being kissed in the Rothko chapel. Going to a motel on Route 29 in midday.

And then he never spoke to her again.

The term "ghosted" was not in use then, at least not to Mrs. Blossom's knowledge. It was the early 1990s; people didn't even have smartphones. They could "chat" online—something she and Michael had done in private "rooms" and, yes, it had gotten rather spicy. People still had landlines, with answering machines and voicemail. She had left him so many voicemails on his work number, claiming, as probably almost everyone claims in that situation, simply to be *worried*. Of course he owed her nothing. Of course she had presumed nothing. But was he OK? Was everything all right?

Of course, she had presumed everything. She had no experience that would have prepared her for the kind of man who courted lonely women, then dropped them as soon as he got them into bed. The thrill of the chase, a coyote who always got his road runner, and left the little bird flattened on the highway.

She had never confided in anyone, not even Elinor. It was too humiliating. One thing to have an affair—one could rationalize that love was a force unto itself, something that must not be denied—quite another to be seduced by such a low-rent Lothario.

Besides, the person she really wanted to tell was Harold. But it would have been unfair to him *because* he would have forgiven her. She suspected, worried, that he had intuited it, anyway. Not the whole story, but a piece of it. Sometimes, she would catch him looking at her and there was a sad wistfulness in his gaze, as if he knew something about her that he wished he didn't.

She was sad, too. Michael Calista was like an inkblot on a beautiful white dress. Small, insignificant, yet the dress was still ruined. Not that he had ruined her marriage. Not that *she* had ruined her marriage. But she had been stupid and foolish, and the one person who might have comforted her must never know how stupid and foolish she had been. It was terrible, living with that secret. But it also was a just punishment for what she had done.

And when Harold died shortly after her fifty-eighth birthday—well, she didn't really believe in God, but karma seemed credible to her. As the song said, you don't know what you have until it's gone. She had paradise and she risked it all for a man who was not that different from a predator. A predator with a Facebook page, but Facebook wasn't around when Mrs. Blossom was forty. Turned out he was married, Michael Calista. He had been married all along. His feed with full of photos of his wife, who was very thin, and his children. This was all news to Mrs. Blossom, news she couldn't use because it was fifteen years later that she stumbled on the page, directed to Calista by Facebook's "People You Might Know" algorithm. Turns out they had a lot of Baltimore mutuals. He sent her a friend request. She accepted because to ignore it would suggest she had been harboring a grudge all these years. She had, but that was none of his business.

One would think that Mrs. Blossom would not have wanted to speak to Michael Calista when he reached out two years ago, asking if they could meet on her next trip back to Baltimore. One would be wrong. She agreed to lunch at the restaurant at the Baltimore Museum of Art—only to be stood up.

And that was the day that she discovered Joan Mitchell's work. She had been so embarrassed to have fallen into his trap again. He had asked her to meet him as a test, and sure enough, she had walked right into it. He must have loved the idea of her sitting there in Gertrude's, waiting for him. Cruel people were Mrs. Blossom's kryptonite. She simply could not understand anyone's desire to be unkind for the sheer kick of it.

She was too self-conscious to get through eating a meal by herself. The waitstaff had seen her there, chugging glass of water after glass of water for almost forty-five minutes. She put down a ten-dollar bill, walked out of the restaurant and up the stairs to the Mitchell exhibit, where the exuberance on display felt healing. There may be cruelty in the world, but there also was beauty.

With the MS *Solitaire* rocking gently beneath her, she quit the Facebook app and connected her phone to the bedside charger. Then she went one step further and removed the app from her phone entirely. Oh, she would put it back eventually—she liked seeing photos of people's grandchildren, enjoyed sharing her own—but not until this trip was over.

Only now she was even more awake. Would she ever learn the cost of looking at screens during a bout of insomnia? She checked her email. Good lord, why was Tess emailing her so late? Then she remembered, it was six hours earlier in Baltimore.

Tess, as promised, had sent all the articles. Mrs. Blossom chose to read the "appreciation" of the late Constance Saylor. Yes, there was the photo that Tess had described and, yes, the quality was terrible. Constance Saylor looked miserable, hawk-nosed and beetle-browed. One could almost see a resemblance between her and the bird, at least in profile. She had a large, soft body, not unlike Mrs. Blossom's.

There was another, later photograph of Saylor in her epony-mous museum, about the time she was in her fifties. This photo was taken from a great distance, the better to showcase the art, so all Mrs. Blossom could tell was that Constance Saylor had spent three decades dieting her body into submission. Oh, and here was an interesting tidbit, in the piece about Saylor's unnoticed death— the insurance company believed the statue had not been in the fire because its sapphire ornamentation was never found. Sapphires apparently can withstand heat.

Mrs. Blossom knew she should get off her phone. Tomorrow was Giverny, it felt like the true start of the cruise, now that the MS *Solitaire* was moving slowly up the Seine. And, again, she did not want to appear to be waiting up for Elinor when—if—she made it back to the room.

Too late. Here was Elinor now, shoes in hand, creeping back into the room like a teenager who had stayed out past curfew.

"You don't have to tiptoe," Mrs. Blossom said. "I'm awake. You're back earlier than I expected."

Elinor sank onto a corner of the bed with a sigh. "I took my shoes off only because they hurt. But my legs look so good in them. Ah, vanity. Not that he seemed to notice."

"Did he try to inveigle you back to his cabin?"

"*Inveigle?* What a delicious word. It sounds so . . . nefarious. Anyway, no. It turns out he and his sister are sharing a cabin." Mrs. Blossom couldn't see her friend's face in the dark, but she could hear the frown in her tone. "Is that weird? It seems a little weird to me."

"Not if they're close."

"So close that they're staying in the same cabin?"

"The cabins can be made up so that the beds are apart, with the nightstands between them."

"But if you really have the money to travel this way—"

"*We're* sharing a stateroom."

"It's different for two female friends. But the more curious thing is that, well, he didn't try anything. I assumed he would want to kiss me at the end of the night, at the very least."

"How do you know he didn't want to? He could be shy."

"Because I took matters in my own hands, stretched up to kiss him—and I basically caromed off his face. I don't usually misjudge so badly. He blushed and said I had caught him off guard. Then he walked me here and gave me a little shoulder squeeze." She took off her earrings and watch, put them in a tray on the bedside table. "I expected some feistiness. A kiss or two on the deck, maybe some groping in a dark corner."

"Elinor, that would look—ridiculous. At our age."

"*Everybody* in real life looks ridiculous kissing. Have you ever seen young people? They look like they're trying to *eat* a melon with their hands tied behind their backs. Even the best-looking ones look dopey. Kissing only *looks* good in movies." Elinor sighed. "What matters is how it feels."

"I suppose that's true." Still, she had no regrets that she and Allan had been discreet. They had not even held hands in public; she had been pleasantly surprised by how demonstrative he was once in her room. Good lord, what if *he* were married? What if his death in Paris had nothing to do with a statue, and everything to do with a woman scorned? Tess was right. There were all sorts of possible explanations here.

Tomorrow, they would have put real distance between them and Paris. They would see Giverny and walk through Monet's gardens.

"Good night, Elinor."

"Good night, Muriel. You know, I heard this doctor on the radio the other day. He said you need eight hugs a day to release oxytocin, which is essential to healthy aging. Eight! When was the last time you were hugged eight times?"

"I probably got that many from my granddaughters." But who would hug her now?

"Would you hug me eight times a day, Muriel? If I can't find anyone else?"

"Of course." She did not attempt to do it just then—it would have been awkward, given how the beds were made—but she reached across the blanket and gave her friend's hand a squeeze.

She felt a little guilty at how glad she was that Marko Polo wasn't head over heels for Elinor, not yet. She wanted her friend to be happy, of course. But it seemed a little unfair, how easily Elinor had always attracted men, while Mrs. Blossom seemed destined to meet one only every twenty years or so—and there had only been one good one, Harold.

Whom she had betrayed.

"IT'S LIKE A fairy tale," Elinor kept saying the next morning, as they traipsed—because that's how one walks through a fairy tale, after all, one traipses or gambols—down garden paths and across green Japanese-inspired bridges. Monet the painter meant little to Elinor, but she could appreciate a beautiful garden, a charming house, the nineteenth-century version of a dream kitchen.

But if it was a fairy tale, then it was one in which a sad old hag hovered over the prince and princess as they made their way through the beautiful gardens. Elinor's hand was tucked into the crook of Marko's elbow, not Mrs. Blossom's. They were a good-looking couple, even from behind, Mrs. Blossom had to concede. One could imagine them in an ad for an erectile dysfunction medication. *I'm not being bitchy,* she thought, defending her id to her superego. *The people in those ads are extremely attractive!*

Hart Tours had arranged early access to the gardens, so the paths were not yet thronged as they would be later in the day. This perk was one of the reasons she had chosen the MS *Solitaire*. Mrs. Blossom stopped to take a photo of the celebrated water lilies. They were not, of course, what they would be later in the year, but Mrs. Blossom decided she was glad she had chosen early spring for her visit. The air was fragrant with hyacinths, the jonquils were like little yellow soldiers, standing proud and straight in the rays of morning sun.

"A photo of water lilies?" inquired a voice from behind her. "You really aren't afraid of clichés, are you?"

It was Paul. He wore a sweater with a pink-and-green argyle pattern today, a V-neck over a crisp white shirt unbuttoned just enough so that she could see a few curly chest hairs. Still no socks.

"And to think," she said, "you weren't even sure of the difference between Manet and Monet two nights ago. Now you're lecturing me on water lilies."

"I'm a fast learner," he said. "And even a rube like me knows that the water lilies are famous. Do you want company, or are you happy alone?"

"I'm with—" But Elinor and Marko had walked far ahead, not realizing she had stopped. She could see them on the bridge—and she could tell that Elinor, by the incline of her head, was all but daring Marko to kiss her. And then he did! They did not, Mrs. Blossom realized, look the least bit ridiculous.

"Yes," she said. "I would love company."

They walked slowly through the garden, enjoying the last few uncrowded moments before the gates opened to the general public. Once the gardens began to fill with people, they retreated to the gift shop, where Mrs. Blossom admired the blue-and-yellow Limoges dinnerware. She even considered buying a set for her new place until she saw the price—$570! Per place setting! A mere mug was $130! Who could eat from such plates, even on a special occasion?

"You should buy them," Paul said.

Normally, Mrs. Blossom had no problem saying she couldn't afford something. But Paul was so clearly wealthy, maybe even born to wealth. He probably assumed everyone on this trip wouldn't think twice about Limoges china.

"I'm being careful to make sure I can get everything I buy in my carry-on," she said, which was true.

"I'm sure they ship," he said.

Mrs. Blossom considered it. After winning the lottery, she had decided to work with a financial adviser, a somber young man— well, younger than her—who said her money, even invested conservatively, could yield about $200,000 a year. It seemed shocking to her, almost shameful, to earn money that way. And she had never really wanted for anything. Harold had been the kind of practical man who had been prepared for death despite its early arrival. *Tell me what you want,* her young adviser had said, *and I'll tell you if we can make it happen.* Should she call him up and say, "Hello, can I buy dinnerware at $570 per place setting if I need only one?"

She said truthfully, if a bit misleadingly: "I'm saving my money for art for my new apartment."

"New apartment?"

"I'm moving back to Baltimore after several years in Arizona and I've decided to start practically from scratch. The place I've chosen is actually a Mies van der Rohe building." Paul looked a bit blank, but she couldn't expect a man who had trouble with Monet/ Manet to know architects. "As pretty as the china is, I don't think it's exactly my *aesthetic.*"

Mrs. Blossom had never in her life spoken of having an aesthetic, but maybe she did? She resolved in that moment to make her home as nice as possible, which didn't have to mean spending a lot of money. But she was sixty-eight. This would probably be the last place she lived, God willing. She thought of all the things she and Harold had put off while waiting—what had they been waiting for? They got their daughter through college without debt. They paid off their house. They put money away for rainy days, but money couldn't really do anything to save you from the rainiest day of all. She did not, in fact, want Limoges china; her heart would break with every chip or scratch.

But she could probably afford a set of Russel Wright. Again, something else her mother had owned, and that Mrs. Blossom had packed up and sold on eBay.

"What did you say you did," she asked Paul, "up in Ardmore?"

"Finance," he said. "Relatively low-key—I'm too old to keep up the pace in today's financial world."

"And your wife—"

"Gone," he said. "My kids sent me on this cruise to cheer me up." He made eye contact with Mrs. Blossom, his gaze steady and warm. "I think it's working."

"There's a small museum in the town and we have time to visit before we report back to the bus. Would you like to—"

"I would love to," he said, holding out his arm. "But only if you explain everything to me. Mrs. Blossom—"

"Muriel."

"Muriel, I'm going to be honest. I'm not sure I even understand what impressionism is. But you have made a wonderful impression on me."

She laughed. It was a terrible joke, what her grandkids would call a dad joke.

It was the best joke she had ever heard in her life.

Sometimes, a day can turn as quickly as an avocado. Less than eight hours after the magical trip to Giverny, Mrs. Blossom was sitting in a café in Les Andelys, hating herself and hating herself for hating herself. If it's bad to exclude people, it's not much better to volunteer for exclusion. But that's what she had done, in a moment of self-consciousness, and now she regretted it.

And things had been going so well.

After Giverny, and the wonderfully quiet interlude in the museum—Paul turned out to be someone who could regard art in solemn contemplation, which Mrs. Blossom enjoyed—it had taken the MS *Solitaire* three hours to make its way up the river to Les Andelys. Paul had joined Mrs. Blossom, Elinor, and Marko for lunch, and he balanced the table nicely, finding ways to get the laconic Marko to speak, teasing Elinor so easily that Mrs. Blossom worried for a moment that he might become enamored with her. But, no, his attentions seemed focused on Mrs. Blossom. There were raw oysters for lunch, and he had a dozen, with champagne. Mrs. Blossom was tempted, but she feared the champagne would make her logy, and they had been warned that the afternoon expedition was physically taxing.

"Don't worry, I'll switch back to my usual iced tea after I take a power nap," Paul said. "You, Muriel?"

For a moment, she thought he was inviting her to join him. Then she realized he was simply asking her intentions for the next couple of hours. "I can't nap," she confessed. "If you ever see me napping, it means I'm coming down with something."

"I will see you in Les Andelys," he said.

Yet when they gathered in the parking lot near the dock, Paul was nowhere to be seen and she didn't feel she could inquire of anyone where he was. The staff had been so explicit on the first day that they would not go looking for people who failed to join the tours. Maybe Paul had changed his mind? Or maybe there was an urgent business matter back home?

Or maybe he had just kept sleeping. She tried not to take it personally, but she was so sure that he had been borderline flirting with her at lunch.

While Hart Tours usually depended on local guides, this afternoon's activity had been entrusted to the staff TDs—tour directors. Two of the three were jovial, big personalities, a man from Croatia and a Polish-born woman who reminded Mrs. Blossom of her younger self, curvy and seemingly unaware that she was a knockout.

The third TD was a native Frenchman, one of the few French natives among the entire staff of the MS *Solitaire*. He also was the least popular, with a face and manner that suggested a state of perpetual constipation. Mrs. Blossom privately thought of him as Gaston-with-a-puss-on. So far, Mrs. Blossom and Elinor had managed to avoid him, but today their luck ran out and they were assigned to his group, the Blue group.

"Shouldn't that be *Bleu*?" Elinor said, attempting to get Gaston to smile. It didn't work, but Marko gazed at her as if she were the most scintillating woman alive.

Gaston droned through his introductory remarks, mentioning over and over that it was an extremely steep climb and that anyone who doubted their ability to manage the grade and the rocky paths would probably be best off in town. "It's really just a view of the river, and it's overcast today," he said. "Besides, you'll see Richard's burial place in Rouen tomorrow. There are no traces of Richard at his old fort."

Throughout this speech, Gaston made constant, unnerving eye contact with Mrs. Blossom, who was standing toward the front of the group, ever the apt pupil. (Elinor and Marko had slowly drifted to the back, the better to hold hands. Really, it was like being on a junior high school field trip all over again. Cool kids in the back, flirting, the studious little brownnosers at the front.) Mrs. Blossom didn't fear the climb, but the guide was clearly skeptical of her. Each time he reiterated that the trip was not for those without stamina, it seemed as if more and more eyes focused on her.

She moved slowly to the back of the group as unobtrusively as possible, whispered into Elinor's ear that her stomach was bothering her, then turned and walked quickly toward what appeared to be the small town's main street.

There were some interesting shops, including one with antiques, but Mrs. Blossom had never cared for antiques. She started to buy some cute stuffed animals for her grandchildren, then remembered that her daughter had cautioned against sending the girls new possessions for a while. Their Tokyo home was so small they had been forced to put almost half their things into storage. She yearned to buy something, anything, for her new home, but nothing she saw was quite right. Granted, it was only five hours ago that she had announced loftily that she had an aesthetic, but she didn't want to buy something just for the sake of buying something.

She could have gone back to the ship, but she felt the staff would judge her, too. No, not judge—pity, which was far worse. *The fat old American woman could not climb the hill.* She was nowhere near the oldest woman on board. Pat Siemen, thin as she was, was much creakier and moved more slowly than Mrs. Blossom. Of course, Pat hadn't attempted either of today's excursions. But there were other men and women as large and old as she was. Why had she been singled out as the fat one, the old one? Maybe she hadn't been. Again, Harold had forever been cautioning her about her self-consciousness.

She ended up killing time at this café, although she wasn't really hungry. She drank hot chocolate and ate a very good pastry, feeling self-conscious with every bite. Were the locals looking at her? Were they *judging* her? France was a confusing place to Mrs. Blossom, full of so much wonderful food, yet also full of women who seemed intent on being thin above all things. She was shocked at how many people here still smoked.

A tall, slender figure, one she wished was not so familiar to her, came ambling down the main street. Danny.

"I thought you were going to see where Richard the Lionheart lived," he said.

"*I* thought we had an understanding that I wanted you to stay away from me."

"Look, why are you mad at me? So I didn't tell you the exact truth about what I do. The parameters are more or less the same. A statue was stolen. I'm trying to return it to its rightful owners."

"You're trying to return it to an insurance company."

"As I said, the rightful owners. They paid for it. If it exists, they should have it. Anyway, why are you here instead of exploring the ruins of the castle?"

Did the tracker bring you to me? Probably so. Now that she was sure that Danny was using it to follow her, she would have to find a way to get rid of it.

"I decided I wanted to explore the town."

"Not much of a town."

She didn't disagree, but Danny brought out her contrariness. "It was good enough for Richard the Lionheart."

Danny frowned; he really did seem in a foul mood today. "I'm not sure that's much of a recommendation, although there are many who believe Richard was a gay icon."

It was the closest Danny had ever come to revealing anything about his own sexuality. Or was it? It was so hard to tell with him. Mrs. Blossom decided to pry, just a little.

"And that's important to you because—?"

Danny shrugged. "It's not. His sexuality is up for debate. His cruelty is an established fact."

"His cruelty?" Mrs. Blossom knew of Richard the Lionheart largely through films, and always as a force for good. All the Robin Hoods, from Flynn to Costner, had pledged their loyalty to King Richard.

"He was barbaric, even by the standards of his time. The most famous incident involves a negotiation with Saladin, over thousands of Muslim prisoners. Saladin kept stalling the talks and Richard finally flew into a rage. He had three thousand prisoners, including women and children, taken to a hill, and there, in full view of Saladin's army, all the prisoners were beheaded and disemboweled. No, I shall not be visiting his castle here, nor his grave in Rouen, which means I'll be skipping the cathedral. I do not wish to pay tribute to Richard the Lionheart. I wouldn't mind seeing his actual heart, though."

"Is that possible?"

"Not really, but they have preserved it, in a vault in Rouen, embalmed with frankincense, myrtle, mint, poplar, bellflower, and lime. If I saw it, maybe I could be convinced that he actually had one."

Mrs. Blossom, stared into her cup of hot chocolate. "I'm sorry, you must think I'm ignorant, not to have considered that there's always another side to history, that anyone who goes to war has caused pain and destruction to others."

"At least you're willing to listen and think about it. So many people now—it seems to me that they just double down when we ask that they reconsider that there's no universal history, that there's no version where someone doesn't get left out, or marginalized. The

Crusades are of great interest to certain elements in the alt right, which speaks volumes. Hey, I noticed you've been hanging out with that guy who wears bright sweaters. What's that about?"

Why did he care, what *that* was about? How could he even know? Danny hadn't been at Giverny, nor had he been at lunch. The tracker may allow him to keep tabs on her location, but it couldn't reveal the company she was keeping. Was she still under surveillance? Were Danny's minions driving from port to port? Had he set up that attempted robbery? Her brain was racing.

"His name is Paul," she said. "He seems nice enough. And, no, he's not traveling with a stolen statue, or looking for one."

"That you know of. What are you doing?"

"Taking a selfie," said Mrs. Blossom, who almost never took selfies. She held her phone up, pretending to vamp for it, but it was focused on Danny, not her. She had promised to send his photo to Tess, but she was sure he would be suspicious if she asked him to pose for one. Yes, there he was, captured nicely in the frame, even if he was frowning.

"You should be careful," Danny said. "You're not the best judge of people."

"I know," she said. "After all, I was taken in by *you*. At first. Oh, here come the others, down the hill. If I don't go back to the ship, Elinor will expect me to visit all the shops I've already visited."

Elinor was holding Marko's hand, staring up into his face, smiling like the proverbial cat who had swallowed the canary. She probably hadn't missed Mrs. Blossom at all.

Back on board, Mrs. Blossom managed to lure Elinor from Marko long enough to sit in the lounge for a predinner drink. The ostensible mission was for the two of them to go over a coffee-table book about the cathedrals of Rouen, tomorrow's destination. She tried not to keep stealing hopeful looks at the door, but Paul continued to be missing. He wasn't much of a drinker, she reminded herself. The champagne at lunch may have hit him hard. Had he been trying to impress her? It had felt that way at the time.

But he didn't appear in the lounge and he didn't show up at dinner, although she lingered as long as she could. Oh yes, she was definitely third-wheeling now. She almost—almost—missed Danny because at least when he was filling the fourth chair, she didn't feel as superfluous.

Finally, after a drawn-out dessert of profiteroles and ice cream, Marko asked Elinor if she wanted to go for a stroll on deck. "Of course you are welcome to join us," he said to Mrs. Blossom.

His lovely manners, his sincerity, only made it worse, somehow.

"You go ahead," she urged them. Then, because she wanted her friend to have an opportunity at the privacy that had eluded the couple so far: "I'm going to have a digestif in the bar and finish this novel I've been reading. It's quite long, but I'm determined to get to the end so I can leave it behind in the ship's library. I have about a hundred pages to go."

"That's a lot of pages to read in a bar."

"Not so very many for me. I can read at least fifty pages in an hour."

That was her signal to Elinor that she wouldn't return to the cabin for at least two hours. If it was a private place Marko required to be romantic, they could have it.

She kept her promise, although it was a stretch for her, dallying over a glass of port for that length of time while reading a book that bored her. The people in the bar tonight seemed so very coupled up, uninterested in making conversation with anyone else. Gaston-with-a-puss-on moved among the groups, but he ignored her.

Paul was nowhere to be seen.

She dutifully finished the novel that had been vexing her—Mrs. Blossom always finished every book she started—then left it on a bookshelf in the lobby, which was full of left-behind books. Her timing was perfect. As she entered the corridor on the Platinum Deck, she saw Marko Polo slip from her room and down the stairs. Ah, so he was Gold Deck.

Or lower.

She decided to take a stroll along the Gold Deck. Paul also was on the Gold Deck, she believed. OK, she had noted his room number when he signed the check at lunch. But there was a DO NOT DISTURB placard on the door. She lingered, much as she once rode her bike, oh so slowly, past the home of a junior high crush. There was no sound coming from within, no light shining beneath the door. Was that a line from a song? Almost. She began humming the Elvis Costello ballad that she was thinking of—such a sad, romantic song. She had always been a fan of Costello, from the first moment she saw him on *Saturday Night Live*, bespectacled and almost knock-kneed. She felt as if they had grown up together, in a sense. Mr. Blossom didn't get the appeal, so she had never seen Costello in concert. She still could she supposed; Costello continued to tour. But who goes to concerts alone?

She impulsively pulled a piece of paper from her handbag and scrawled a quick note: "Hope you're feeling OK? Call my room or my cell if you need anything."

Mrs. Blossom went to her room, expecting to find Elinor in postcoital contentment, but she was cranky and irritable.

"We fooled around a little," she said, "but he was so distracted, as if he expected someone to burst in on us. He kept getting up and wandering around our cabin, remarking on our view, how lucky we were to have a balcony, and he was in the bathroom for a long time, quite the mood killer. Maybe he's not actually attracted to me?"

For Elinor, this was no less than an existential dilemma. Who was she if not someone whom men found attractive? Mrs. Blossom felt obligated to comfort her.

"He's probably just shy. Plus, he couldn't be sure when I would return, which would put a crimp in any man's style. Maybe tomorrow, you should convince him to skip the excursion altogether, stay behind on the ship with you."

She hoped Elinor would say, *Oh no, we must see Rouen together.* But she merely nodded. "I think that would work, he'll be fine, missing Rouen. But probably not the D-Day lecture, later that afternoon. What is it with men and D-Day? I won't even watch those movies and miniseries with Tom Hanks. Too graphic."

"I didn't watch them, either," Mrs. Blossom confessed. "But I did like the podcast, by the man who got fired from that Tom Hanks HBO show before he even started."

"Podcasts," Elinor said. "My, aren't you modern. Next thing I know you'll be telling me you're doing TikTok dances."

"I had to drive so much in Arizona, I needed podcasts to keep from going insane. In Baltimore, I'm not going to own a car at all."

"Not own a car? Are you crazy?"

"I'm *ecstatic*. I hate driving. I've run the numbers—between delivery services and Zipcar and Lyft, I can get by without owning a car at all, and spend about the same amount of money it would cost to insure a car in Baltimore City."

"Driving at night is the worst," Elinor conceded. "I try to avoid it when possible. Oh, Muriel, when did we get old?"

"Speak for yourself," Mrs. Blossom said, laughing, but the fact was—she *didn't* feel old. If the trip had started off with a bit too much adventure to suit her—Allan's death, the bizarre interest in her possessions, the attempted mugging—it was now taking on the shape of what she had imagined, all those months ago during the planning stage. The scenery was everything she had hoped for, the food was good, her eyes were almost drunk from the beauty she had seen, in the countryside and the museums. And she sensed she was making at least one new friend, in the eccentric Pat Siemen. A shipboard friendship was more meaningful than a shipboard romance. A shipboard friendship had a greater chance of continuing.

Still, she wished Elinor had thought to assure her that *her* crush was reciprocal, that there had to be a reason Paul had disappeared so abruptly after their lovely morning and lunch. But that had never been their dynamic. Elinor was Doris Day and Mrs. Blossom was Audrey Meadows. Or, worse, Elinor was Grace Kelly and Mrs. Blossom was Thelma Ritter. Mary and Rhoda. Veronica and Betty. Why did the culture pair—pit—women this way? She remembered again Pat Siemen's comforting words about everyone being the main character in their own life.

She climbed into bed. OK, so she wasn't the femme fatale of the MS *Solitaire*. But she was beginning to see that much was still possible, even at the age of sixty-eight. She might not be able to afford to travel at this level every year, not unless she continued finding lottery tickets in parking lots. Maybe it would be even more fun strategizing how to travel on a budget. She could rent a house in a foreign city for a month or so, or do an apartment exchange. Eventually, she would make her way to Tokyo. Where else would she like to go? The Galápagos, Cape Town, Barcelona, Rio . . .

How did the Lewis Carroll couplet go? *The world is so full of a number of things / We all should be as happy as cabbages and kings.*

No, no—that wasn't it. *Of all the words of mice and men*—No, wrong again.

She laughed at herself in the dark, realizing she had mashed together Carroll and Robert Burns—and then she recalled that the Walrus and the Carpenter were using their conversational wiles to lure succulent baby oysters into being devoured.

Oysters made her thoughts circle back to Paul. She hoped he wasn't tossing and turning behind his DO NOT DISTURB sign. *Cabbage* made her think of cabbage roses, and cabbage roses reminded her of a skirt she had worn in the 1980s, when in thrall to the romantic trends of the day, and her cabbage rose skirt made her think of—nothing. She was asleep.

TRUE TO HER word, Mrs. Blossom tackled Rouen alone, although she did linger at breakfast, wondering if Paul might show up. It was a small ship and it was strange to go almost two days without seeing someone, but then—Pat Siemen was never in the main dining room. Mrs. Blossom was beginning to wonder if the whole thing with Paul was some fantasy she had cooked up. Not Paul himself, of course—he existed, he had interacted with Elinor and Marko, they could vouch for that. But his kindness, his interest in her—perhaps that was all in her mind. Was this another kind of ghosting?

She took the morning tour of the cathedral—pausing to give a harsh frown to the resting place of Richard the Lionheart's heart in the cathedral, now that she knew the monarch's cruel history— then decided to eat lunch in town while everyone else in the group headed back to the ship. It was important to embrace doing things alone. That was her reality, after all.

Besides, the longer she stayed away, the more time Elinor had to spend with Marko.

After lunch, she found the site of Joan of Arc's execution, marked by a simple sign, not too far from an open-air market. She wandered happily among the stalls, marveling at the beauty of the produce, the briny fresh smell of the seafood. She was in France, it was a beautiful day, she was seeing new things, learning new things. What more could she ask for?

Back on the ship, she was immediately aware that something was amiss. The usually amiable staff seemed harried and distracted; passengers were whispering among themselves. She wished she had tried to make more friends among the other travelers, then she might feel comfortable asking what was going on. Maybe Pat Siemen would be taking in the air on the upper deck?

She was, her face tilted toward the sun, her eyes shielded by enormous and—Mrs. Blossom had to assume—very expensive sunglasses, possibly vintage.

"And how was Rouen, city of churches?" she asked.

"Very pretty," Mrs. Blossom said. "Things are so old here."

Pat laughed. "That's why I prefer to live in Europe. I fit right in."

"Did something happen on the ship today? I know you spend most of your time in your room, but—everyone seems so agitated, yet I can't figure out why."

Pat raised her sunglasses. "Yes, there was a kerfuffle of sorts, but the ship is keen to keep it under wraps. A passenger was taken away this morning, while everyone was in Rouen."

"Taken away?"

"In an ambulance," Pat Siemen said. "I saw it through my windows. And when the maid came to make up my room, I asked her if she knew what was going on. I think she confided in me because I speak French. She said there was a passenger who had left the DO NOT DISTURB placard on their door for more than a day and the staff finally decided to check, found someone in great distress. I wager it's either food poisoning or a virus, and neither one is good for a cruise. Either way, I feel validated by my choice to avoid the dining room."

"Did the maid tell you which passenger was stricken?"

"No, and I couldn't see from here whether it was a man or a woman on the gurney."

Mrs. Blossom thought back to the oysters, the champagne. April had an *r* in it, but she wasn't sure if that rule about which months in which to eat oysters applied in France, or if it applied anywhere anymore, given the changing climate. She felt awful, hoping for food poisoning, but she also didn't want to get a virus in the middle of her dream vacation. Wouldn't it be just her luck to flirt with a man and end up with nothing but his germs?

"I wonder if the ship staff will fill us in later today, at the briefing on Normandy?"

"I doubt it," Pat said. "They'll want to keep this quiet. Wash your hands frequently and use soap and water—if it's a norovirus, alcohol-based sanitizers won't stop it."

"Norovirus?"

"An intestinal bug. I've read that the incidence of them is increasing on cruise ships, but don't be too concerned, as they're still generally rare. Is tonight the night you're going to invite me to a sunset drink on your balcony? The weather is relatively good and the ship will be moving, which is always nice."

"Let me check with my friend," Mrs. Blossom said.

"Oh, I keep forgetting that you're traveling with someone," Pat said.

So did Elinor.

"Any night will do," Pat continued. "I'm always here! Oh, do you remember that other cartoon, the one that became a movie about the cartoonist's life—a wheelchair in the desert, a posse inspecting it and saying, 'He won't get far on foot.' That's me. I can't get far on foot."

"Is it—I'm never sure if it's polite to ask—what is—?"

Pat's smile was at once gentle and rueful. "Why do I use a cane? I'm just a little rickety. I took a bad fall off a horse several years ago and I was never quite the same again despite multiple surgeries. But, mainly, I'm old. I try to tell myself there's no shame in it—"

"There's *not*." Said fiercely, swiftly because she wanted to believe it was true.

"Isn't there? The world seems to suggest otherwise. To be an old woman—I know people complain about being invisible, but that's not what bothers me. It's the sense of being an affront."

"An affront?"

"An offense, almost like a bad smell. People don't like the old because it reminds them that they will get old and, eventually, die. Aging is seen almost as a disease, something to be fixed or arrested. All those tech billionaires trying to 'hack' their bodies— what a waste of money. You know, I would have been an excellent billionaire. Certainly, I'd be a better one than these silly men obsessing over their abs."

"You said that before," Mrs. Blossom said. "The billionaire part, not the abs part. I don't think I would be a good billionaire."

"You seem to be doing pretty well as a little old millionaire."

"How do you know I'm even that?" Mrs. Blossom felt as scandalized as if someone had commented on the color of her underwear.

"First of all, a million dollars isn't what it once was. Almost nine percent of Americans have at least a million dollars. And while this cruise isn't the priciest option, it isn't cheap. You don't strike me as someone who would spend a disproportionate amount of your savings on pleasure."

Pat probably was trying to be complimentary, yet her assessment stung. To be a person who others perceive as not being willing to pay for pleasure—how dutiful, how dull. Mrs. Blossom was the country mouse to Pat's glamorous city mouse. Of course, according to Aesop, it was better to be the country mouse, but who was Aesop kidding?

"I'm—OK," Mrs. Blossom said. "Not as well-fixed as you, obviously. But OK." The conversation was making her uncomfortable. She had experienced less shame years ago, flirting explicitly with Michael Calista in a chat room.

"Obviously?" Pat smiled. "If my wealth is obvious, I must be doing it wrong."

"Oh I didn't mean—you're not showy at all. Except for your ring, perhaps. You've got that quiet-wealth thing going on, classy and subdued. Honestly, I think it's your posture. You walk like someone who went to etiquette class and had to balance books on her head."

Pat leaned across the space between their lounge chairs and fixed her hand on Mrs. Blossom's forearm. "Guess what? I *did*."

This struck them both as wonderfully funny despite not being that funny at all, and they ended up in a laughing jag, that meta moment when one laughs at the fact that one is laughing so hard for no good reason, which only makes one laugh harder still. When they finally contained their giggles, Mrs. Blossom fetched them hot chocolates and a plate of sweets from Cedric's and they sat for a little while longer, looking out at the steeples of Rouen while establishing another friendship milestone: the ability to enjoy a companionable silence.

Back in her room, Mrs. Blossom found something truly disturbing: a somberly happy Elinor. She had been steeled for a postcoital Elinor, dreamy and self-satisfied, her ego fluffed by male attention.

Instead, her friend was standing in front of the mirror in her robe, her face grave, yet her eyes clear and bright. The light in the room showed every line, every imperfection—and she had never looked more beautiful.

This is a woman who is falling in love. If she's not already there.

"Was it better today, then?"

Elinor—chatterbox Elinor, always ready to dish—didn't answer right away.

"The sex was good and it will get better," she said at last. "It always does, the more time you spend with someone. But it was more about how we spoke, *after*. Muriel—he's thinking about moving back to the States."

"To Kentucky?" Her voice squeaked a little, as if Kentucky were an unfathomable choice. As if *Elinor* were an unfathomable choice, which wasn't what she meant at all.

"We didn't get too specific. Even I know it's too soon to make concrete plans, that we'll have to find out how this translates to real life, on dry land. My inference is that he would be OK with New York or Washington, DC—he says it has to be an East Coast city with a good international airport. He loves to travel."

"DC," Mrs. Blossom echoed stupidly.

"Wouldn't that be great? That's what I'm hoping for. Then we could see each other all the time, you and I. The truth is, I was already wondering if I should move back east. There's really nothing keeping me in Louisville except my garden."

This was the first that Mrs. Blossom, her oldest friend, had heard that Elinor had ever thought about relocating.

"Marry in haste—" she said, then realized she had echoed what Danny had said to her earlier in the week. It had been mean when he said it and it was mean now.

"What's 'haste' at our age? Besides, you married quickly, and that turned out pretty well."

Elinor turned from the mirror and faced her. One of the good things about knowing people over many decades is that you can see every person they've been. Here was the little girl with pigtails on a slide in Herring Run Park, the teenager who couldn't quite fathom the attention she was suddenly getting from boys. A soigné twentysomething on her first wedding day, the forty-year-old who had cried off her mascara on the day of her first divorce thinking she would never love again, the sixty-year-old who finally had found a good match. All those people lived behind these careworn blue eyes and had formed the smile lines on either side of her mouth.

"Muriel—I've never had what you had. I never will. That's just math. Almost forty years with a man who adored you, when you were in the prime of your life, while I made two bad marriages in a row. And then when I met Richard"—Elinor's third husband—"I got a glimpse of how good marriage can be, only to lose it. I feel *unfinished*. Is it so wrong to want to be loved, to want a partner?"

"Of course not." She wanted to add: *But please don't leave me behind.* She could never say that, however. It was too naked, too vulnerable. Besides, Elinor was right. Mrs. Blossom had thirty-eight years with a loving partner. She was being a bit of a dog in the manger here.

"Do you still want to come to the D-Day lecture with me?" she asked. "It's OK if you don't."

"Of course I want to come. And I want to hear about Rouen, I really do. Did you pay your respects to Joan?"

"I did," she said. But her day, which had felt adventurous, now seemed drab and ordinary, a consolation prize.

The D-Day lecture was a popular one, and the lounge was almost full. Mrs. Blossom and Elinor might not have been particularly interested in war per se—they were the products of a generation who had believed, however briefly, that war might become a thing of the past. But they recognized that it was almost disrespectful not to tour the beaches and the cemetery while in Normandy.

Much to Mrs. Blossom's surprise and delight, even Pat had decided to attend the lecture.

"Does this mean you're considering the excursion tomorrow?" Mrs. Blossom asked Pat.

"Oh, no, I'm here to soak up the highlights and pass them along to my brother. He wanted to come, but he's in desperate need of a nap. I have no idea how he managed to wear himself out so thoroughly when he didn't even do anything today."

"I can't believe I haven't met him yet," Mrs. Blossom said.

"Oh, but you have. He spent yesterday with you both in Giverny." Mrs. Blossom could not quite clock the look that Pat gave Elinor. It was neither approving nor disapproving, but it was definitely an inspection, a sizing up. "He said he had a *wonderful* time. But *Normandy* is what really excites him."

Maybe it was Mrs. Blossom's imagination, but Pat's words seemed to be full of ironic curlicues.

"Your brother is—" Mrs. Blossom knew the answer, but what if, hope against hope, Pat's brother was *Paul*? How perfect would that be?

"Emmanuel Markowitz, but everyone calls him Marko."

Mrs. Blossom envisioned the wheels turning in Elinor's mind: *Did she need to beguile the sister as she had charmed the brother? Did Pat know how quickly and intimately her brother had become involved with Elinor, the implicit promises he was already making?* Although Elinor had always loved men, she knew it was important to win over any other women in their lives—sisters, mothers, daughters.

"He has lovely manners," Elinor said at last. "A true gentleman."

"His mother was a big believer in manners," Pat said, adding with a wink directed at Mrs. Blossom. "Mine not so much."

Oh, good, maybe she was warming to Elinor.

"Were you always close?" Mrs. Blossom asked. "As children, even?"

"No. But as adults, we found we enjoyed one another's company. We travel together, we even share a place near Lake Como when we're not traveling. He has a lot of wanderlust. It's hard to pin Marko down."

Now *that* sounded almost like a warning. But then, Pat was probably quite dependent on her brother. If he was serious about moving back to the United States, she would probably have to follow him. Maybe they would settle near DC—hadn't Pat said she had grown up near there?—and Mrs. Blossom could visit her from time to time.

Or maybe Pat was a little jealous of Mrs. Blossom's friendship with Elinor? They had, after all, been forming this lovely bond.

The program was late getting started, unusual for the MS *Solitaire*, where schedules were strictly adhered to. The staff kept conferring, coming together in little groups, breaking apart and forming new groups.

"I bet they're talking about the sick passenger," Pat said.

"Sick passenger?" Elinor asked. Mrs. Blossom had forgotten to fill her in on this minor intrigue.

"Yes, a passenger was taken off the ship today while you two were in Rouen." No one bothered to disabuse Pat of the idea that

Elinor had been in Rouen. "Maybe they'll make an announcement before the film, finally tell us what happened. But I doubt it."

She was correct. Gaston-with-a-puss-on simply reminded them that tomorrow's journey would start relatively early and that they should bring water bottles. They would be on their own for lunch. Mrs. Blossom could have sworn he looked at her when he said "lunch."

The lights went down for the screening of a short film narrated by Tom Brokaw. Mrs. Blossom adjusted her chair to get a better view and noticed Pat's large leather bag plopped carelessly on the floor beneath her seat. An Hermès bag, but a beat-up one, which, Mrs. Blossom knew from reading the *New York Times,* was now considered more prestigious than a brand-spanking-new one. Not a Birkin, but a tote, and it was an absolute jumble inside: a mess of Kleenex packets and Altoid tins, notebooks, pens, paperbacks. Mrs. Blossom was shocked that the fastidious Pat Siemen could have such a messy purse.

On impulse, she slipped the cube tracker into the bag, aiming for the unzipped interior pocket. Given Pat's disinclination to leave the ship, it would create some confusion, but not *too* much. All day today, she had been looking over her shoulder, expecting Danny to show up in Rouen as he had in Les Andelys. He hadn't, but the awareness of being tracked had kept her from being fully in the moment. Yet, come to think of it, she hadn't seen him at all today, not even on board.

What if Danny were the person taken off the ship? There had been more than one DO NOT DISTURB placard hanging on the doors along the Gold Deck last night.

Well, that would solve all her problems, wouldn't it? Still, she was surprised at the pang she felt, thinking of Danny on an ambulance gurney. She didn't like him, and she didn't respect him, but she didn't want him lying in a foreign hospital with stomach pains.

Seconds after Mrs. Blossom dropped the tracker, Pat began fishing around in her bag. For a panicky moment, Mrs. Blossom thought her impulsive act would be discovered, but Pat pulled out her cell phone, which she left on her lap, glancing down at it occasionally, typing short messages. She was probably taking notes for Marko.

The lecture over, Elinor suggested drinks and snacks on the deck. Mrs. Blossom invited Pat to join them. She shook her head and said: "This is about as much social activity as I can take in a day."

Maybe it was sheer ego on her part, but Mrs. Blossom couldn't help feeling that Pat didn't want to share her with Elinor. Well, Mrs. Blossom didn't want to share Elinor with Pat's brother, so they were even.

"I'm eating so much on this trip," Elinor said, licking mayonnaise from her fingers after devouring a club sandwich they had fetched from Cedric's. Pat had not oversold it. "I'll have to diet when I get home."

Mrs. Blossom winced. It was a comment she had heard many times, in many variations, from almost every woman she knew. Sometimes men as well. It wasn't personal, and yet—it wasn't *not* personal. And if she couldn't make that point to her oldest friend— then what was the point of friendship?

"I wish you wouldn't talk about dieting, Elinor. For one thing— you're a twig. Always were. I know you can't eat as you did when you were a teenager, but you're still awfully thin. And for another—" She faltered.

"And for another?" There was an openness to Elinor's expression, an invitation to keep going, be candid.

"Is it so awful to be fat? Would it be unbearable for you to have a body like mine? And isn't that what you're saying, when you talk about diets and having to lose weight while we're sitting here eating the exact same sandwich? That being fat—looking like me—is the worst thing you can imagine?"

Elinor opened her mouth, then appeared to think better of what she was going to say. She took a sip of white wine, trained her eyes on the shoreline. The MS *Solitaire* had stopped, waiting for a lock to open, and the view was of the countryside, green and lush, relatively flat. Her cheeks were pink—possibly from embarrassment, but it also could be the air. The breeze was getting sharper as night approached.

"When we were young, all the boys liked you best," she began. "Your big blue eyes, your hair, your skin. Your boobs! All I had was my thinness."

"I don't remember it that way." Well, she remembered the boobs, which had arrived suddenly, making her even more self-conscious about her body.

"Being thin was my one real accomplishment. I wasn't particularly clever, I had no ambition beyond marrying a nice man and being thin, and staying thin seemed key to that. Although, as I found out, men leave skinny women, too." Elinor's second husband had left her for a larger, but much younger, woman; it had been akin to a crisis of faith for her at the time. "Besides, being thin is healthier—"

"Not necessarily. In fact, premature mortality is more common among underweight people than overweight people." Another fact gleaned from a podcast. "And you're the one who takes blood pressure medication, not me."

Elinor smiled ruefully. "My doctor is worried about my bone density now. But I've noticed your pillbox isn't that small, old friend."

That was because of the hidden compartment, but not even Elinor knew about that.

Mrs. Blossom said, "I take a statin and progesterone because I have an estrogen ring and an estrogen patch. The other pills are supplements—calcium, vitamin D. The big horse pills, which I take four of every day? They're for my hair. There's hard science behind them, too, evidence that they really do improve thinning hair."

"Your hair isn't thinning."

"Exactly. Because I started taking these pills. That reminds me. I met a woman, the person who designed my caftan, in Paris. She said I should wear it very short or grow it out. I think I'm going to grow it out. It's been six weeks since my last haircut and it's already just long enough to do a wispy updo."

"That would be absolutely chic," Elinor said. "Speaking of changes—growing your hair out is a good first step, but it's not enough. I know you, Muriel—you're in danger of letting your life get smaller. For everything that's happened—the money, the move—you're curling in on yourself, the way you did right after Harold died. I want you to start dating again."

Mrs. Blossom shook her head. "That ship has sailed for me. That ship is farther up the Seine than the MS *Solitaire*."

"Well, if that's your attitude, that's how things are going to be." Elinor looked at her watch. "Gah, dinner is only an hour away, and there's apparently a special dessert tonight. I feel like we just go from one feeding to another and"—she took a deep breath—"and there's absolutely nothing wrong with that. It's what vacations are for."

"It's what life is for."

"Life is a banquet and—oh, I can't finish the quote, help me—"

"It's from *Auntie Mame*. 'Life is a banquet and most poor'—was it sons of bitches or bastards?—'are starving to death.'"

"But not us." Elinor dragged a *frite* through what the staff called aioli and Mrs. Blossom believed to be mayonnaise. "Never us."

Back in their room, changing for dinner, their rapport was no different from what it had been when they were teenagers. They chatted easily, made recommendations on how to tweak their outfits. Mrs. Blossom hated to admit it, but she preferred the black pants that Danny had given her to almost anything she had packed, especially when paired with the Isabel Marant ankle boots. She urged Elinor to try one of her scarves, and they ended up laughing at their inept attempts to knot it, going back to the YouTube tutorials to figure it out.

"Definitely wear the earrings you wore night before last," Mrs. Blossom told Elinor. "You need a bit of dangle with that outfit."

"You think? Wait—where are they? I'm sure I put them in that little ceramic tray by the bed. I remember thinking that I shouldn't leave them there. Oh dear, you don't think—"

"No, I can't imagine the house cleaner taking them. I mean, I know they outfit the rooms with safes, but it's unthinkable to me that anyone on board, guests or staff, would steal anything."

"They're not valuable, but they're my favorites. And maybe I didn't close the door all the way when we went to the presentation? You know how the doors don't shut completely if you don't make sure to pull them close—"

"Let's look carefully before we jump to worst-case scenarios."

It took a while, but they found them—in Mrs. Blossom's zippered jewelry pouch in the bathroom, where she kept everything but her diamond earrings.

"Ah, the housekeeper was simply overly solicitous, I guess, putting them where she thought they belonged," Elinor said, fastening the earrings.

It was almost as if the barometric pressure in the room shifted. Mrs. Blossom felt her actual hackles rise, strange pains in her joints. It was the same sensation she had experienced in Paris upon encountering her neatly ransacked room. When you are accustomed to order, your mind argues for the status quo, tells you that you are imagining things, that nothing is amiss.

She looked around the cabin. It was like playing that game Spot the Differences in the old *Highlights* magazine. Earrings in a jewelry pouch when they should have been in a tray. Curtains open, but Mrs. Blossom always pulled them shut during the day. The novel she had started this morning was closed on her bedside table; Mrs. Blossom was in the habit of leaving her books splayed open, indifferent to their spines.

Someone had been in their room, and it wasn't the housekeeper. Her things had been searched yet again, but whoever had done it had gotten confused and put Elinor's earrings away in the wrong place. This time, she wasn't supposed to know that anyone had been there. She thought about the tracker she had slipped into Pat's bag. They had sat together through the D-Day presentation, almost an hour long. How precise was the tracker? The marketing materials claimed they could pinpoint a tagged item within a hundred feet.

Well, tomorrow would be an interesting test, then. Let's see what happened when she left the ship, and the tracker stayed behind with Pat, enjoying the view from the upper deck and the occasional club sandwich.

PAUL WAS GONE. And no one wanted to talk about it. Mrs. Blossom couldn't even confirm that he was the person who had left the ship by ambulance. She asked their friendly waiter, Esteban, and he simply shrugged. "Some people find the sailing life is not for them." The attendant at the front desk stared blankly, her heretofore perfect English forgotten. "Monsieur Pat-er-akis? *Je ne sais pas.*"

Marko had confirmed at dinner last night that he had not seen Paul since lunch after the trip to Giverny. "We had a smoke on the upper deck and then he went to his room for a nap." The concierge asked sternly *why* Mrs. Blossom wanted to know. "Was he a friend, madame?" This put her on the defensive, as if she were being a horrible snoop, and maybe she was.

She walked slowly through the corridors, passing by the room she was sure had belonged to Paul. To her amazement, the door swung open, and for a split second, she almost believed she had willed Paul into appearing. But it was Gaston-with-a-puss-on. Strange, she could have sworn that was Paul's room. And she hadn't known that any staff members were housed among the guests.

Perhaps her surprise showed on her face, because Gaston offered an explanation, his nose up, as if he smelled something offensive: "When the ship is undersold, some of the staff are allowed to use guest rooms." He drew himself up to his full height, which was maybe five foot six at the most. "I have seniority, so I was given this cabin."

"Have you been staying there all week?"

Gaston was quick with a comeback—but not quick enough that Mrs. Blossom didn't pick up on his split second of hesitation. "Where else would I have been? Swimming behind the boat?"

She laughed, as if she found this hysterically funny, thinking it might endear her to Gaston. It did not.

"The bus leaves in fifteen minutes," he said, heading toward the stairs. "Don't be late."

"I never am," she said, which was simply factual. But she stood, staring at the closed door as if she were a bloodhound who could pick up the faintest of scents. That had been Paul's room, she was sure of it. Paul was the one who had gotten sick. How sick? That was not a question one asked lightly in these times. She casually placed her hand on the door—as Elinor had noted, the doors did not automatically lock unless one tugged hard upon leaving. But this was firmly shut. Besides, what would she see if she could enter? It was Gaston's room now.

At least Paul hadn't stood her up that afternoon in Les Andelys. She tried to take comfort in that. She wandered up to the registration desk, stole a glance at the passenger list. Some, if not all of the passengers, had included their email addresses. (Pat Siemen had not. She probably didn't even have one. Wouldn't that be the biggest flex of all, not even having email?) Ah, there was Paul—he used an AOL address, which Mrs. Blossom found endearing. She shot him a quick email, similar to the note she had left the day before. **I hope you're OK? Can I do anything for you? Call or email me.**

Mrs. Blossom was far more moved by Normandy than she had anticipated. This part of the trip had seemed obligatory to her, something every dutiful American tourist should do.

But standing on the beach under much better weather conditions than the troops had encountered not quite a century ago, she finally grasped the magnitude of the invasion. The distances that soldiers had to travel under sniper fire, the claustrophobia of the bunkers, the unforgiving cliffs. How did people go to war? It was not the first time Mrs. Blossom had pondered this. She could imagine putting herself in the line of fire for her loved ones, but to march toward death for anyone or anything else—it was unthinkable to her. She could never muster that kind of bravery.

Maybe she would finally get around to watching *Saving Private Ryan*. Mr. Blossom had always liked a good war movie and she had watched most of the classics with him: *The Great Escape, Stalag 17, The Bridge on the River Kwai, The Longest Day*. She had enjoyed some of them, but she had never understood Mr. Blossom's passion for war. He had certainly not regretted being spared from serving in the Vietnam War. (Mrs. Blossom's mother had been unkind enough to suggest that was why he wanted to marry Muriel, to avoid the draft, but that was simply untrue. He had flat feet and wasn't eligible.)

After a respectful silence, Elinor said: "You're right, I'm glad I didn't wear my heels today."

"I thought it was because Marko wasn't joining us."

Elinor squeezed Mrs. Blossom's arm. "I'm not that vain," she said. "I do feel awful for him, though. The whole point of this trip was for him to see Normandy and now *he's* got that weird stomach bug. That's why he missed breakfast."

So it was a virus, not oysters, after all. And it had felled half of their lunch table from Saturday. Worrisome.

"Maybe the two of you will come back here together one day, to commemorate how you met."

Mrs. Blossom yearned for Elinor to knock down the idea, to tell her that she was assuming too much. But Elinor nodded, as if she had already considered this possibility.

They found the American Cemetery even more affecting than the beach. Mrs. Blossom liked how egalitarian military cemeteries were; the identical headstones reminded one that everyone was the same in death. (Although Theodore Roosevelt Jr.'s grave was allowed patriotic touches of red, white, and blue.) Mindful of Harold's Jewish roots, she collected stones to leave at several graves with Star of David markers, with Elinor helping her through the prayer.

"My father was too young to fight in World War II," Elinor noted, her arm linked with Mrs. Blossom as they walked back to the bus. "He ended up in Korea."

"Mine served—although as a typist in New Jersey." Muriel's father had been in his forties when she was born, older than the other fathers. "What's interesting to me is that all the people on this trip who did have fathers or grandfathers active in the European theater say they never spoke of it. And now the so-called Greatest Generation is all but gone. Soon there won't be anyone to tell the stories."

Their guide, a young Frenchman born in Normandy, had told them on the long drive to the beaches that he spent his winters in the States, taking oral histories from World War II veterans. He had even ended up marrying an American woman from Bedford, Virginia, the town that had lost the most men per capita on D-Day. Mrs. Blossom admired his enthusiasm but also was baffled by it.

He was only thirty, so even the Gulf War was history to him. But maybe she was the odd one for never thinking to ask her father a single question about his life. He had been only sixty-three, younger than she was now, when he died.

"Do you think," Elinor said, "that we talk more about generations than we used to? I mean, you and I are boomers, but I don't remember thinking it significant growing up. Just as my father always felt wistful about World War II, I always felt I didn't really experience the 1960s. We were in junior high in 1968! We never went to Woodstock, never protested anything. The 1960s absolutely passed us by. When people say, OK, boomer, I want to say, no, I missed the good times."

"Oh, I don't know," Mrs. Blossom said, bumping her friend's hip playfully. "You did know a lot of free love."

"Not *free*," Elinor said, preening a little. "I got alimony from the first two, and now Richard's Social Security is mine." Her smile faded. "I'd give it all back, three times over, to have even one more year with Richard."

"I know how you, feel. There's no amount of money that can make up for Harold being gone."

Mrs. Blossom was thinking once again about the source of her good fortune, that errant lottery ticket. If someone had been in her room, what was he—or she—looking for? Her diamond studs remained hidden in her pillbox, her charm bracelet was off her wrist only when she slept. Besides, the bracelet's value was largely sentimental.

Danny had asked about the charm bracelet. So had Allan. Unusual in a straight man, she thought, to be interested in a woman's literal charms. She fingered the latch on the golden fortune cookie.

She and Elinor ended the day at a café in Honfleur, where Elinor managed not to make a single comment about how much she was eating on this trip. People in Normandy seemed friendlier than Parisians, but maybe that was a country-versus-city thing. Or perhaps, even all these decades later, they still had a soft spot for Americans. The wait service indulged Elinor's broken French, insisted on giving them glasses of wine they had not ordered.

"I can't believe how much I've been drinking," Mrs. Blossom said. "I think I've had more to drink on this trip than I've had in my entire life."

"When in Rome—well, France." Elinor raised her glass. "I can't believe how quickly this week is flying by. It's been a perfect vacation. Thank you for arranging it, Muriel."

Mrs. Blossom knew that the thing that had made Elinor happiest on this trip had nothing to do with her careful planning. And if she could do it all over again, she would have said "no" to the man in the polo shirt when he asked to sit with them that first night. It was small of her, she knew, perhaps the only type of small that wasn't considered positive. She must try harder to be happy for her friend.

Although Mrs. Blossom had been on the MS *Solitaire* for only six days, it now felt like home, familiar and cozy. It was like living in a little village, its routines and rhythms second nature now, all faces known to her, if not all names.

Perhaps that was why it was immediately evident that something was amiss again when Mrs. Blossom and Elinor returned late that afternoon. Yes, there was the usual tray of cucumber-infused drinks and lavender-scented hand towels for the passengers to freshen their faces and hands. But the atmosphere was charged, buzzy.

"I wonder if another passenger has been forced to leave the ship," Mrs. Blossom whispered to Elinor, who looked stricken at the thought. Marko, after all, had canceled the trip to Normandy because he was feeling unwell. And perhaps it was just her imagination, but the dining room had seemed a little emptier this morning.

But, no, Marko was in the middle of the buzzing conflab at the concierge desk—alongside his sister. The usually easygoing Pat looked angry and tearful. She kept both hands on her cane, as if she needed more support than usual, but she still towered over the seldom-seen captain of the MS *Solitaire*, who appeared to be trying to comfort her. Mrs. Blossom took her time cleaning her hands with the damp towel, sipping her tea. She wished she could hear what they were saying, but they kept their voices low.

A scowling Danny arrived in the lobby and made a beeline for Mrs. Blossom and Elinor, looking like a father whose children had broken curfew.

"Where have you been all day?" he asked. "I searched for you on the ship but couldn't find you."

Ah, then the tracker had done its job: Danny had thought she was on board all this time, then panicked when he realized she wasn't. Was he worried for her safety, or keeping tabs on her for another reason?

"We went to Normandy, of course."

"But—"

She saw him realizing that he could not speak further, lest he reveal that he had been tracking her since Vétheuil, or earlier. "But, I thought you were going to give that a skip."

"Plans change," Mrs. Blossom said. "Even mine." A reminder that she was not the stick-in-the-mud he had accused her of being.

Pat Siemen suddenly shrieked.

"That's the man! That's the man I saw in my room. He thought I was sleeping and I pretended to be because I was so scared. He took my ring from my nightstand. I watched him from beneath my lashes. I was terrified."

She was pointing to Danny.

"What the—" Danny sputtered.

Mrs. Blossom, glancing at Pat's left hand, saw it was, in fact, ringless. The enormous pink diamond was gone.

"I was napping and I left the door ajar because Marko had gone to Cedric's to fetch me some tea. I awoke and saw this man standing over my bed. He didn't realize I was awake. Most of my jewels are in the safe, of course, but I take my ring off when I sleep and place it by the bedside as it tends to twist and dig into my flesh."

Mrs. Blossom remembered how Elinor's earrings had gone missing from the bedside table, only to be found in her jewelry pouch. But that wasn't quite the same, because nothing had been taken. Maybe their jewelry simply wasn't up to Danny's standards? Or had Danny gone to Pat's stateroom because the tracker told him that Mrs. Blossom was there?

"I just popped my head in—" Danny began, only to be interrupted by the captain.

"Wait, so you were in Ms. Siemen's room?"

"I was looking for someone. I—I just had the wrong room. It's no big deal. I apologized and left."

"That's not how it happened at all," Pat said. "Search his room! I bet we will find it there."

"Madame," the captain said gently, "we cannot simply search a guest's room on your say-so. Everyone here is entitled to privacy."

"Go ahead," Danny said. "It's not like you're going to find anything. Let's put this matter to rest as quickly as possible. She probably lost it or put it somewhere for safekeeping and now can't remember where it is."

"How dare you?" Pat said. "Just because I'm old doesn't mean my memory's faulty."

"Doesn't mean it's good, either."

Mrs. Blossom couldn't believe how nonchalant he was in the face of such accusations. No, wait—she could. Ever since she had known him, Danny's reaction when caught in a lie was either to deflect or change up his story. Tess had urged her to think of the most obvious explanation for the strange things that had been happening to her. Wasn't Danny the constant, the throughline? Perhaps everything he had told her was simply a pretext to follow her onto this ship in order to steal from the other passengers. She wouldn't be surprised if he was connected to Paul's sudden leave-taking somehow.

Mrs. Blossom and Elinor trailed after the group to the lowest level. The rooms on the Silver Deck were noticeably smaller than those on the Platinum and Gold Decks; Mrs. Blossom would not have wanted to share one of these with anyone, not even Harold. Given the size—and, Mrs. Blossom couldn't help noticing, Danny's austere tidiness—it took almost no time to search his quarters. Pat opened every drawer, had her brother look under the bed. They even felt inside Danny's shoes and the pockets of every pair of trousers; there were only two. Nothing turned up, not even a stray euro.

"What about the safe?" Marko asked.

"What about it?" Danny replied. "I've never used it."

"Then why is it locked?"

Danny seemed credibly surprised to see that the lock on the safe had been set. But then, as Mrs. Blossom knew, Danny was good at faking all sorts of emotions and personae. "I have no idea. I swear to you, I've never used it."

"Well, someone has," Pat said.

"Would you tell me the password, monsieur?" the captain asked Danny. But he just shook his head.

"Try one-two-three-four," Marko suggested, and then did that on his own, without waiting for anyone to affirm it was a good idea.

"I'm not brain-dead," Danny said. The safe remained locked.

"What's your birthday?" Marko asked.

"What's it to you?" Danny said. "But it's December fourteenth."

Marko punched in 1214. Again, the safe held its ground. Pat said: "Try one-four-one-two. That's how a European would convey it."

"I'm not European," Danny pointed out.

"No, but you've spent quite a bit of time here, no?"

"Not really."

The door swung open. There was Pat's ring, the large pear-shaped pink gem. There also was a large stack of colorful bills—not euros, but similar-looking.

And a statue. The prettiest little bird, carved from a marble more gray than white.

At the sight of it, Mrs. Blossom had the most ridiculous thought: the Quqnoz, like most celebrities, was so much smaller in person. It was simpler than she had imagined, too. She had expected something in solid gold, encrusted with jewels, but there was no ornamentation at all. Still it seemed to radiate with its age, its history. If she had seen it in a museum, she would have paused at its case, charmed by the directness of its shape, the suggestion of power in its wings.

Danny gasped, but did not speak. Finally, he was at a loss for words. "That's not mine," he said at last. "Not the cash, at any rate."

"Are you saying the ring *is* yours? Or that statue?" Pat asked. There was something in her tone that Mrs. Blossom couldn't identify, almost a note of offense.

"The ring isn't mine either, of course. But whoever stole it also stole the statue, then put them both here to frame me. Do you know what we are looking at? Do you understand the importance of that bird?"

"It looks like marble," Marko said. "How valuable could it be?"

"There's no need—" Danny began.

"Call Interpol!" Pat said, cutting him off. Unlike Mrs. Blossom, she wasn't going to give Danny the chance to start spinning his tales. "I don't know to whom the cash belongs, but you can bet it's not his. And the ring most definitely is mine. People have seen me wearing it" She indicated Mrs. Blossom, who nodded. "As for the statue, maybe its rightful owner will show up, assuming this miscreant hasn't killed him. Put him in the brig!"

A ring, a statue, cash in foreign currency. Danny had quickly disavowed the cash and the ring, but the bird held his eyes. He claimed he was being framed. But by whom, and to what purpose? Mrs. Blossom was the only person on board who knew of his quest—wasn't she?

Pat had seen him take her ring, and it was locked in his safe, with a code based on his birthday. How did one explain that?

Simple. Danny was a thief. Not a stylist, not an FBI agent, and not even a self-interested investigator working for a soulless insurance company. A garden-variety thief. For all she knew, he had killed Allan back in Paris, thinking he would find the statue among his things and be able to sell it for his own profit.

But if he had the statue all along, why was he still following her?

The captain was trying to calm Pat, who was visibly shaking, although Mrs. Blossom wasn't sure if it was from anger or relief. "Madame, we are still in port and we're not pulling anchor for several hours. We can simply turn him over to the police here in Caudebec."

"Jesus Christ, I didn't *do* anything," Danny said. "I didn't take her ring, this is all preposterous. All of this was planted here—the ring, the cash, the statue. If you tested them for fingerprints, you wouldn't find mine." He stared hard at Mrs. Blossom, pleadingly, as if she could rescue him. But how could she? *Why* would she?

Still, it was unsettling to watch crew members escort Danny from the boat, to hear the captain instruct two of the cleaners to pack up his room. She had the feeling of a near miss; she had spent so much time in his company over the past week. Lord knows what his intentions were toward her.

"What will happen to the things you found?" she asked the captain. It felt close in the tiny cabin, which could barely hold the five people who remained. Yet no one made any move to leave.

"We will place the money and the statue in the ship's safe, assuming for now that they, like the ring, were taken from other passengers, although we've had no reports of missing items. I will make a discreet announcement at dinner tonight that, if anyone has, um, lost anything they should report to the front desk and describe the items. I would appreciate it if you and your friend do not reveal what you have seen here. Only the rightful owners would know about the statue—or the fact that the currency is Swiss."

"But the statue—I think—I'm not sure—I think it's an antiquity that was stolen long ago." Mrs. Blossom was racking her mind, poring over the passenger list, trying to think who might have brought it on board. The family from Sonoma? The grandmother and grandson from North Carolina, who had taken the trip because her father had received the Bronze Star for his D-Day bravery? "If it is what I think it is, it's very valuable."

"Are you saying you know the owner?"

"No—I mean, maybe the Pakistani government. Or it should be. But its last 'rightful' owner—that person died several years ago and left no heirs. And its most recent owner—well, I guess it's Danny and he stole it, but from someone who didn't really have clear title to it. Although, come to think of it, I only have his say-so for that and—"

The captain held up his hands to stop her, and really, who could blame him. "We will treat it as we treat any lost-and-found item on board. Again, please do not speak of it to the other passengers. I would hate for someone to claim it when it is not theirs. The fewer people who know, the better."

He looked at Pat and Marko, who was patting his sister's back, urging her to calm down. "I can say definitively that the money is not mine," she said.

"Are you sure it's not yours," the captain asked. "After all—"

Pat cut him off: "Quite sure. I am not one to lose track of my money. Or my jewels."

Mrs. Blossom and Elinor walked back to their cabin to prepare for dinner.

"Well," Elinor said. "An international jewel thief. Who would have thought it? I'm rather insulted my earrings didn't rate."

Mrs. Blossom found her heart oddly heavy. Fool me once, shame on you, fool me twice, shame on me. Although this thing with Danny wasn't the same as with Allan. She'd picked up on Danny's lies, his glibness. *I'm a stylist. No, I'm an FBI agent. Would you believe, a private investigator?*

The statue lingered in her mind. Such a pretty thing, but she couldn't imagine dying for it. Had Allan ever actually had it in his possession? Was his death just another coincidence? But if Danny had the statue, what was he doing on the MS *Solitaire*? It didn't strike her as the best use of a thief's time. Certainly, a larger cruise ship would yield far more opportunities, yet also more anonymity.

Darn it—she had to assume her black chiffon pants were stolen, too. She'd return to the store on her last day in Paris and offer full restitution. After all, she had worn them several times and, well, she really liked them.

Pat Siemen made her first appearance in the dining room that night. The ship was abuzz, a cliché that had never seemed more apt to Mrs. Blossom, because there was a literal, audible hum, one that had risen in volume when she and Elinor had entered the dining room, then rose again with Pat's entrance. Did people think Mrs. Blossom was connected to Danny? Was she now suspect in their minds?

Given her self-consciousness, it meant a lot when Pat, with Marko at her side, made a beeline for the table where Mrs. Blossom and Elinor sat.

"If everyone's going to talk about me, I'm going to make them do it to my face," Pat joked. She looked almost overwhelmingly elegant, in a matching silk top and flowing pants, the pink diamond back on her finger. Mrs. Blossom couldn't help noticing that her outfit was riotous in both color and print, with huge daises running in a row down one side of the shirt and the right pants leg. *Flowers can be stylish*, she said to Danny in her head. So there!

Then she wondered why she was still bothering to talk to Danny in her head.

"I love what you're wearing," Elinor said.

"Marni," Pat said, and Mrs. Blossom needed a second to realize she wasn't referencing the Hitchcock film.

"It's perfection," Elinor said, clearly still on a mission to butter up her beau's sister.

"Well, yes, but one has to be tall, like Muriel or me, to wear big patterns and prints," replied Pat. Even as Mrs. Blossom registered Pat's coolness toward Elinor, she couldn't help enjoying how Pat seemed to think she and Mrs. Blossom were a team of sorts.

Pat glanced around the dining room. "Do you think," she asked, "that people *are* talking? Or has the, um, disturbance with that young man been kept quiet, the way they handled the guest who fell ill in Rouen?"

"Some people inevitably saw that a man was escorted from the ship by police," Mrs. Blossom said, for that had been Danny's fate. "But I don't think anyone knows why, and even if they did, they wouldn't be unkind. You're the victim."

Pat smiled, but it wasn't a happy smile. "Don't kid yourself, Muriel Blossom. People can be particularly nasty about anyone they perceive to be a victim."

"I know what you mean," Elinor said. "I think it's because people fear being victims so much that they're always trying to rationalize why it's the victim's fault, somehow. But anyone might have left their cabin door ajar if someone popped out for just a moment."

"Who said I did that?" Pat asked. Elinor really brought out the frost in her. She must have discerned that her brother's interest in Elinor was getting serious.

"Well—you did."

"Oh, of course. I thought you were talking about a third party, not one of us. I feel we four are coconspirators in a sense because we know about the other things that were taken. The money, that little bird. But as the captain said, we must keep it to ourselves." She held a finger to her lip and winked.

Mrs. Blossom was so tempted to brag—to tell them that the bird had a name and a specific, strange history that had left dead men in its wake. That Danny had been following her—well, Allan—

since Baltimore in search of that bird. She wasn't often the person at the center of a story, the one who knew more than others. It was tempting to speak, but she worried that it would make her sound like Danny's accomplice. Besides, how would she ever explain to Elinor all the secrets she had kept this week?

"That was not an insignificant amount of money," Marko said. "How can someone just let something like that go?"

"Maybe it's no one on the ship," Mrs. Blossom said. "The captain said it was Swiss currency, and I don't know of any guests from Switzerland."

"Why would someone steal Swiss currency?" Elinor wondered.

"Money is money," Pat said.

"Yes, but you think he would have been able to steal more," Mrs. Blossom said. "Overall, I mean. One ring and a pile of cash—not a good take for a week's work."

"And the statue," Pat reminded her. "Maybe that has some value, too."

"Oh, yes. The statue." What had Danny said? Was it $4 million or $5 million? Definitely worth enough to lock in a safe. "So strange that he used his birthday as the code. That seems like a dumb move and whatever Danny is, it's not dumb."

"Did you know him that well?" Pat asked.

"Do we ever know anyone well?" Mrs. Blossom countered.

Pat gave her happy bark of a laugh. "Fair point. No matter how long we know someone, there are always discoveries to be made. Between friends, between lovers. Even between spouses."

She looked pointedly at Elinor on the word *lovers*, while Mrs. Blossom flinched at the word *spouses*, fingering the clasp on her fortune cookie.

Elinor, perhaps sensing that she wasn't winning Pat's affection, reverted to her candid self: "How much is your ring worth?"

Mrs. Blossom was aghast, but Pat didn't seem to mind the question at all.

"To me, it's worth everything. I'm sentimental about it because of who gave it to me. It's the one piece of jewelry I wear every day. And now I don't think I'll ever feel safe taking it off again. Such a coincidence, him coming to my room as I napped."

Mrs. Blossom squirmed, wondering if it was a coincidence at all, if Danny had thought he would find her in that cabin. "Have you noticed the doors don't always shut all the way? Maybe he was just wandering the halls, testing them, while most people were in Normandy."

"Or maybe," Pat said, "he had assistance from someone on the staff. He has a rogue's charm, your friend."

"He wasn't really my friend. Just a man I met in Paris."

"Ah, the men one meets in Paris seldom become friends, but they can be entertaining for a bit."

Mrs. Blossom wished she were as worldly as Pat assumed. "It wasn't like that, either. We shared a table at a restaurant and then he helped me with a, um, dilemma that came up."

"Stolen travelers checks?" Pat asked.

"No, but—something like that."

"My dear, I was *kidding*, of course. No one stills travels with traveler's checks, not with ATMs everywhere."

Mrs. Blossom blushed because she did have five $100 traveler's checks, along with five $100 bills. Her son-in-law, who worried obsessively about the grid going down, thought one should always have some cash on hand.

"He kept telling me I was in danger," Mrs. Blossom said. "But maybe he was the danger, I don't know—"

"With all due respect," Pat said, "I'm not sure you're the mark I'd pick if I were a jewel thief."

With all due respect—another phrase that usually indicated some-one was intent on offering the opposite of what they we're saying. But Mrs. Blossom couldn't take offense at something so obviously true, not when it was the forthright Pat. The only valuable jewelry she had were her charm bracelet and her diamond earrings, but, precious as they were to her, they weren't jewel-thief bait.

The ship's all-purpose entertainer was noodling on a small key-board in the corner. It took Mrs. Blossom a second to recognize the tune.

"'Leaving on a Jet Plane,'" she said delightedly. "Remember, Elinor, when we sneaked out to see that Chicago punk band at the Marble Bar and they played a cover of this?"

"We told our husbands we were going to the movies," Elinor said. "And then we had to explain why we came home so sweaty at two a.m., smelling of cigarette smoke and beer."

"You went to the Marble Bar?" Pat asked.

"You know of it?"

She shook her head. "Oh no, but just the way you speak of it—it sounds quite disreputable. In the best possible way. Was it a dive? Did it have lock-ins?"

Mrs. Blossom loved Pat's curiosity. "It was a bar in the old Congress Hotel, the epicenter of Baltimore's punk scene in the 1970s."

"You were—into punk?"

"Muriel has always been very avant-garde in her tastes," Eli-nor put in. "Music, films. She was forever dragging me to movies with subtitles. I hated them. Now I have them on for everything I watch."

"Even shows in English?" Pat asked.

"*Especially* shows in English. It helps me focus."

"I suppose you speak only English?"

Elinor laughed. "I studied German in middle school and French in high school. I can speak a tiny bit of French, but the only thing I remember from German is how to order a beer—and I don't even like beer. I have no facility for languages."

"Oh, that's just an excuse. Anyone can learn a foreign language if they try. And they should. It's the mark of a truly well-rounded person."

A silence, a strained one. Pat probably meant no harm, but she obviously had hurt Elinor's feelings. Mrs. Blossom decided to cut the tension by making a joke. "Well, if there's one thing we can agree on, it's that I'm a very well-rounded person."

She puffed out her chest. Elinor laughed, but Pat turned grave, as if the little bit of self-deprecation had revealed something almost, well, sordid about Mrs. Blossom. "You know, if it bothers you, there are things that work, even at our advanced age. And now these shots that everyone is getting—"

"It doesn't bother me," Mrs. Blossom said shortly. "I was just being silly."

Pat seemed baffled. Obviously, she was a woman who prized thinness. But at what cost? Mrs. Blossom wondered. She noticed that Pat had barely touched the food she had ordered tonight, pushing it around on her plate and taking only a bite here and there. Frankly, Mrs. Blossom was surprised that Pat's beloved ring wasn't at constant risk of sliding from her bony finger. If it fit better, she wouldn't have had to take it off for her nap. Good lord, what was it like to walk around with a million dollars on one's finger, barely secured?

They stayed up quite late, the four of them. Mrs. Blossom kept thinking that Pat would tire of socializing, and then she could make excuses, giving Elinor and Marko a chance to be alone. But Pat was in high spirits, insisting they go to the bar after dinner, ordering champagne and fancy brandies. She asked the bartender to put out cocktail peanuts for them, then leaned into Mrs. Blossom as if she had an extraordinary secret to share: "Do you know why you have to ask for the peanuts here, whereas bars always have them available?"

Mrs. Blossom didn't have a clue. "Are peanuts expensive in France?"

Pat laughed. "You are *precious*. No, it's because the drinks are free and when people eat salty nuts, they drink more. So, in a bar, it helps them sell more drinks, but there's no point in making people thirsty here." She took a sip of her drink, an austere vodka martini—no olive, not even a twist. "I know you think I care too much about money—"

"I don't!" Gracious, could Pat read her thoughts?

"But money is the root of everything. Not evil, as the saying goes. *Everything*. It's all we have, the final religion, the only score-card that matters. Everyone wants it. Everyone needs it. There's nothing else like it."

"What about love?" Mrs. Blossom asked. From where she sat, she could see Elinor's hand on Marko's knee, but Pat could not.

"Love lets everyone down, eventually. Tell the truth—hasn't love disappointed you once or twice?"

Mrs. Blossom could not tell the truth. *She* had let love down. Instead, she looked at her watch. "It's almost midnight! I never stay up this late. I will be a wreck tomorrow if I don't go to sleep soon. When we get back to Paris, I'm going to an exhibition of Robert Doisneau's wartime photography."

"I thought you were more art history buff than history buff," Pat observed.

"I am. But on this trip—I felt that I should enjoy the things my late husband would have enjoyed. He was obsessed with the

History Channel, especially World War II history. I owe him that much."

"Do you believe in life after death?" Pat asked. Oh, dear, Mrs. Blossom had not meant to engage her in some deep philosophical discussion; her goal was to set an example by heading to bed, hoping Pat would follow.

"Not really," she admitted.

"Then how can we owe the dead anything?"

Mrs. Blossom was stumped. Elinor removed her hand from Marko's leg before she spoke. "In the Jewish faith, there's a saying when someone dies, 'Let his—or her—memory be a blessing.' I do think we owe the dead our memories because that's how they live."

Pat shook her head. "I loved my father, but I don't think I owe him anything. In fact, he shuffled off this mortal coil owing me more than any inheritance could compensate for."

"Pat—" Marko, usually so laconic, seemed emotional, almost angry. Did they share a father or a mother? A father, Mrs. Blossom believed, but then—why did they have different surnames? She had assumed "Siemen" was Pat's married name, yet she had never spoken of a husband. Well, not everyone gabbed about their spouses all the time. And half-siblings often experienced their parents differently. Heck, even siblings experienced their parents differently. Her son-in-law was much easier with the twins than he had been with their older sister.

"Anyway, to bed!" She was trying to make it a rallying cry, at least for Pat and herself, but Pat insisted she was having too much fun to leave.

Back in the cabin, she checked her phone before leaving it on the bureau to charge, determined not to repeat the mistake from earlier in the week. Tess had texted in all caps. Tess often texted in all caps. CALL ME. DANNY JOHNSON IS NOT A PI.

Ha, Mrs. Blossom already knew that. For once, she was well ahead of her former boss. There was no need to call. Besides, it was dinnertime in Baltimore and she remembered all too well what it was like, trying to get a meal on the table—although Crow did most of the cooking in that household—then putting children to bed. She would check in later. Oh, how she would regale Tess with the story of the would-be jewel thief who had the bird all along.

He had used her as a pretext, a cover, Mrs. Blossom had decided. Having stolen the bird from Allan, he had followed her onto the boat, thinking he might steal even more. He wasn't a stylist, an FBI agent, or even a freelance investigator. He was garden-variety thief, nothing more.

Her phone vibrated in her hand, shocking her. Who would be calling her? Her iPhone had an answer of sorts: May be Paul read the caller ID—and the number had a 215 area code, which she believed was Philadelphia.

"Paul? Where are you? Are you OK?"

His laugh was the buttery rumble she remembered. "I'm in Paris and I'm fine. Really, everyone overreacted to my little stomachache. It felt more like food poisoning than a virus, and I think they just wanted to get rid of the very literal corpus delicti. I'm back in Paris. Do you think we could meet up here when the ship returns?"

The ship was scheduled to leave Caudebec just after midnight, then dock in Paris for the final day. Mrs. Blossom had made plans, as she had said at dinner, but she had no problem scuttling them.

She almost stuttered in her delight. "S-sure. Why not? Where would you like to have dinner?"

"I have a suite at La Réserve—it's one of the few places in Paris with a smoking lounge, can you imagine? Would you be OK dining in my room?" She inhaled sharply, and he must have assumed she was shocked by the offer. "It's a suite, but if that makes you uncomfortable, we can dine downstairs. Or on the balcony, which has a view of the Eiffel Tower and a table for two. Whatever suits."

"I'm not sure—"

"I know it's a lot, asking you to skip the farewell dinner on the ship, but I had hoped to get to know you better, and we were robbed of two days."

"I'd be happy to have dinner with you, Paul. As long as it's not on the late side. I am flying home the next day."

He laughed again, although she didn't see how she had been particularly funny. "I'm glad you checked in on me, as I didn't have any of your contact information. I wasn't sure how I'd find you again—and there you were, in my email."

Mrs. Blossom felt like a cartoon character dumbstruck by love, or at least attraction—stars circling her head, angels singing joyous syllables, her pupils heart-shaped. It took her an hour to fall asleep, and it felt as if she had been dozing only a minute or two when Elinor finally came in.

She had never realized that footsteps could sound disappointed, but Elinor's did. Pat must have stayed with them until the bar closed.

MRS. BLOSSOM WAS still so full of starry daydreams at breakfast the next morning that she barely registered that Gaston was moving from table to table, addressing the diners. Then she began hearing the moans of disappointment from others in the dining room.

"Can't you make up the lost time?" one asked.

"Couldn't we cab to Paris and return before you set sail?"

Cab to Paris? Weren't they in Paris? Mrs. Blossom looked out at the shore. It was a familiar landscape, but it wasn't suburban Paris. This was a village with a few businesses and rows of pretty houseboats. They were back in Vernon, where they had docked the morning they visited Giverny. And the ship appeared to be slowing down.

"I'm sorry, this is beyond everyone's control. We were not allowed to leave Caudebec for some time because of, um, a paperwork situation. There was no way for us to make Paris by morning, so we have hit on an excellent compromise plan—a visit to La Roche-Guyon, the former home of Rommel."

"Rommel? He's a Nazi," said the patriarch of one of the larger clans on board.

"Yes, but as Nazis go, he was not so bad," Gaston said. Not even he seemed convinced. "And no one is required to take the trip, but it is the best we could do under the circumstances. It's a new tour for us, and we are very excited."

Paperwork, Mrs. Blossom thought. It was probably related to Danny. Even under arrest, he could still spoil her chance at a good time. Her eyes filled with tears, but she quickly dabbed them away, embarrassed. It was just a dinner with some preppie from Philadelphia, a man who didn't even like art that much. She texted him the update, afraid that too much emotion would show in her voice if she called him. He sent back a sad-face emoji, then added: Where there's a will, there's a way. Maybe I'll make my way to you, become a stowaway.

Resigned to the change in plans, she went back to the room and grabbed her headset for the tour, telling Elinor what had happened. Elinor, who was still in bed, announced from behind her sleep mask, in an imitation of their waiter at Le Bristol, "I have hit zee wall!" Despite the little joke, Mrs. Blossom worried that Elinor was hiding heartache behind her mask as well.

No one chose to sit next to her on the bus, and Mrs. Blossom told herself that she was fine with that. She hadn't really tried to make any friends beyond Pat. She listened with half a mind to Gaston droning on about the challenges of climbing to the top of the castle keep.

"It's extremely steep," Gaston warned repeatedly, his eyes fixed on hers. "There are two hundred and fifty-five steps, and the passageways are narrow. If you're the least bit, uh, *claustrophobic*, it's best not to try it."

Ah, memories of Les Andelys—a steep climb, now with the bonus of her nemesis, claustrophobia. But she was on a bus, part of a tour, she couldn't slip away unobtrusively into the town and sip coffee or chocolate while the others toured the château. Besides— *she didn't want to.* There was more to La Roche-Guyon than the castle keep. She could take the tour without committing to the climb.

But the château itself was a bit of a bust, echoingly empty with no real sense of how the rooms had functioned at any point in its history. The "library" was filled with fake books, all covered in white paper, as if waiting for some Instagram influencer to take a selfie. Giant tapestries that told the story of Esther in the Bible were clearly not part of Rommel's decor, Mrs. Blossom deduced; the guide confirmed that they were medieval items that had been donated many years after Rommel's death.

As they neared the staircase to the keep, Gaston repeated his admonition that it was not for the claustrophobic, his eyes again lingering on Mrs. Blossom. To be fair, she *was* claustrophobic, but he didn't know that, and it really applied only to under-water tunnels. She looked up the passage. It was fairly wide here at the bottom, but it probably narrowed toward the top. If other people were trying to descend as she ascended, she would have to flatten herself against the wall. Oh dear—what if it was so small at the top that she became stuck, like Pooh at Rabbit's tea party, and she had to stay there for weeks until they could finally wrest her out.

No, she told herself. She was entitled to climb these stairs if she wanted to. In fact, she was entitled to try and fail, to abandon the trip midway if it was, in fact, too challenging for her. Hart Tours actually rated its tours on an activity level of 1–5, and this trip was a 2, accessible to people with limited mobility. That was another reason why she had chosen the company: it wanted to make travel possible for people of all ages and capabilities.

She started up the stairs. When she was a child, people had still been allowed to climb the Washington Monument, and it had far more than 255 steps. She had made the trip once with her beloved father, the only person besides Harold who had ever loved her unconditionally. He had rewarded her with a Good Humor toasted almond bar when they finished.

True, she was huffing and puffing a little now, but she noticed everyone breathing heavily, even seemingly fit people with sinewy limbs and T-shirts that boasted about 10k runs.

At one point, which she thought was about halfway, a woman coming down smiled at Mrs. Blossom as she turned sideways to make more space. "Don't worry," she said, "you're almost there," and Mrs. Blossom was proud to think she had made such swift progress. Then, as the woman rounded the curve in the staircase, her laughter and words floated back. "The poor thing, I'm not sure she's going to make it, but I wanted to offer her some encouragement."

"I'll probably get up there faster than you did," Mrs. Blossom muttered under her breath. Then, in a much louder tone, one she hoped would echo through the stairwell: "SO THERE!"

She kept going, pausing from time to time. The winding stairwell was a trickster: Just when she thought she must be at the top, she would turn and find another flight of stairs. Even when she glimpsed blue sky overhead, there were still two more flights to the actual summit. But she kept going, and it's not as if she was impeding anyone. No one had to wait patiently behind her, no one had been slowed by her pace, no one had passed her on the way up.

And every visitor who arrived at the top after she did was just as winded as she had been, many bending over and grabbing their knees as they panted.

Their reward was a view of the river that had been their home for the past week. There were the red roofs of La Roche-Guyon as well and a huge, perfect sky, cerulean with white fluffy clouds. It was possibly the most gorgeous sky that Mrs. Blossom had ever seen, and she believed part of its beauty was that she was closer to it here.

"What a beautiful country," she said, then realized she had spoken aloud. But who cared? It was a harmless, inarguable sentiment. Could she live here? Would she live here? At this moment, looking at the huge sweep of the countryside, anything seemed possible.

"You made it," said a woman from the boat. She was perhaps in her fifties and string bean thin, her skin deeply tanned. Mrs. Blossom had seen her in the dining room, but she was part of a large family group that kept to itself.

"So did you," Mrs. Blossom said shortly, inferring condescension.

"Where are your friends today?"

"Oh, Elinor preferred to sleep in. I think she's going to take a walk in the village later, maybe with her friend Marko." She wasn't sure if Danny was included in "friends," and she certainly wasn't going to claim him as such.

"His wife is such a good sport about letting him hang out with other women on the cruise, given her mobility issues," the woman said. "I'm not sure I would be as gracious."

His *wife*? "They're brother and sister. They have the same father, but different mothers."

"But they're sharing a room."

"Some siblings like each other." It was a borderline rude thing to say, as this woman's family members were forever squabbling.

"I'm so sorry. When you assume, et cetera et cetera. She just didn't look like a Markowitz." Mrs. Blossom wasn't sure what *that* meant, and she preferred not to find out. Harold's tell-nothing surname had often exposed them to anti-Semites who presumed they shared their views. "Obviously, you know them better than I do."

"No worries. I guess a river cruise is a bit like a small town. You see the same people day in, day out; you begin to speculate or fill in the gaps without realizing what you're doing. It's funny, here we are on the last day, and I realize that I've spoken to so few people. I hope I didn't seem standoffish."

"No, not at all. It's very much an experience where there's no right or wrong way to do it—you can mingle aggressively, or stay self-contained. I confess, I thought that young man I saw around you in the early part of the trip might be a gigolo, but I guess that's better than a thief."

The early part of the trip—without intending to, this woman had pointed out something Mrs. Blossom should have noticed earlier. On the first two days, Danny had stuck quite close to her, joining her for meals. Once the tracker was in her purse, he had more or less disappeared, avoiding everyone. She hadn't really seen him again except at the café in Les Andelys. Then she had put the tracker in Pat's bag and he had been fooled into thinking she was on the ship, instead of in Normandy. Why had he gone into Pat's room? Was he looking for her, as she first suspected, or trying everyone's doors, looking for things to steal?

"I'm sorry," the woman said, mistaking her silence for offense. "I didn't meant to be rude. I mean, if he was your friend—"

"What? Who? Oh, no, I was just going down the rabbit hole of my own thoughts."

"Well, here I go back down those steps," the woman said. "The trip down will be easier, but it's also easier to fall. Be careful!"

The return trip was, in fact, more treacherous. The steps were of varying heights, so one had to move carefully. Mrs. Blossom smiled encouragingly at those making the climb, hoping to convey: *I did it and you can, too.*

Even after her slow and deliberate trip downward, she had thirty minutes to kill in the small village. She stood on the sidewalk, admiring the early spring produce in the small grocery store on the main street. Was everything more beautiful in France, or was it simply that the lives glimpsed on vacation always seemed better than what awaited one at home? She gave herself a pep talk about the coming weeks. Her new apartment was lovely, and it would be fun to pick out art for the walls, even if they were just framed museum posters. She would be spending time with Tess and her family. Maybe Marko would prevail on his sister to relocate stateside, and she would see Pat when she visited Elinor.

But the mere fact that she needed a pep talk was dispiriting. She felt like the sad little millionaire in that Cole Porter song, the one who was down in the depths while living on the ninetieth floor.

She needed something money couldn't buy. It was tempting to think that love was the answer, to bounce from Cole Porter to the Beatles. Look at how happy Elinor had been since meeting Marko. But also—look at how dejected she seemed this morning. Look at how her own mood had plummeted when she had to cancel her dinner plans with Paul. So, no, not money, not love. What was this itch she felt, what was keeping her from being contented? What would give her life *meaning*?

She found herself reaching for her charm bracelet, checking the time, then fondling the latch on the little fortune cookie.

The tour directors had been talking up the mentalist all week, but Mrs. Blossom couldn't help assuming the act would be rather cheesy. Still, it was the last night of the cruise, and she had no intention of staying up for that late-night dance party with the crew, so she felt she must put in an appearance at the farewell dinner. She realized she had appeared standoffish all week, missing opportunities to mingle with the other guests. She had started the cruise assuming she would be spending all her time with Elinor and now here she was third-wheeling again. Mrs. Blossom sat silently through dinner, listening to Elinor and Marko speak elliptically about the future. She didn't think she had ever heard the word *we* used so many times.

If the ship had made it to Paris this morning as planned, would she be having dinner with Paul right now? Would they be *we*-ing? No, that would be premature. He had made a joke about sneaking onto the ship before it left Vernon, but of course it was nothing but a joke. She had googled his hotel and learned that a suite there cost almost as much per night as one week on the MS *Solitaire*. She couldn't expect him to leave that splendor for an evening with her.

The mentalist stopped by their table as they were beginning dessert, demonstrating his schtick. He spoke very rapidly and made intense eye contact. He asked everyone at the table to think of a three-digit number and Mrs. Blossom chose "249"—she had once won a big jar of candy at a Halloween party by guessing that number, and the jar held 250 pieces. Of course, her mother locked it in the pantry and parceled it out, one piece a day, and even the sturdiest, shelf-stable candy begins to get a little grim seven months out. Yet it was the only prize she had ever won and the memory still shone. She had thought she might have a chance at best costume—she was dressed as Margaret Dumont, with Elinor as a game Groucho—but that was perhaps a little too high concept for Hamilton Elementary School. Besides, the prize for best costume was simply a ribbon. The candy came in a blue-glass jar that she kept in her kitchen to this day, filling it with sweets on which there were no limits.

Once she thought of her lucky number, she tried to block it from her thoughts, although she didn't believe he was reading her mind. He was staring so intensely—there must be some kind of ocular clue, combined with questions more leading than they seemed. Sure enough, when he showed her the scrap of paper on which her number was written, it said "249."

She wondered what else he could intuit about her?

Intrigued by this demonstration, she stayed for the entire act, and it exceeded her now-high expectations. She knew it was a trick, but he wasn't using an assistant with a hidden mike, so it wasn't rigged. She wondered if one's pupils contracted or expanded in some way that tipped the mentalist off. She couldn't help thinking it was all in the eyes.

The eyes. A stray line of Shakespeare flitted through her mind. *Those are pearls that were his eyes.* The statue had no eyes, just divots where eyes had been. That wasn't so strange. But it was supposed to have sapphires around the head and tail. *Ornamentation* was the word the newspaper had used, but that could mean eyes, could it not? Where were the sapphires? The article about the death of Constance Saylor said they had not been found in the fire's wreckage, which is why the insurance company doubted the statue had been there at all.

A very nice lady, Allan had texted to a mystery number. *She has your eyes.* Allan, who had two phones that day in London, one for US calls and one for Europe. Which one had the police found?

He had sent someone her selfie from the train. At the time, she had been pleased because it was much more flattering than the photo with the Paddington statue. But it also was a better, clearer photo of her face.

Allan was trying to help someone find her. Because she had the *eyes*. Plan A, Danny had said, was to stop him in customs. But, no, that was a story told by Danny when he was pretending to be an FBI agent. Still, maybe Allan had hidden the gems, the statue's "eyes," in her luggage, which would explain the endless fascination with her things. But when, where? Why had he gone to Paris ahead of her? He knew which train she was on; he had made the reservation for her. If he was so desperate to find these sapphires, why was he having a smoke and a cigar on his balcony, when she was only a few blocks away?

Cigars. She and Allan had kissed deeply. He wasn't a smoker, not a regular one, she was sure of that. *I like to have a cigar and a brandy.* That was Paul, who had wanted her to come to a Paris hotel for dinner tonight. Just the two of them. On a balcony. What had started the fire in which the handyman died? "He lit up a smoke—" Tess had said. A smoke could be a cigar.

Sometimes a cigar was just a cigar. And sometimes—

Mrs. Blossom clapped absent-mindedly at the climax of the mentalist's act. "Elinor, I think I'm going to go back to the cabin and pack."

"I thought you were packed."

"Mostly. But I want to be able to put my suitcase out tonight, before I go to sleep, just to be sure, so there are a few more things I need to do. We're in the eight a.m. group, after all."

She went back to her room and sat on the bed. Sapphire eyes. Was the statue worthless without them? No. But they were probably intrinsic to its value.

Still—*sapphires*. There were obviously no sapphires among her possessions. She would have noticed even the tiniest blue stones. Unless—On a hunch, she typed into her phone's Google app: What hues do sapphires come in?

Sapphire is generally known as a blue gemstone but surprisingly it comes in a wide range of colors and quality variations. In general, the more intense and uniform the color, the more valuable the stone.

Sapphires that are not blue are known as fancy sapphires, and may be any color—except red (which is a ruby). The fancy sapphire colors are: yellow, green, purple, violet, pink, and orange. Within the pink-orange gems, there is a vast range of shades, from pale pink to salmon.

Oh, Mrs. Blossom knew what, among her things, were salmon-colored.

She retrieved her pillbox from the safe. She had not worn her diamond earrings once on this trip. She almost never wore them, these love-hate earrings, the ones that Harold gave her on the anniversary after her affair with Michael Calista. What was that expression young people used? *Tell me you know I had an affair without telling me that you know I had an affair.* With that gift, Harold had been issuing a silent plea. *Stay with me.* It broke her heart that he thought he had to ask.

It also broke her heart that he had been prescient: they didn't make it to their diamond anniversary.

She carried the pillbox into the bathroom, sliding open the hidden compartment. There were her diamonds, sitting jauntily on the bed of pink-orange gummies that had kept them company since that first night in London. She began poking and prodding—yes, two of the gummies were rock hard, larger than the others, more heavily crusted. She worked her way through the rest—here were five smaller ones, also hard. Perhaps these had been on the tail. When she held them under a stream of hot water, the sugar coating melted away.

She had someone's eyes, all right—the Quqnoz. She was getting ready to return them to her pillbox when she heard a knock at the door. She slipped them into her pocket and left the pillbox on the bathroom counter.

It was Pat Siemen, holding a bottle of champagne aloft. "You promised me we were going to drink on your balcony, and now here it is the last night. I will not be denied."

"Oh—OK." It's not as if she could do anything about the probable phoenix eyes she had just found, although she would have liked to have been alone with her own pinballing thoughts. *Allan had planted the eyes on her. He must have figured out that he was going to be detained at customs. He insisted she take his bottle of gummies. He had slipped her the cannabis gummy and set her watch, then used her confusion to keep her from boarding her second flight. He had been glued to her side all day. He insisted on staying and watching her fall asleep, probably planning to retrieve the gummies. But she had put the pills in her hidden compartment and pocketed the bottle in her nightgown, in order not to hurt his feelings. He could have searched the room all night and not have found them. Someone had searched her room in Le Bristol, and on this boat. Someone had tried to steal her purse. It was always about the eyes. He had removed the eyes from the statue. But where had the statue been all this time, how did Paul and his cigars fit into this—*

"Muriel," Pat said, "do you have glasses?"

"Oh, of course. But the ones here in the room are just wineglasses, not proper champagne glasses, and this, of course, is proper Champagne."

Pat squeezed her arm. "Look at you. Eight days ago you were a nice woman from Baltimore who barely drank and now you're someone who knows that Champagne is not a generic, and it should be sipped from flutes or coupes. I *really* do like you, Muriel."

"I like you, too, Pat." She wondered at Pat's need for emphasis, why she stressed the word *really*. Was she such an unlikely friend?

She sat on her balcony with Pat, sipping what she supposed was excellent Champagne. The sapphires in her pocket felt at once heavy and delicate, a burdensome secret that raised as many questions as they answered.

"So, where do you go next?" Pat asked.

"One day in Paris, then home."

"And will you go back to Le Bristol?"

"No, I've booked a different hotel—how did you know I was at Le Bristol?"

"You mentioned it, when we met."

"I don't think I did."

"Oh, you absolutely did. We talked about the hotel cat."

No. No, she had not, she was sure of that. She had been shy about discussing her splurges, fearful that Pat would be dismissive of her choices.

"Have you stayed there, then?"

"A few times. I prefer the Crillon or the Ritz, but it's a good option when one is lying low."

Lying low. An interesting turn of phrase. "But you live in—"

"Near Lake Como."

"So in Italy?"

"Yes, Lake Como is in Italy."

"But it's also very near Switzerland." She was thinking of those Swiss francs. The captain had started to suggest they might belong to Pat because—and she hadn't allowed him to finish the sentence.

Switzerland was somehow relevant to the bird and its origin story, but Mrs. Blossom couldn't pin down the one darting, elusive fact that would tie everything together.

"Well, I am impressed by how well Baltimore schools teach geography," Pat said with her drawling vowels, teasing Mrs. Blossom yet again. "You've caught me out. We actually live in Lugano, which isn't that far from Lake Como. It's just easier to say 'Lake Como' because more people have heard of it. Oh look, someone is joining us."

The door had opened and there were Elinor and Marko, although Elinor looked confused, possibly drunk. She turned to Marko, slurring her words: "I thought you said Pat and Muriel were meeting in the bar and you wanted to be alone with me here—"

"Oh, I wanted us all to be together on our final night," Pat said with her smooth, impeccable manners, as if it were a party. Mrs. Blossom's own thoughts echoed back to her—*as if it were a party.*

This was definitely not a party.

The balcony had only two chairs, but the room had two small upholstered armchairs. Marko pulled one toward the open sliding doors. Pat moved to that chair and indicated Elinor should take the seat she had vacated on the balcony. Mrs. Blossom couldn't help noticing that she and Elinor were blocked from getting back into the room, unless they wanted to crawl over Pat, or push past Marko, who was standing like a sentry behind his sister. If they both ran at the same time—but Elinor was in no shape to run. She was slumped in her chair, her eyelids fluttering.

Pat sipped her Champagne and Mrs. Blossom pretended to.

There had been a few tiny glimmers of light left in the western sky, but now it was pitch-black. Pat sighed in satisfaction. "Well, at last, we must come to the end. Muriel, I am genuinely fond of you, but you have something that belongs to me."

"Something that belongs . . . to you?" The sapphires belonged to the statue. The statue had belonged to a woman, Constance Saylor. The statue had disappeared from her museum before a fire, stolen by the handyman who set the fire. The handyman had died. Constance Saylor had died, a drowning death.

In Lake Lugano.

Marko put his hands on Pat's shoulders. The gesture was at once loving yet controlling; Mrs. Blossom could swear that Pat flinched at his touch. "We want the sapphires," he said. "The statue won't fetch as much without them."

"Statue? Sapphires? I'm sure I don't know what you're talking about."

"They're pink, not blue," Marko said. "Perhaps that's why you're confused."

"And they're *mine*," Pat said. "As is the statue." Her words seemed almost plaintive, meant more for Marko's ears than Mrs. Blossom's. Elinor was beyond hearing anything, she could barely keep her head up.

"How are they yours?" Mrs. Blossom wished to take the words back the second she said them because she had now all but confirmed that she did have them. She felt them in her pocket, resting against her thigh. "They could only be yours if you are Constance Saylor. Patience Siemen. Constance Saylor. I get it now. You do like wordplay."

Pat laughed, but wanly. "Yes, I do. Constance drowned, and then Patience Siemen arose from her ashes. Like a phoenix. Or a Quqnoz."

Mrs. Blossom remembered her fleeting thought that the statue was cursed—all those accidents. But there were no *accidents*. Constance Saylor was alive. The handyman, Allan—those were murders. She and Elinor were going to go over the side of the balcony, just as Allan had, leaving behind *two* glasses of champagne. Elinor, already in an altered state, would not be capable of saving herself. But how would they make Mrs. Blossom's death look like an accident? Would everyone assume she had tried to save Elinor? But Marko had to ensure that she died, no small thing. It was a short drop to the water, she was a strong swimmer, the shore was close—

"Let's go," Marko said, producing a gun. Ah, he would hit her with the gun and then push her. The contusion would probably be consistent with a fall. And then he would gently, or not so gently, ease Elinor over the rail. Two old ladies, undone by drink, one falling to her death, the other dying in an attempt to save her friend. So insulting. So—she was just going to allow herself to say it—so *fucking* insulting.

The music from the sun deck, where the party was in full swing, was so loud—even if someone heard her screams, they would assume she was upset about Elinor going overboard. By the time anyone arrived, it would be too late.

"Your friend is going over the side if you don't give us what we want now," Marko said. "Tell me the code for the safe."

"I thought you"—she paused for the right word—"*liked* her."

"He likes money," Pat said. "If it's any consolation, your friend could never have afforded him. I can barely afford him."

Ah, so Tess Monaghan had been right: rich old ladies are vulnerable to fortune hunters.

If she could get back into the room and into the hall—but, no, she couldn't risk leaving Elinor behind. She had to think of another distraction.

"The sapphires aren't in the safe," she said. "They're in my pillbox, in the bathroom."

"Are you sure?" Marko asked. "I searched in there the other night and didn't find anything." Ah, his night with Elinor, the one in which he had spent so much time in the bathroom.

"It has a secret compartment," she said. "And it wasn't in there the night you searched."

She went to the bathroom, Marko hovering at her elbow, and picked up the pillbox. Marko grabbed it from her and directed her back to her chair on the balcony, but he couldn't figure out how to access the hidden compartment. He handed it back to Mrs. Blossom, who slid it open with ease. Her diamonds on a pile of gummies. She should have worn them more often. They were, in this moment, almost painfully precious to her.

But she knew Harold would insist that her life was more precious.

"Here you go," she said, holding the box up—and then, with a flick of a wrist, she poured its entire contents over the side, two shining white lights in a shower of pink.

"No," Pat gasped, and Marko pushed past Mrs. Blossom to look over the balcony railing, craning over it, as if he could grab them before they disappeared into the river, dark and impenetrable under a starless sky. This was the opportunity she had hoped for, the reaction she had bet everything on. Mrs. Blossom stooped, then pushed her weight up and out against his backside, upending him. *Is this what you did to Allan?*

"Man overboard," she shouted, hoping her voice would carry to the sun deck and that someone, anyone, might hear her over the noise of the party. She had no desire to kill anyone, even someone who had been on the verge of killing her. Before she could shout again, Pat/Constance rose unsteadily from her chair, screeching as if she thought the sound of her voice could intimidate Mrs. Blossom, raising her cane as if to strike her.

Mrs. Blossom calmly and sternly pushed Pat with great force, aiming her toward the bed, but Pat twisted as she fell and ended up hitting the bedside table. Mrs. Blossom believed it was that impact, not the slide to the floor, that was responsible for the sharp, cracking noise she heard.

"I'm sorry," she said. She was. She was sorry Pat was in pain, sorry Pat was not the friend she had hoped for, sorry her diamond earrings were sinking to the bottom of the Seine while a set of salmon-colored sapphires that meant nothing to her were safe in her pocket. She was even sorry that her friend's shipboard romance was a ruse.

But she was, as Pat had prophesied, the main character in her own life. And that felt pretty good.

It took several hours for the captain to sort out what had happened. First, of course, they had to stop the boat and retrieve Marko, who was found on the riverbank, angry and sodden.

They did not bring him back to Mrs. Blossom's room, where Pat Siemen—Constance Saylor, but Mrs. Blossom's brain could not stop thinking of her as Pat—had been instructed to stay on the floor until the boat could dock and proper EMTs could arrive. (The passengers had been asked if there was a doctor among them on board and there was only one, a lovely gentleman from Michigan who cheerfully announced he was far too drunk to provide any assistance.)

So Pat Siemen remained on the floor of Mrs. Blossom's room, while Mrs. Blossom and Elinor were instructed to sit at the end of their bed. They did, like the dutiful schoolgirls they once were. Pat spoke from time to time, almost as if trying out different versions of her story, but her heart didn't seem to be in any of them.

"These two women lured me here, determined to steal my ring," she said at one point. Later, more tentatively: "They were trying to kill Mr. Markowitz and I feared I was going to be next. It's all a terrible misunderstanding."

The captain listened and nodded, but he seemed unmoved and unconvinced by Pat's story, perhaps because the still befuddled Elinor kept drifting in and out of consciousness. He told Pat that the first thing they needed to do was get her to a hospital and that Marko should probably see a doctor as well, for the cuts and bruises suffered in his fall. Mrs. Blossom did not know where they were keeping Marko, but she doubted he would be clever enough to intuit the version of the story Pat was now telling—and the captain had pocketed everyone's phones, making it impossible for anyone to confer.

"We're going to stop in Conflans, the nearest town. But the ship must continue on—I have passengers who have flights out of Paris tomorrow, starting at noon, and then we have to ready the ship for its next voyage. I cannot inconvenience the others because of this . . . incident. Everyone will be handed over to the authorities in Conflans and they can sort out who did what to whom."

"Everyone?" squeaked Mrs. Blossom.

"Yes, I'm sorry, Madame Blossom, but you will have to disembark at Conflans, too. Please gather your things and wait in the lobby. It will be almost midnight by the time we arrive."

"But what will we—why do we—?"

The captain held up a hand. "This is a matter for authorities above me. I control my ship, nothing more. You must disembark and let the local police take over from there."

The paramedics arrived first, lifting Pat Siemen onto a gurney. "Please don't forget my cane," she said, almost meekly. The captain then returned Mrs. Blossom's and Elinor's phones and told them to be ready to depart in thirty minutes. Thank God they had both done most of their packing earlier in the day.

Mrs. Blossom and Elinor were waiting in the ship's lobby with their luggage when they saw Marko escorted off in handcuffs, damp but otherwise looking not too much worse for wear. He really was a dapper man, even wet and dripping. The handcuffs made Mrs. Blossom nervous. Would they be arrested, too? Were they to be put in restraints?

"Whoa," Elinor said between yawns, "we really do have terrible taste in men."

We, Mrs. Blossom wondered. But she let it pass.

"Maybe I should move to Baltimore, anyway," Elinor said, her drugged mind following its own logic. "I don't need a man to move. I'm tired of Kentucky. I want to come home, now that you're there."

Mrs. Blossom patted her hand. "We can talk about this later." *When you're not roofied.*

Once Marko had been taken away, they were allowed to make their way down the gangplank unshackled; the police who escorted them were even kind enough to take control of Elinor's roller bag, given how unsteady she was on her feet.

Danny was waiting onshore. And it was at the sight of him that Mrs. Blossom knew everything was going to be all right. They would not be spending the night in a French jail, they would not be detained and forced to miss their flight home. Danny, whoever he was, would take care of them.

"We are entrusting these women to you, Agent Johnson," the captain said. "We have given the statue to the police, as you asked, along with the Swiss currency. Mr. Markowitz is in custody, and Ms. Siemen has been sent to a Paris hospital, where she will remain under police oversight. But we're sorry—even after searching their cabin, we have not unearthed the other objects you described to us."

"I'm just glad everyone is safe," Danny said. He loaded their luggage into the back of a black SUV. They put the still spacey

Elinor in back, where she could stretch out and nap. Mrs. Blossom chose to ride up front with Danny.

"We have a hotel for you tonight. It's not Le Bristol, but it's nice enough."

"Agent Johnson?" she asked. "So the one true thing you told me was that you were an FBI agent? Why would you then lie and claim to be a de facto mercenary?"

"Well, technically, I was working for myself. I do work for the FBI special art task force. Or did. The agency never would have allowed me to work on the case of the missing Ququoz, so I took a leave of absence. When you threatened to check on me—it seemed better to pretend I was a soulless PI, rather than risk having you alert the Bureau about what I was up to."

"But why would you try to do this on your own?"

"Constance Saylor's handyman, Daniyal Hassan, was my father."

It was as if a dozen different vectors in Mrs. Blossom's brain suddenly lit up and showed how everything connected. Tess's text. The fire. Danny and the statue.

"So your real name is—"

"Danny Johnson. My father and I had a difficult relationship, and when I was a teenager, I refused to visit him anymore. We fought bitterly over my decision to attend MICA—so bitterly that I legally changed my name to Danny Johnson. Johnson was my stepfather's surname. It was a spiteful, hurtful thing to do, and I regretted it. When my father was released from prison late last year, I reached out to him to make amends. And he immediately compromised me by telling me he had the statue all this time."

"Then your father did take the statue before setting the fire for Constance?"

Danny sighed. "He said it was a last-minute impulse. He rationalized that he was assuming a disproportionate amount of the risk—and he wasn't wrong about that. But Constance had agreed to pay off my student debt, so if he implicated her, she would probably renege."

Mrs. Blossom worked this through in her head—a prodigal son, in a sense, reaches out to his father to repair their relationship, only to be burdened with a secret that could cost the son his career. It was an impossible choice.

"You were trying to figure out a way to get the statue back to Pakistan without your father being arrested again."

"Exactly. It wasn't enough to set up a sting operation, even an unofficial one. I wanted to make sure that my father wasn't there when the deal went down. I set up the meeting in London because my father, as a federal parolee, couldn't leave the country, so I knew he would need a coconspirator. To my surprise, he turned to Allan, Constance's longtime lawyer—and apparently one of the few people who knew Constance had faked her own death. I assume it was Allan's idea to let Constance compete for the statue—he knew she was fond of it, that it had sentimental value for her. Allan was greedy. Until he was killed, I believed he was greedy enough to kill my father."

"There's a big difference between being greedy and being a killer." Mrs. Blossom still felt a knee-jerk loyalty to Allan.

"Fair enough. But look at it from my side. I knew from security footage from my father's storage unit that Allan had visited the facility the day after the fire. And Allan was greedy enough to create a bidding war for the statue; it didn't seem like a stretch that he would want to keep all the money for himself."

Those two phones, buzzing away in synch throughout their day in London. She wondered how Allan felt negotiating for the statue, knowing its sapphires were in the melatonin bottle he'd tucked inside her purse. And where was the second phone? To her knowledge, the French police had found only the one, which included the cryptic text about her eyes. Forget the phone—where had the statue been all the time?

"Did Allan even have the statue? You said it wasn't found when he went through customs."

"Allan had sent it to the hotel ahead of him, using one of those luggage delivery services, but he kept the jewels on him, not entrusting them to couriers. Then he hides them on you. So imagine how he's feeling that Sunday morning in London—"

"He had to call an audible!" Mrs. Blossom said, adding: "That's a sports term."

"I'm aware," Danny said dryly. "From here, everything is conjecture. Allan texted someone—probably Marko, using a burner phone—that afternoon in Paris. He meets Marko in his hotel room and shows him the statue, explains that you have the sapphires, since he had to sneak them through customs. But I don't think Marko ever had any intention of paying for the statue. He killed Allan and took it, figuring he could track you down and find the sapphires."

Mrs. Blossom shivered. Not even four hours ago she had been on a balcony, facing the same fate. She could imagine Allan's surprise, then his fear, as he toppled over.

But why had Allan given her the sapphires, when he had already gone to the trouble of hiding them in his bottle of melatonin? How did Allan know he would be detained in customs?

Danny had been on the plane; Danny told her that from his seat in economy he had seen her use the lavatory. Allan had used the same bathroom only minutes before. She took out her phone and searched through the articles Tess had sent her. There was a photo, grainy and small, with the article about the death of Daniyal Hassan, possibly his mugshot. She used her fingers to enlarge it, looked back at Danny. The resemblance was pronounced. If Allan had seen him—that must be the moment when Allan decided to give her the gummies.

Which meant that everything that happened before that moment could have been out of genuine kindness. He hadn't *planned* to use her.

Making excuses for a thief—maybe Elinor was right about their taste in men.

"I can believe that Marko killed Allan—after all, he was going to kill Elinor and me. But why? Surely, Pat—Constance—could have afforded whatever price he was charging."

"I honestly am stumped by why they wanted the statue but didn't want to pay for it. Constance was always odd, but never cruel or cheap. I knew her when I was a little boy, before my mother left my father and took me to Atlanta. She sent me a gift for my birthday every year before she moved to Europe—hence the code on the safe. She paid off my college debt, although I didn't know she was my anonymous benefactor."

"That's pretty noble."

"Of him or her?"

"Both."

"I wish I could see my father as noble. All these years"—Danny stopped, started again—"all these years, I wanted to believe that my father hadn't set the fire, then I learned that he was not only a willing coconspirator with two other men, but that he also had stolen something from the museum. And when I found out that he still had the Quqnoz, I tried to convince myself that he had saved it in order to return it to Pakistan. I tried to persuade him to do just that, but he wasn't having it. I saw a chance for him to rewrite his story, to transcend his mistakes and redeem himself. But he felt that he was entitled to the money."

Mrs. Blossom was in that giddy frame of mind in which the exhausted body cannot shout down the adrenaline-charged brain. Who was Marko? Constance Saylor had no brother, not according to the articles Mrs. Blossom had read. Did Allan realize he was at risk? No, the death of Hassan had been reported as an accident. Tragic, but a deal had been set in motion. Why wouldn't Allan follow through on it?

"You should check Marko's passport and see if he traveled to the United States around the time your father died."

"We will," Danny said. "I am sad, of course, that the sapphires are at the bottom of the Seine, but at least we have the Quqnoz."

"But they aren't in the river, Danny."

She told him about the gummies, and why she had hidden them, then forgotten them until tonight, when she realized that sapphires come in a variety of hues. His gasp, when she told him about tossing her diamonds into the Seine, was particularly gratifying, as was his laugh about the way she shouldered Marko overboard.

At story's end, she slid her hand into her pocket and brought out the gems.

"Your service is appreciated, Mrs. Blossom. Maybe the Pakistani government will buy you a new pair of diamond earrings."

She shook her head. "They can't be replaced, for any amount of money. Besides, it was a small price to pay to save my life, and Elinor's."

She was shocked to realize that Danny's eyes were filmed with tears. "If anything had happened to you—I really was just trying to keep you safe. I put the tracker in your bag—right before you were mugged in the café. You left it unattended when you went back to the counter for a napkin. Do you think Marko orchestrated that, too? Or was it just a coincidence? Anyway, then it stopped moving, and when I tried to find you on the day of the Normandy trip, I ended up poking my head in Pat's room. Which is probably what gave her the idea for framing me."

"I put the tracker in Pat's tote. I didn't trust you."

He laughed. "Fair enough. I didn't deserve to be trusted. Look, you should feel free to sleep, as your friend Elinor is doing. It's another hour to Paris. Anyway, it will take some time to disentangle everything. The FBI is pretty unhappy with me, as you can imagine. I might lose my job over this. But I don't care. That statue cost my father so much, including his life. The least I can do is see that it gets home safely. Now allow yourself a catnap. Tomorrow will be quite busy."

"Oh, I couldn't possibly sleep," Mrs. Blossom said.

But she could. And as she began to nod off in the swiftly moving car, she realized how relaxed she felt for the first time in two weeks. No one was chasing her. No one wanted anything she had. She giggled softly to herself.

"What's so funny?" Danny asked.

"When I invited Elinor on this trip, I promised her it would be the vacation of a lifetime. I think I ended up providing that at the very least. Romance! Intrigue! Adventure!"

"How will you ever top it?"

"I think"—she yawned—"I think"—two more yawns—"that next year, I'll just go to Ocean City."

THE HOSPITAL TO which Constance Saylor had been taken seemed chicer to Mrs. Blossom than any American hospital she had ever visited, or maybe it was just that Constance Saylor always got five-star treatment, even with a police guard stationed outside her door.

The room was spare, but full of the loveliest light, and there was a vase of white tulips on the bedside table. The white bed, the crisp white linens—it would not have been out of place on one of the home-improvement shows that Mrs. Blossom loved.

The woman in the bed, however, looked like someone in a depressing film, the kind with very little dialogue and when there was dialogue, there were subtitles.

"I suppose you're here to gloat," she said. Her voice was wan, so different from the jolly woman who had befriended Mrs. Blossom. But then, the woman who had befriended Mrs. Blossom didn't actually exist. Or did she? Who was the "real" person, Pat or Constance?

"Of course I haven't come here to gloat," Mrs. Blossom said. "I'm very sorry about your pelvis." That was the diagnosis, a fractured pelvis. "It's terrible thing to fall at our age. Then again"—she couldn't help herself—"it's worse to be thrown over the side of a ship."

"You probably would have survived, now that I think about it. If you're anything, you're buoyant. The unsinkable Muriel Blossom."

"No need to be rude."

"It was a sincere compliment. I don't think anything can keep you down. I wish I had your resilience."

She seemed sincere. Mrs. Blossom drew a chair close to the bed and sat, remembering the look on Pat's face as Marko had gripped her shoulders. She loved him.

She also was scared of him.

"I need to understand what happened, Pat. Everything, from the beginning."

"What does it matter to you?"

She was prepared for this question. "For two weeks, I've been at the center of strange events through no fault of my own. I was almost killed, along with my friend. I was attacked on the street—probably by someone you or Marko hired. My privacy was invaded over and over. At the very least, I'd like to know why it mattered so much. You're rich. Why did you want a statue that you once left to burn?"

Pat looked thoughtful. Thoughtful and a little blurry; they probably had given her serious pain meds. "I suppose you do deserve to know. But my story's only for you, OK? Between two friends? I really do like you, Muriel."

"I liked you, too."

She wondered if groggy Pat noticed the difference in their tenses.

"The first thing you need to know is that the fire wasn't my idea."

"Are you saying Hassan acted alone?"

"Oh, no. I'm saying that it was Marko who insisted that we burn it all down. I had lost so much money, you see, and Marko is—expensive. He needs things."

"You mean he *wants* things," Mrs. Blossom said. "There's a difference."

Pat sighed. "The semantics are not important. My finances were under siege. The museum was covered for fire, but not theft. And Marko was tired of life in the Baltimore exurbs. He had no affection for Maryland, Muriel. He certainly wasn't going to stay there if I no longer had money. He wasn't going to stay with me, wherever I was, if there was no money. Marko's always been quite clear that he requires significant upkeep. In that way, he's not unlike a piece of art. Proper temperatures, low humidity, the occasional restoration—"

"Restoration?"

"He's had more work than I have, my dear."

"I didn't notice."

"That's how you know it's *very* good work. Anyway, Marko arranged the fire with Hassan and Allan. Hassan didn't expect to be caught—no one ever does, I suppose—but whatever happened, Allan was in charge of making the payments we agreed on. The museum burned down and Hassan's arrest didn't void the insurance, as long as he kept my name out of his mouth. I paid off Danny's college debt through my foundation, collected the payout, and moved to Switzerland with Marko. Everything was fine until the insurance company reopened the case, noting that the sapphires had not been found and raising doubt that the statue had ever been there at all."

Mrs. Blossom pondered this. "That's when you faked your death."

"Again, Marko's idea. My money was in a Swiss bank account with both our names. He thought that if Constance Saylor was dead, it would be harder for the insurance company to reopen the case and demand compensation for the statue, which was the most valuable piece in the museum. The thing I didn't anticipate was that it also meant that Marko controlled the money. And he was . . . not careful with it."

Tess had told Mrs. Blossom that the payout for the museum had been "a pile." What was a pile? Ten million? Twenty million? Mrs. Blossom wasn't clear if such a windfall would be taxable—she thought not—but even if it had been reduced by half, it seemed unfathomable to her that someone could run through that much money in less than ten years.

"I can feel you judging me," Pat said.

"No, no—it's just—" She kept doing the math in her head.

"Life in Switzerland is expensive." A sigh. "*Marko* is expensive. That baseball cap he wears on sunny days?"

"Is it from The Row?" Mrs. Blossom had learned about the Olsen sisters' luxury brand from reading *Succession* recaps.

"Zegna. Almost two thousand dollars. He has at least three. And he's forever losing them. Don't get me started on how much he spends on sunglasses. Anyway—so there we are, sitting in Switzerland, worrying about our funds, and Hassan gets in touch with us. Someone wants to buy the statue from him, but he's willing to 'let' us have it for a higher price. Well, as Marko pointed out, it belonged to me, not Hassan. Why shouldn't we bypass the middlemen and sell it ourselves, which would help our financial situation?"

Mrs. Blossom kept doing math. The offer for the statue was a fraud, but Pat and Marko couldn't know that because Hassan and Allan also believed it was genuine. By competing for the statue, they could figure out how much it might be worth on the black market.

She also noted that it was Hassan, not Allan, who had drawn the couple into the bidding. It was Hassan's greed, not Allan's, that had led to his death.

"Marko went to visit Hassan, to make the case that the statue was really ours. He came back empty-handed." *And Hassan died*, Mrs. Blossom thought. How could Pat be so blind to his true nature? "I thought, well that's that. But then the last week of March, Allan got in touch. He had a meeting in London, but he was willing to let the two parties keep bidding until five p.m., Baltimore time, April first. We 'won,' and Allan asked us to meet him in Paris, saying there had been a slight 'hiccup.' Marko went to his hotel to collect the statue and they quarreled about who was responsible for getting the sapphires from you. There was . . . an accident."

An accident. So many accidents when Marko was around. Mrs. Blossom had almost had an accident, too. There had been a cigar, a snifter of brandy on Allan's balcony. That seemed an odd thing to be having in the middle of a fraught discussion over how to retrieve the sapphires. Could Pat really not see what was happening?

Had Pat had an accident, too?

"Your cane—"

Pat glanced at her bedside, where it stood sentry. "I look forward to using it again. For now, I'm quite immobile. I fractured my coccyx, and only time can heal that kind of injury."

"You told me you used a cane because you hurt yourself in a horseback riding accident."

"Yes, that's what I usually say. Because it sounds glamorous and no one ever asks any follow-up questions."

"Oh, Pat."

"It wasn't intentional. Just a little push, but I lost my footing and fell down a flight of stairs."

"Pat—"

"You don't understand, Muriel. He loves me. He always comes back to me. He was only romancing your friend to get access to your room. And that part of our life has slowed down. But he loves me, I'm sure of that."

"Did Marko recognize Danny on the ship?"

"Oh, yes, that's why he joined you for dinner that first night. Keep your enemies close, et cetera, et cetera. We didn't know why Hassan's son was on board, but we knew it couldn't be a coincidence. We feared he might be the other bidder, and Allan had told him about you and the sapphires as well. But that didn't make any sense because he clearly couldn't afford it."

"How could you know that?"

"It's my super power: I can tell a person's net worth by looking at them." She regarded Mrs. Blossom. "Maybe seven million, with all your assets combined."

Mrs. Blossom felt as if someone had told her they could see her underwear through her skirt.

"I can see why you framed him, but why risk putting the statue in his safe? You might not have gotten it back."

Pat looked almost embarrassed. "Marko tends to overthink things. He was mad at me for insisting that we put that stack of Swiss francs in the safe, he thought it was wasteful, but I wanted it to look as if Danny had robbed at least two people on board. Truthfully, I think he put the bird in the safe because he's always been a little jealous of my affection for it. It was a gift from a suitor, the same man who gave me my ring." She held up her bony finger and looked at the pink gem, which Mrs. Blossom now understood was a sapphire. "I'll probably have to sell it just to pay for all the lawyers we're going to need."

Lord, Mrs. Blossom felt terrible for everyone in this story. Well, not Marko. But at least another question had been answered: Pat had told Marko to use Danny's birthday when he put the money, ring, and statue in the safe. It was Marko, who had been living overseas for years, who transposed the month and the date when he had set the safe's code, European style. Pat had projected the error onto Danny, claiming he was the one who had flipped the numbers.

"Did Marko overthink his way into hiring someone to mug me? Was Marko somehow responsible for Paul getting sick?" They had shared cigars right before Paul got ill.

Pat gave a helpless little shrug. When it came to Marko, she was overall helpless.

"Pat—Pat, listen to me. You can cooperate. You didn't really do anything. If you tell them that it was Marko—that he killed Hassan and Allan, that he was the one who insisted on getting the statue in order to sell it—they'll cut a deal with you."

Pat's voice was fading, her chain of thought drifting. "My father thought I was going to waste my fortune, that I would be vulnerable to horrible men, fortune hunters. The man who gave me the statue—and the pink ring to match—my father chased him away. Offered him $500,000 *not* to marry me. He didn't take the money, but he also didn't stay. He saw the rot at the heart of my family tree. I met Marko the year after my father died, when I was swimming in money, more money than I thought anyone could spend in a lifetime. Everything was his idea. The vineyard. The museum as a tax write-off. Burning down the museum to collect the insurance. But I had to make him happy. Because without him, I would be miserable."

"Pat, you deserved so much better."

"No one deserves what they get in this life. Not even the wicked."

"It that another line from a cartoon?"

"Willa Cather, although I probably mangled it a bit." Pat smiled wanly. "I was a serious person, Muriel. Once. Love made me foolish."

"You're only foolish if you keep protecting this man."

Mrs. Blossom realized she didn't believe that love made one foolish. *Love* was never a mistake. Her own mistake had been the consequence of ego and boredom, not love. She had risked love, real love, yet that love was there waiting for her when she recovered from her reckless stupidity. Harold's early death was not karmic retribution for her brief betrayal of him. That's not how life worked. We make mistakes, we pick ourselves up, we start over—the better to make more mistakes. But love, if you are lucky enough to know it, can never be a mistake. And the possibility for love was a constant, every day, if one could broaden one's scope beyond the romantic. There are so many ways to be loved in this world, if we allow ourselves to be.

"Pat—just think about it, OK?"

"There is no Pat." She turned her face to the window.

"I disagree. I met a woman named Pat, and she was smart and lively and wonderful company. She told me that I deserved to be the main character in my own life. I wish she would take her own advice."

Mrs. Blossom left the room, but not the hospital. She took a seat in the corridor and pulled her phone from her pocket. At Danny's instruction, she had hit record before entering the room. He had told her that it wasn't legal, in France, to record without consent, but he wanted a transcript of their conversation. If Pat had any information about his father's death, he needed to know.

But Pat didn't know anything about Hassan's death, or Allan's. Worse, she had made it clear that Hassan had set in motion the events that led to his murder. Mrs. Blossom wasn't sure how that would make Danny feel.

As for the other things Pat had said—they seemed so private, so painful. Mrs. Blossom remembered the photo of the beetle-browed young woman sitting next to a statue of a bird. That woman had been loved; she should have chased the man who rejected her father's money to the ends of the earth. Instead, she had transformed her body and her face, through diet and surgery, only to lose herself, to live under the spell of a man who made it clear that her money was the only draw.

Mrs. Blossom looked at her phone, pressed a button, then walked downstairs, her tread heavy. Danny was waiting for her in the lobby.

"Well?"

"I'm not sure she can be of any help at all. She truly doesn't know anything, and she seems determined to protect Marko." She pulled her phone from her pocket. "I can tell you this much— Marko definitely met with your father before he died. But—" She fumbled with her phone. "Well, drat, I guess I never pushed record. Anyway, that bit about Marko—that's all you need to know."

June 11

"**DID YOU SAY** one for *Book Club: The Next Chapter*?" the young ticket clerk asked Mrs. Blossom.

"No, *All the Beauty and the Bloodshed*," Mrs. Blossom repeated, wondering how anyone could confuse the two titles. It was hard enough not to be seen in the world, could she not at least be heard?

"It's twelve dollars either way."

"I believe," Mrs. Blossom said, "I qualify for the senior discount? I'm sixty-eight."

"We don't ask," the clerk said. "Anyone who wants to say they're a senior can get in for ten."

It was fun, broadcasting her age. True, she had never disguised it, but she had never been one to shout it in public. But why not? She found herself wanting to announce everything about herself— her age, her weight, her shoe size, her full name, Muriel Hummel Blossom. She wanted to shout to the world, *I foiled an international art crime.*

But, for now, all she wanted was to go to a matinee and then have dinner by herself.

"I'm happy to be my age."

"Great. Pick a seat."

Mrs. Blossom stared at the proffered screen that showed which seats were available. She liked this relatively new practice. With ten minutes until the 4:00 p.m. screening, only five people had reserved spaces. She chose an aisle seat in the fifth row, as it had extra legroom and was far from everyone else.

The first trailer showed a plane streaking across the sky, and just like that, she was back at the British Airways ticket counter, being asked if she wanted an upgrade. Despite all that had happened, she was glad she had said yes. She was sorry Allan was dead, but his death had been, in a sense, foretold before she met him. Allan was on his way to being dead the moment he told Hassan that Constance Saylor was still alive and might want to pay them more for the statue.

She stretched her legs. It was her fourth solo trip to The Charles since she had returned from France and settled into her new apartment. She hoped Elinor, who had decided to move back to Baltimore later this year, would come to the movies with her. But it was OK if she didn't. No one friend could be everything to you.

She wasn't sure yet if Paul liked going to the movies as much as she did. They somehow hadn't gotten around to texting about movies yet. So far, it was life stories, their children and grandchildren, the occasional aches and pains endemic to their ages.

He had emailed her a week after her return from France, expressing regret over their missed encounter in Paris. They emailed back and forth, then started to text, a progression in intimacy. A face-to-face meeting seemed implicit, but Mrs. Blossom didn't feel particularly urgent about it. She had a sense that Paul, a relatively new widower, might be looking for a wife—and she didn't want to be anyone's wife. But she was confident that he wasn't a fortune hunter at least. His net worth appeared to be far greater than hers.

No, not a wife, never again. Someone's lover, however—could that happen? Would that happen? She could imagine it, but—she could imagine just about anything, that was her superpower. Was it ridiculous to think one might find passion at her age? It was probably ridiculous at any age, and she had beaten the odds once, with Harold. But she also had found a piece of paper worth more than eight million dollars in a Circle K parking lot. She had saved her own life. Clearly, anything was possible.

The previews at The Charles always ended with a short film about a dog coming to the theater to see *Lady and the Tramp*. Mrs. Blossom was never going to tire of seeing that good boy's sweet face staring up at the screen in intense anticipation. She sighed contentedly, sprinkled a box of miniature Butterfingers into her popcorn, and, as she had been instructed, sat back and prepared to enjoy the show.

The other four people in the theater left as soon as the credits started rolling, but Mrs. Blossom felt it was important to watch to the very end. A lot of people had worked hard to make this movie; she owed it to them to sit here and watch their names scroll by.

She emerged into the soft fading light of a perfect spring evening. There were several good restaurants within walking distance, but she decided to try and see if she could get a seat at the counter at Le Comptoir du Vin, the place where Allan had once promised to take her.

"The counter is full, but we have a table downstairs," the host told her. She was delighted to be delivered to a two-top on an open patio, a secret garden of sorts behind this otherwise nondescript rowhouse in a part of Baltimore that didn't really have a name. Oh, they were forever trying to give it various names—Penn North, Station Arts—but the area was a no-man's-land, defined by what it wasn't. Not Charles Village to the north, not Midtown to the south. Mrs. Blossom felt a kinship. She, too, could be defined by what she was not. A mother, but no longer a hands-on mother or grandmother. No one's wife. She was just Mrs. Blossom.

She ordered the sourdough and "Normandy" butter, asked for the pâté as well. The menu advised that its food was designed to be shared, but she would have to make do with a solitary meal. If there were leftovers, she would enjoy them at home. She could make a savory bread pudding, eat pâté on crackers.

"Were you on my train today?" A man's voice, with a hint of a southern accent.

She turned and saw Danny. "Your train?" she said. "Do you own it?"

"This place is very popular," he said. "It would be a courtesy if you let me join you at your table, rather than take up a seat at the bar, which they could use for a walk-in."

Mrs. Blossom glanced at the waiter, assuming he would be mystified. He simply looked bored. This nonsensical banter between a sixtysomething woman and a fortysomething man was of no interest to him. What did he see when he looked at them? Did he think they were a mother and son? A gigolo and his client? She was forever cataloging the differences between them—in age, in looks, in ethnicity, but, really, no one else cared. Perhaps the world's general incuriosity was a gift. If no one was ever truly looking at you, what was there to be self-conscious about?

"Are you following me again?" she asked.

"Only for the last ten minutes or so, and it was rather spontaneous. I had just left a screening at The Charles and I saw you walking out ahead of me."

Well, Smalltimore, Mrs. Blossom thought. It was entirely plausible. Still, she wasn't sure she believed him. "What did you see?"

"The *Book Club* sequel. I love Jane Fonda."

OK, who would lie about that?

"Why are you even in Baltimore?"

"I see they say their butter is from Normandy—let's use our recent experiences to judge it imperiously. Ah, and sweetbreads. I love sweetbreads. And treacle for dessert. Treacle! No offense—" He looked up, smiled apologetically. "Strike that. As a wise woman once told me, that phrase is nothing but a clever way to offend."

"Danny—I asked you a question. Why are you here? What happened with your job? Did you get in trouble?"

"Oh yes, quite a bit. Quite. A. Bit." He tried to play it off with his usual glibness, but Mrs. Blossom could hear the pain beneath his words.

"What did they do to you?"

"They didn't fire me—I guess a dead father gained me a little sympathy—but I'm no longer assigned to the stolen art task force, and there's a disciplinary period before I'm allowed to return to work. I've been reassigned to DC, but after looking at the cost of renting down there, I've decided I'm better off in South Baltimore, or maybe someplace up here, near the train station. I was scouting apartments before I went to the movies. I could walk to the commuter train from either location, which is fine, because my job is going to be a straight nine-to-five desk gig." He sighed. "Lord, I'm going to be miserable."

"Why don't you leave?"

"My dad always said that a boss can punish you only so long. Which is funny, because he was an engineer in Pakistan and he ended up as a handyman for a pain-in-the-ass rich lady. But he was actually happy, working for Constance Saylor. She was good to him, and funny in her way."

She was *funny*, Mrs. Blossom thought. She had enjoyed her company. She remained mystified that this smart woman, a woman with real intelligence and exquisite taste, could come under the thumb of such a vapid man, who cared only for the things that money could buy him—and didn't even take good care of them.

Their bread arrived and Danny buttered his lavishly, as did Mrs. Blossom. "Pretty good," he judged. "Lord, when I went to MICA, I never would have dreamed that a place like this could be on Maryland Avenue. Back then, it was mainly Korean restaurants."

"So you *did* go to MICA. I still get confused about what was true."

"Why, almost everything. Yes, I went to MICA, and although I've never been a professional stylist, I've always helped my friends—and my mother's friends—dress. I've also helped them avoid counterfeits. I am an FBI agent, albeit one who was on leave when we met. And while I might not have been a private investigator working for an insurance company, I was a private citizen working for a private client—myself. But I was never the thief you believed me to be."

"I didn't—" Mrs. Blossom began, somewhat disingenuously.

Danny held up a hand. "Who would blame you if you did? Like father, like son. You know, all I wanted to do was redeem him. Problem was, he didn't want to redeem himself."

"Didn't the Quqnoz end up in Pakistan?"

"Not yet. Its provenance is a bit of a mess. You see, when Constance Saylor's museum burned, all the records also were destroyed. But I'm confident it will eventually make its way to Chitrali. It cost me a lot, in terms of my job. But it cost my father his life, so I'm not going to complain. Enough of that. How is Baltimore? How do you spend your days? Outside of going to matinees?"

"I am studying French," she said. "Because I want to go back. Not on a cruise. I want to find a little place I can rent, preferably in the countryside, and try to just live for a month or so. I have been babysitting for my old boss, but she told me today she needs an investigator, not childcare. She can't afford to put me on the payroll, but she wants me to take on surveillance on a per-case basis."

"They'll never see you coming."

"They never do," Mrs. Blossom said, adding, "you know I'm very good at what I do."

"That," Danny said, "is one thing I never doubted."

She shook her head. "You thought I was an incompetent, that I wore my heart on my sleeve. If you had told me the truth the moment we met—and if you had described the statue in detail— maybe I would have understood that text, the one that was alluding to the statue's eyes."

"We were like the blind men—"

"I think we're supposed to say visually impaired," she corrected.

He doubled down: "Like the *blind* men, patting an elephant. I was looking for a statue, which I assumed was intact because it was in the photos that Allan shared when I set up the buy. Constance and Marko knew they were looking for the gems. Meanwhile, you thought you had cannabis gummies!"

"Which I hid, to be on the safe side. And yet—"

She thought about that night in London. She pictured Allan, watching her sleep, then trying—oh so silently, as she wasn't drugged this time—to find the pill bottle he had put in her purse. How stymied he must have been, how nervous. He wasn't the most honest of men, but that didn't void the chemistry they clearly had.

She thought about Pat—she would always be Pat to her—far more often than she thought about Allan. Pat finally had agreed to testify against Marko, but it was tricky—the attempted attack on Mrs. Blossom and Elinor was the only crime for which any government, the US or French, had a solid case. Pat hadn't been there when Allan had fallen from the balcony. She had no first-hand knowledge of Hassan's death. If Marko hadn't tried to kill Mrs. Blossom and Elinor in front of her, she probably would have remained convinced that he wasn't a dangerous man, merely an expensive one.

Danny said: "I like your hair. It suits you."

She put a hand to her head, confused, then remembered: she now wore it in a chignon almost every day. It was effortlessly chic, especially when one's hair was dirty. And, as Danny had prophesied, she also wore her expensive sunglasses every day. Disappointed in the clothing selections available to her even when she traveled as far as DC to shop, she had been corresponding with Cece about adding one or two more custom-made dresses to her wardrobe. As for the black chiffon pants, which Danny had *not* shoplifted—she was wearing them now.

"I've decided," she said, "that fashion isn't entirely frivolous. Or simply for the young."

"Everyone is entitled to beauty," Danny said. "If I could rewrite the Declaration of Independence, I think I would add that, although I guess it's implicit in the pursuit of happiness."

To pursue happiness—yes, exactly. That was how she had de-cided to live her life. She was going to do things that made her happy. It was wonderful. It was terrifying. She thought often of the day she'd bent down to pick up that lottery ticket twisting in the wind. A piece of paper had changed her life. It was now her responsibility to make sure it was a life worth living.

A piece of paper. She found her fingers caressing the fortune cookie charm.

"Do you think," she asked Danny now, "that we could be friends? Since you're going to be living in Baltimore. We both like art museums and going to the movies in the middle of the day, two things that Elinor detests. Besides, I'm beginning to see one needs a deeper bench. It's a sports term," she added.

"I *know*," Danny said, and they laughed. They had their first inside joke. They toasted to their friendship with a nice Chablis that Danny had chosen. She wondered if he expected her to pick up the check.

"You see this charm on my bracelet, the fortune cookie? There's an actual fortune inside, from my late husband, but I don't know what it says. He wrote it not long before he died, but he didn't know that, of course—that it would be his final words to me. I need you to open it, read it, and tell me what it says, word for word. Even if you think it's cruel or unkind, I need to hear it."

He didn't ask any questions, simply held out his hand for the bracelet. His fingers worked quickly at the cookie's clasp, but it seemed as if centuries passed while he carefully opened the piece of paper. After all, it held ten years of creases, tight and worn. Her *fortune*. Ten years of creases and the final word on her marriage, if merely by default. Danny read it to himself—like a judge, Mrs. Blossom thought, accepting the verdict from the jury before passing it back to the foreman—then lifted his eyes from the paper and met hers.

Everything was fine, she realized. Everything had always been fine. She had been living in the past, sad and troublesome as parts of it were, because she didn't think she had a future, or even much of a present. When Danny unfolded Harold's note, she realized her world had already unfolded, expansive as a canvas she had stretched for herself, a space for her to fill corner to corner with whatever colors she chose.

AUTHOR'S NOTE

MRS. BLOSSOM FIRST appeared in the novel *Another Thing to Fall* (2008), and if her biography now does not gibe exactly with how it was presented then—well, I blame Tess Monaghan for getting so much wrong about her new employee.

Over the years, an occasional reader has called me out for being ageist—that was in response to a specific reference to Mrs. Blossom being low-tech—and antifat. (The latter involved a rather toxic POV in a 2005 novel, but I think the reader had a valid point.) I took those admonitions seriously, and I saw putting Mrs. Blossom at the center of a novel as an opportunity to do better. It helps that I am now almost as old as Mrs. Blossom, a character I created when I was still in my forties. It also helps that I have spent the past few years trying to educate myself on antifat activism, relying on writers (and podcasters) such as Aubrey Gordon and Virginia Sole-Smith, to name only two. And, of course, I relied on sensitivity readers. The point was to write about a character who happened to be fat in the culture in which we now live. Is she sometimes self-conscious? Yes. Is she strong, sexy, smart, and vital? Also yes. Does she have any desire to change her body? Absolutely not. As someone who often writes about terrible people, I loved every minute I spent with Muriel Blossom, and if she really existed, we would be side by side at The Charles Theatre this weekend, sprinkling miniature Butterfingers into our popcorn.

I took two trips to France to research this book—three days in Paris in February 2023 and then a Seine river cruise in June 2023. I have never doubted the powers of my imagination, but I also have no regrets that I chose to see much of this itinerary in person. Alas, my cruise with Tauck was practically perfect in every way, so I felt obligated to create a cruise company with the occasionally pissy employee, doors that don't always lock shut (a detail actually taken from another cruise line with which I traveled several years ago), and a possible norovirus outbreak.

There really was a Marble Bar in Baltimore and it was amazing, but I was living in Texas during its glory days. It was my older sister, Susan, who happens to be the same age as Muriel Blossom, who took me there to see The Fabulous Thunderbirds, circa 1980. And it's Susan who had the avant-garde record collection, although I was a bit of a punk poseur in Chicago, hence the reference to The Swingers' cover of "Leaving on a Jet Plane."

I am lucky enough to have an amazing team, there really is no other word. It includes my agent, Vicky Bijur; my new editor, Danielle Dietrich; publicist Sharyn Rosenblum; Molli Simonsen, who is so much more than an assistant; my publisher, Liate Stehlik; and my daughter, who accompanied me on the cruise and rolled her eyes at my embarrassing existence only seventeen thousand times. I have many writer friends, so please excuse me for naming an emblematic few who got me through this book (and the last couple of years): Megan Abbott, Alafair Burke, Kellye Garrett, Alison Gaylin, Greg Herren, Wendy Corsi Staub, and Sarah Weinman.

This is the first book I've written that my mother won't read; she died Sept. 7, 2024. She was a much savvier traveler than Mrs. Blossom; she had been to Europe five or six times and when I returned from my 2023 tour, she wondered if she would have been able to enjoy such a trip. We both decided she probably did have the necessary stamina and had hoped to find a "three-generation" cruise for her, my daughter, and me. Alas, that trip is never to be.